FRONTIER WOLF

Frontier Wolf

Rosemary Sutcliff

Front Street
Asheville, North Carolina

Other books by Rosemary Sutcliff
Dawn Wind
The Eagle of the Ninth
Knight's Fee
The Lantern Bearers
The Mark of the Horse Lord
Outcast
The Shield Ring
The Silver Branch
Warrior Scarlet
Rudyard Kipling (Walck Monograph)

Copyright © 1980 by Rosemary Sutcliff
All rights reserved
Printed in China
Designed by Helen Robinson
First Front Street paperback edition, 2008

First published in the U.S. 1980 by Oxford University Press

The Library of Congress has cataloged the hardcover edition of this book as follows:
Sutcliff, Rosemary.
Frontier Wolf / Rosemary Sutcliff.
196 p. : map ; 22 cm.
Summary: As punishment for his poor judgement, a young, inexperienced
Roman army officer is sent to Northern England to assume the
command of a motley group known as the Frontier Wolves.
[1. Great Britain—History—Roman period, 55 B.C. – 449 A.D.—Fiction.] I. Title.
PZ7.S966 Fr 1981
[Fic] 19   80039849
Paperback ISBN 978-1-59078-594-2

FRONT STREET
An Imprint of Boyds Mills Press, Inc.
815 Church Street
Honesdale, Pennsylvania 18431

To Phil Barker, Ted Bishop and Wallace Bream
—R.S.

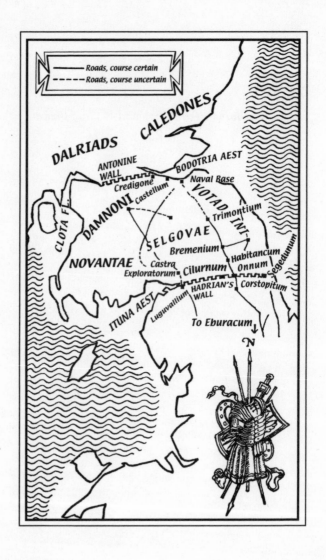

Author's Note

ALMOST IN THE FRINGES OF EDINBURGH, WHERE THE RIVER Almond joins the Firth of Forth, there is a village called Cramond; and where the village now stands, there was once a Roman fort. Its Roman name is lost, and so I have called it Castellum, which is simply the Latin word for a fort. When I first wanted to write a story about a unit of Frontier Scouts based here, I learned from the archaeologists who had excavated the site that there was no trace of any Roman military occupation at the date that I needed it—A.D. 343—or for nearly a hundred years before. So, sadly, I put the whole idea aside.

But twenty-five years ago, when *The Eagle of the Ninth* was just published and it was too late to do anything about it, I found to my horror that there was no trace of any Roman military occupation at Exeter. And now, twenty-five years later, traces of the Second Legion are being dug up all over the city! So maybe in twenty-five years' time they will be digging up traces of the Third Ordo, Frontier Wolves, all over Cramond!

Anyhow, after thinking it over for a long while, I decided to go ahead with the story I wanted to tell, playing fair with you who read it, by telling you that up to now, no traces have been found.

According to the *Notitia Dignitatum,* which lists the whereabouts of every unit of the Roman Army around ad 420, a crack light infantry unit of Attacotti was part of the Field Army in Gaul at that time. It would be hard to think of anything much more unlikely than a force of Irishmen serving in the Roman Army, and it seems to me that, allowing for the changes of frontiers and military needs over eighty years or so, they might well be descended from the First Attacotti Frontier Scouts of this story.

Contents

1 | *Decision at Abusina*

THE ORDERLY SET DOWN THE PLATTER OF COLD MEAT AND bread and the cup of wine on the end of the clothes chest, cast one half-contemptuous, half-sympathetic glance at the slight dark young man who sat hunched on the edge of the narrow cot with his elbows on his knees and his head in his hands, and went out, shutting the door behind him.

He was glad he was not Centurion Alexios Flavius Aquila.

And Centurion Alexios Flavius Aquila went on sitting with his head in his hands, staring at the floor but not seeing it. He felt dazed, as though he had taken a blow between the eyes; as though the past few days were all part of some monstrous nightmare from which he might wake up if only he knew how, to find himself back in his own quarters at Abusina. But the nightmare went on and on, and there was no waking up from it.

Life had gone so well for him, until those past few days; not always easily, but well. He had joined the Eagles at eighteen, and come up through the ranks, as most officers of the Roman army must do nowadays, in this region of the Emperor Constans. But he had served barely a year "below the vine staff" before being promoted centurion; and from there he had gone up steadily from the Tenth Century to the Ninth, to the Eighth, until just short of his twenty-third birthday, he had found himself in command of Number Two Century, of the British Cohort of Abusina where the old frontier defences came down to the Danubius. That was what it meant to have an uncle who was Dux Britanniarum, Governor of Northern Britain. Well, one couldn't be blamed for having an influential uncle; one couldn't be expected to throw his influence back in his face...

All that was over, now. There was nothing more his uncle could do for him. Nothing more he wanted him to do. He wished it was himself and not Centurion Crito who had taken that tribesman's spear under the breastbone.

For the hundredth time, his mind went back to the beginning of the nightmare. Only at the time it hadn't seemed to be the beginning of anything at all. It had been simply that Tribune Tetricus the fort Commander had been ordered back to Head-quarters at Regina to meet the new Governor; and the senior centurion had taken over in his absence in the usual way, so that Alexios was now second-in-command.

And before dawn, two days later, the Marcomanni had attacked the fort.

They had had a few hours' warning, from the bloody survivors of a frontier patrol, who had got back to them with word that the Tribe was on the war trail. Why, there was no knowing; there was seldom any knowing, with the German tribes; usually a god spoke to them, or they remembered their wrongs at a beer-drink. Centurion Crito had sent off three gallopers to Regina, with the report and an urgent request for reinforcements—it was heavy thundery weather, with low cloud massing along the hills, and no smoke signal could have risen clear of the high ground between Headquarters and the outpost fort—and they had evacuated and burned down the native settlement under the walls that might give cover to an enemy, and made ready in whatever ways they could, for what was coming.

They had beaten off the first attack; and when it was over, one of the senior optios had come to Alexios in the southwestern shooting-turret, and said, "Sir, Centurion Crito—"

"What about Centurion Crito?"

"He's dead, Sir."

Alexios stood and stared at the man, while his belly slowly turned cold and clenched like a fist within him.

It was not the first time he had seen fighting, known men killed. You did not serve five years with the Eagles along the menaced frontiers of the Empire without seeing a certain amount of action. But always, before, there had been somebody else to give the orders; somebody else to make the decisions and take the responsibility for them.

Now it was for him and no one else, to give the orders and take the decisions for a fort with well over a quarter of its garrison dead, or wounded, or down with the fever that the long wet summer of the German forests had let loose among them, and the surrounding country crawling with hostile tribesmen.

He heard a voice that did not seem quite his own, giving the needful orders for getting the wounded under cover and issuing a morning ration of barleycake and raisins, and letting him know the instant any sign of movement showed among the trees. Then he went down to the Principia, the Headquarters building.

God knew how long they had before the next attack was upon them, and there were matters that he must see to while the breathing-space lasted. In the heart of the Principia, the Sacellum, part-shrine, part-office, housed both the Cohort's standard and the Cohort's pay-chest. And there also were kept the muster-rolls and official correspondence; all those papers which must not be allowed to fall into rebel hands. And it was for the fort Commander to make sure that they did not. Barbarians, the Marcomanni might be, but officially, like all the rest of Empire, they were Roman Citizens, and there were those among them who could read Latin.

Not that it would come to that, of course. They could hold off several more attacks if they were lucky; and the relief force would be through to them by nightfall; by next morning at the latest. Still, there were the things that must be done, in case. Alexios, with the help of the military clerk, was just finishing making an orderly pile of papers on the floor, where a torch could finish the work in a few moments if need be, when one of the optios came running.

"Movement on the forest edge, Sir, north-west sector."

Alexios nodded, and turned to the doorway, re-knotting the cheek-guard thongs of his crested helmet which he had slackened off, and with the optio at his heels, headed across the Principia forecourt and down the main street of the fort between the barrack rows. High on the signal tower the trumpeter was sounding the alert, and in the open space behind the walls, the reserves were massing. He took the rampart steps two at a time, and at the top Centurion Clovius stood aside for him without a word. From all along the ramparts came a ripple of movement that was scarcely movement at all, the quickened breath, the grip tightening on the spear-shaft, the feet shifting into fighting stance.

For a short while that was all; then, away north-westward, where the road to Regina plunged into the crowding woods, his questing gaze picked up a kind of dark shimmer under the trees, and the glint of a weapon in the low stormy sunlight. A few heart-beats more of waiting time, and the formless movement spilled out into the open and took shape and substance. A swarm of men, running low and yelling as they came. At the same moment the trumpet coughed its warning from the far side of the fort. From all sides the attack was pouring in; but this looked like being the main thrust, up through the blackened ruins of the settlement, against the Praetorian gate. They carried tree trunks to serve as rams, torches that streamed behind them reddish in the daylight as they ran; and in their forefront they bore standards of some sort, small but oddly sinister, seeming to promise horror even while the distance was still too great to make out what they were.

Beside him, Alexios heard Centurion Clovius catch his breath, and in that instant he recognized those small sinister standards for severed heads upreared on spear-shafts. Three gallopers sent out to carry the message to Regina, three heads coming back!

The attack was upon them now, thundering on the gates, pouring in over the first attack's dead in the ditch, with notched poles to scale the ramparts where the British Cohort stood braced to meet them. In the gate towers, the archers stood loosing steadily into the mob below; and in the forefront of the yelling surge of tribesmen, the three heads bobbed in hideous mockery. One of them still wore a cavalry helmet set on at a rakish angle. For a few moments they disappeared in the press beneath the walls; and then one of them, freed from its spear-shaft, came over the breastwork, and landed on the rampart walk almost at Alexios's feet. It rolled to the edge, and hung there a moment, then toppled over and went hopping from step to step down the rampart stair, leaving thick brownish-red stains like stale mulberry juice behind it. The second followed. The third, maybe weighted down by that rakish helmet, failed to top the breastwork and fell back into the ditch …

The attack drew off at last. And again there was breathing space, in which the defenders could hear the fretful mew of a buzzard swinging lower out of the sky, and a faint mutter of the thunder that had been hanging among the hills for days. The medical orderlies were busy among the wounded below the ramparts, the dead were being hauled out of the way, while men laboured to make good the place where a stretch of timber breastwork had been breached and gone up in flames.

And Alexios was standing at the foot of the rampart stair, looking down at the heads of the two gallopers, hacked and battered and barely recognizable. Fighting down the vomit that rose in his throat, he looked up to meet Centurion Clovius's cold blue gaze.

"Sir?" said Centurion Clovius, as though he had spoken.

Alexios said, "Have them put with the rest of the dead."

The third must be left where it was. Well, it would have friendly company in the ditch; more than one of their own men had gone outwards over the breastwork during the attack; that always happened in close combat, when men grappled with each other on a narrow footing. "Come to me in the Commander's quarters when you have finished here."

Then he went to the latrines and was sick until there was nothing left in him to be sick with; and managed to get it over and reach the fort Commander's quarters just ahead of Centurion Clovius.

They looked at each other a long moment in silence. Then Alexios said, "So—we can rule out all hope of a relief force."

"No, Sir," said Centurion Clovius. "But we shall have to hold out longer for it. The supply train is due in four days. With any luck they'll get wind of the situation well before they reach here, and be able to send back word; but one of the patrols from Regina will almost certainly get the same wind before that."

"Maybe. How many attacks like these can we hold off, Centurion?"

"It would take our late Emperor Constantine's three-fold god to answer that question. We can hold for a while yet."

"But *four days*! We're down to less than two-third's strength, now!"

Centurion Clovius said woodenly, "What do you suggest we do about it, Sir?"

"Pull out tonight, while there are still enough of us for a fighting chance of getting through to Regina."

He saw the centurion's face stiffen. "With respect, Sir, I think that would be a mistake." His voice was formal. "We have plenty of stores and war supplies."

"Only not enough men to use them."

"A few men generally stand a better chance behind a breast-work than out in the open. Also ..." he hesitated.

"Well?"

"Sir, standing orders in an emergency are to sit close and wait for the relief force."

"I have not forgotten. There's a time for breaking orders. A fort full of dead heroes may be to your taste, Centurion; but I intend to get my men back to Regina alive."

"We'll never make it." Centurion Clovius forgot the "Sir."

They faced each other across the table, and after a moment Alexios said deliberately, "Centurion, I am in command here."

And silence came down between them like a sword.

Centurion Clovius, who had grey hairs in his beard, looked back at this puppy, who with nothing to recommend him save that he was a first-class swordsman (and you could say the same of any gladiator who outlasted three fights in the arena), just because he had an influential uncle, had been promoted over the heads of men like himself, before he had had time to learn his job, and said, "I should like to place it officially on record that I disagree with your decision, Sir. If it remains unchanged, then naturally I must accept it from now on and shall carry out your orders to the best of my ability."

"Naturally," said Centurion Alexios Flavius Aquila, control-ling his voice too carefully, so that it came out sounding coldly arrogant. "We shall pull out under cover of first darkness. See that there are litters and baggage beasts for the sick and wounded; and make ready to destroy all war supplies behind us."

They beat off two more attacks that day, watching their dead and wounded grow. But dusk came at last; a soft heavy dusk with clouds banking higher from the westward that promised rain by morning. The tribesmen had drawn off for a while to lick their wounds. The dusk deepened into the dark; and in the Sacellum Alexios had burned the neat stack of papers that he and the clerk had made earlier that day, knowing as he did so that he was taking the first steps on a road from which there could be no turning back. When the last flame died, he ground out under his heel the red sparks that still clung, here and there, to the edge of a charred scrap of papyrus. Then he went out to join his men drawn up and waiting the final orders.

They left the lamp burning in the Sacellum from which the standard-bearer had taken the Cohort standard, and flares wherever lights were normally kept burning, and the wells choked up with dead bodies and bent and blunted weapons, behind them.

They went out through the old north-eastern gate that had been half walled-up many years ago, circled wide to avoid the camp fires massed across the Regina road, and, their scouts going ahead, gained the trees without alerting the tribesmen. Lacking the wounded and the fever cases, they might have kept to the forest the whole way. That would have given them a better chance. As it was, they would have to come down to the road eventually. Fifteen miles of road; less than four hours' march in the normal way of things. How many before the Marcomanni were on their trail? Maybe until the trumpets failed to sound for watch-setting.

The wind was changing, the banked clouds climbing steeply up the sky; and as Alexios, heading the Rear Guard, pulled aside and turned for a moment to look back from the crest of the first ridge, a few drops of rain spattered in his face, blurring the faint blink of light from the abandoned fort. A Roman fort abandoned to the barbarians. Nothing to do now but push on, anyway.

They pushed on, through low dense scrub-oak, the ground becoming soggy underfoot as the rain grew heavier. Now the ridge was between them and the fort. No point in looking back again.

The scouts were thrusting ahead, searching out the best ways for the sick and wounded; but it was a slow business. Too slow. The ground began to rise again, and over the next hill saddle, Alexios left his optio in charge, and hurried forward to the head of the drenched and straggling column, to speak with the centurion in charge of the Van Guard.

"Centurion, we're making desperately slow progress, and it must be past watch-setting—the hunt will be up for us by now. It's time we got down to the road."

Centurion Clovius, who had served five years at Abusina, and knew the woods as well as any scout, ducked under a low-hanging branch. "Aye, we're leaving a trail like a wounded elephant that they can follow as easily as the road, anyway. And with the wounded we'll never make the climb over the Boar's Back before they come up with us. There's a track down to the road not far ahead. If the rain keeps up, it'll be a water-course by morning, but it should be good enough travelling now."

"Right then, we'll take it."

He turned back to the rear of the column, passing the word to the remaining centurions on the way.

They found the track; one of those that wound through the forest, linking village with village among the trees, and headed down it towards the road, slipping and sliding in the mud. They had almost reached it when they heard the first wolf-cry behind them in the rainy night.

All down the straggling weary line of the column, men raised their heads, tensing as they heard it, knowing it for what it was, the hunting call of the Marcomanni. Alexios sensed the sudden tension that echoed his own, breath caught, hands moving of their own accord towards sword-hilts. And then the familar surface of the road was beneath their feet.

He knew that at all costs he must get them quickly into proper marching order. To straggle down the road just as they broke from the trees would be asking for disaster. He gave the orders for "Fall in" and "Full pace," and heard them passed forward, and the ragged sound of weary and random feet steady into the quick regular beat of the forced march. It would be bad going for the wounded, but the hunted cannot choose their pace when the hunt is on their trail.

Before them, as the moon for a moment broke clear of the low scurrying cloud, was the gleam of water, where the road came down to the river marshes. On their left flank rose the dark hunched mass they called the Boar's Back. There ahead, in the narrows where the steep wooded slopes came down to the river was the place where the tribesmen would attack. If the desperate column, burdened by its sick and wounded, could get through the narrows to the open country beyond, they might yet stand a chance of making Regina. But the wolves were crying closer behind them. Closer and closer, wolf calling to wolf in the sodden dark among the trees.

The river drew nearer on their right, the wooded walls of the ridge on their left, closing in on them; and then suddenly the wolf calls, the hunting calls, were on their flanks as well as behind them; the hunt was closing in for the kill. A short way ahead of them, the steep slope of the ridge fell back a little, and between it and the road rose a hillock cut off by a shallow dip from the rest of the mass. If they could gain that, it would at least give them the advantage of higher ground.

The time when silence could matter was passed. Alexios shouted at full pitch of his lungs.

"Make for the hillock!"

And an answering shout came back to him from the head of the column.

They gained the crest, and managed some kind of formation, with the wounded and the Cohort standard in their midst, even as the first rush came; a nightmare swarming-in of shadows across the dip from the wooded ridge, and up from the marshes across the now deserted road. "Here they come!" someone shouted; and the defenders of the little knoll rose to meet them; and all round the defensive circle broke suddenly the clash of blade on blade, and the high battle-cry of the Marcomanni. The rain was passing, and the moon shone remotely down on the savage struggle for the narrow hilltop. The British Cohort was down to less than half strength, hopelessly outnumbered, and the end was beyond all doubt. The small desperate rampart of men round the wounded and the standard grew steadily smaller, falling back step by stubbornly yielded step, to close the gaps torn by the German spears. And for every tribesman who went down, it still seemed that there were two more to spring into his place.

Alexios heard his own voice shouting encouragement to his men; there were no longer any orders to be given. He plunged across to see how things were on the far side of the dwindling circle. "Centurion Clovius?"

But the moon showed him a sprawling shape, and Centurion Clovius's unanswering upturned face, above the ragged hole that grinned blackly in his throat. And somebody lying in a soggy mess of mud and blood turned his head as he passed, and deliberately spat at him.

A tribesman came charging straight in at him. He saw a horned war-cap and raised spear against the moon. And sprang to meet them in the gap left by a fallen man. He took the blow across his sword and turned it; but everywhere the line was beginning to go. Behind him as he heard the trumpeter sounding the call that had sounded over so many last stands. "To the Standard! Rally—Rally—Rally …"

And then, unbelievably, from far up the road towards Regina, came the sound of an answering trumpet.

The door opened again; but lost in his own private nightmare, Alexios did not know that someone else had come in, until the voice of Tribune Tetricus above him said, "Stand up!"

He looked up then, saw who it was, and got stiffly to his feet. "Sir—I'm sorry. I did not hear you."

They stood looking at each other; then the older man turned away and crossed to the window, walking lame with a lashing of bandage-linen round his left knee. Tribune Tetricus had led the relief force, and few had come out from that fight between the Boar's Back and the marshes unscathed.

"I have come to bring you two pieces of news," he said, speaking to the window. "Word has just come in that Abusina is back in our hands."

Alexios said, "Yes, Sir." There was not anything more to say.

"And the Inquiry is fixed for the day after tomorrow."

"Inquiry?"

The tribune gave a twitch to his shoulders. "Name of Light, man, did you not think there'd be an Inquiry? You are extremely fortunate to avoid a Court Martial!"

"I can only say in my own defence, Sir, that when those heads came over the ramparts—"

"Two heads. You never saw the third at close quarters, the tribesmen took care of that. Did it never occur to you that the

Marcomanni might well think it worth the death of, say, a wounded man or an old one past his fighting days, to make you think that none of your gallopers had got through?"

"No, Sir," Alexios said with a kind of quiet desperation, "it didn't."

"And so you lost a complete fort to a pack of rebels, and cost me the lives of twice as many men as you would have lost if you had obeyed standing orders."

"I know I took the wrong decision, Sir."

"You took the wrong decision. You can tell that to the Inquiry."

"I suppose this is where I should fall on my sword," Alexios said after a moment; and was surprised and rather shaken to find that something that had come into his mind as a black jest, had turned as he spoke it, into something that he actually meant. "But they have taken my sword away. I didn't take even that decision until too late. Perhaps you could arrange—"

Tribune Tetricus swung round from the window. "My dear Alexios, don't be so old-fashioned. Heroics of that kind went out before they split the Empire between East and West." He crossed to the door, and turned once more, his face bitter and unrelenting. He was normally a kindly soul, but he loved his men, and he had lost too many of them for kindness or even justice at the moment. "But you might try the suggestion again on the Inquiry Court. Enlist sympathy and create a good impression."

He went out, shutting the door behind him.

Alexios heard the small commonplace sound of the falling latch. He folded up once more onto the edge of the cot and went on sitting with his head in his hands. A small trickle of blood oozed from the knuckles of his right hand, where he had dashed his clenched fist against the rough-cast wall in the moment of the latch's falling. But he did not even know that he had done it.

2 | *Second Chance*

IN THE GREY AUTUMN LIGHT THE HILLS WERE DARK AND sodden and hostile. In places the heather had encroached on the old paved road, and the ponies' hooves fell suddenly soft, their legs brushing through it as through shallow water. High overhead a kestrel hung bivvering against the sky, then dropped on its unseen prey. Otherwise nothing moved but the little knot of horsemen in all the emptiness.

Alexios, already wearing the uniform of the Frontier Scouts, leather tunic over crossed-gartered breeks like any barbarian, a cloak of thick rough wool that was the dark and sullen green of mountain juniper, rode staring straight ahead of him between his pony's ears.

Behind him—more than two months behind him now—lay the Inquiry. Stern faces round the table that had been set up in the cross-hall of the Principia at Regina. Someone drumming on the table with impatient fingers. Voices that went on and on: "Grave error of judgement …" "Lack of experience rather than cowardice or deliberate treachery …" The President of the Court giving the final ruling, "That you receive a severe reprimand to be placed on the records, and that you be relieved of your post forthwith." And afterwards, the voice of one young officer speaking to another in the colonnade: "Of course if it were you or me it would be the end of our careers altogether; but then neither of us has the Dux Britanniarum for an uncle."

Behind him was the summons to Britain. Two days' leave

spent on the family farm in the southern Down Country. His half-Greek mother crying with soft desolation; she was somewhat given to tears; and demanding to know was it for this that she had left her people in Ephesus and come to bear a son and spend her widowhood on this cold rim of the world; saying that what his father would have said she could not think. Telling him again and again how grateful he must be to his Uncle Marius for having applied for him to be transferred back to Britain and found another posting for him. Finally, waving a damp kerchief after him as he rode away.

Behind him also, one long and most unpleasant interview with the Dux Britanniarum in his headquarters at Eburacum.

"Command of the Frontier Scouts up at Castellum," his uncle had said. "Command of an Ordo—two Centuries in place of the one that you have commanded until now—and of the fort itself. Promotion to the rank of Ducenarius. It sounds like advancement, doesn't it? Make no mistake, it's not. You're an incompetent soldier, unfit to serve in a decent auxiliary cohort, so—it's the Frontier Wolves for you. And don't ask me how they came by their fond-name, you'll find out soon enough. They may make some kind of man of you, if they don't arrange for you to have a fatal accident instead. I believe that has happened before now."

Alexios had tried desperately to keep a grip on things, himself included. "Sir, I do not need to be told what I have done, nor what I deserve; I am only too well aware of both, and too bitterly sorry. I can but thank you for all that you have done for me in the past, and for this chance to redeem myself. I will do all that I may to deserve it."

"I suppose your mother told you to apologize and say thank you, like a good boy," Uncle Marius said, not bothering to keep the scorn out of his voice.

Alexios, feeling like a whipped cur, had still hung on to himself. "I hope I should have done both, without her prompting."

"And I suppose she thinks I did it all for her sake, eh?"

"She *is* your sister, Sir. The whole army knows it."

"Half-sister," Uncle Marius said with asperity. "Ah well, even a weeping half-sister is easier to yield to than to withstand. But she is mistaken; the whole army is mistaken. All that I have done for you was done for your father's sake, not hers. He was the best friend I ever had, I never had a son of my own, and I wanted his son to do well. I see now that I was mistaken in my dealings with you, all along. I hope to God I'm not mistaken now. Get out!"

And Alexios had got out, horrified to find himself shaking from head to foot and on the edge of laughter, with most assuredly nothing to laugh about. He must stop it, or he would end in the ultimate shame of tears here in the open forecourt. He had managed to straighten up and get as far as his sleeping quarters. Then he had kicked the door shut and flung himself down on the narrow cot with his head in his arms.

All that was behind him, and falling further and further away with every beat of his pony's hooves; and ahead, as the road crested a shallow moorland ridge, the land changed, and the wilderness fell back as they reached the edge of the crop-lands. Away to the right a man was ploughing, a wheeling, crying cloud of gulls following the heavy ox-drawn plough. And ahead too, crouching like an old scarred hound between the waters of the great estuary that shone sword-grey beyond it, and the brown thatch of the native settlement that huddled on its landward side, Alexios saw the fort that was to be his command.

The optio of the little escort, riding beside him, pointed. "There's Castellum, Sir."

As though he needed to be told.

Alexios nodded. It should have been a proud moment, this first sight of his first command. But it was the end of something, not the beginning. He was going to rust out what was left of his soldiering days here. He was done. Finished. Broke.

He found that he had dropped his gaze from the distant fort, and was staring down at his bridle hand; at the flawed emerald ring with its intaglio-cut dolphin on his signet finger. An old and battered ring that had come down to him through a long and proud line of soldiers. And the only thing he could do for them now, having utterly failed them, was to take his beating in a way that wouldn't shame them still further. The engraved stone was dark and secret, giving back nothing but the cold surface reflection of the autumn sky. It had nothing to say to him. Well he could do without. He straightened in the saddle, bracing his shoulders with a small jerk that was not lost on the men riding behind him.

And so they clattered up the last stretch, between the settlement and the roughly cleared practice ground, between the gravestones of men who had died there, since the Eagles first flew north, and in through the Praetorian gate of Castellum.

Later that evening, supper over, Alexios sat with the outgoing Commander and the rest of the fort's officers over a jug of wine in the Mess. The upward light from the three-flamed lamp on the table threw their shadows far up the roughly plastered walls behind them and brought their faces forward into sharp relief. The red-faced and balding Quartermaster, drinking himself into a quiet stupor, according, as Alexios later found, to his nightly custom; the sallow, long-nosed man with the serpent-staff on the breast of his tunic, who was the fort's Medic. The two hundred-captains, Centenarius Lucius, square, dark and a little wooden, and Centenarius Hilarion, lank, lean and freckled, pale eyes that glinted and flickered under a cap of straight sandy hair. Druim, leader of the fort's handful of Arcani, the "eyes-and-ears in the dark," who, if their reputation spoke the truth, knew when a leaf fell, three days beyond the old Northern Wall. Mouse hair in thick braids, framing a blue-eyed face apparently as open as the day.

Alexios took them in without, he hoped, seeming to stare too closely; the faces of the men who would be his officers in three days' time. Guarded faces that as yet told him nothing of the men behind them. At the head of the table, Ducenarius Julius Gavros, the outgoing Commander, had turned reminiscent, which he supposed was not surprising under the circumstances.

"When I first served with the Frontier Scouts, the whole Numerus was stationed at Castra Exploratorum. We were responsible for patrolling the whole of the lowlands in those days. Now, of course, we are split up—well you will have seen that for yourself, on your way up here. One Ordo doubling up with the regular garrison at Habitancum, for scouting and security immediately in front of the Wall; one at Bremenium, under the Praepositus himself; also doubled up with a part-mounted auxiliary force and the main body of the Arcani, but the nearest thing we have now to a headquarters. One up here at Castellum, almost on the old Northern Wall; something over two hundred of us, counting Druim's lovely lads, rattling around in a fort that was originally built to house a full cohort. We are the forward observation post; our job to keep things quiet in general and an eye on the Picts in particular. It's a flimsy arrangement. None of us could do much about backing the others up if trouble started. The old way was better."

"Why the change?" Alexios asked.

Julius Gavros shrugged. "We've had peace in the north for a good while now. Sea-raiders in the south, yes, but up here things have been quiet, comparatively speaking. And the Higher

Command doesn't much like—or trust—irregular units in peace time. If it can't do away with them, the next best thing is to split them up."

"And let us admit," said Centenarius Lucius quietly into the depth of his wine-cup, "that no unit was ever much more irregular than the Frontier Wolves."

Hilarion had risen and moved across to the window, and stood with his arm along the high sill, listening. Somewhere outside in the night men were singing, without words; raising a strange haunting mouth-music above the rhythm of a softly tapped drum. "The Pack is giving tongue. Aye well, it's the full of the moon." He swung back to the table in one stride, and flung himself down opposite Alexios, grinning. "Your new Command. The tribesmen more than half believe that we swear some kind of kinship with the wolves; and the mothers tell their children that if we bite them they'll end up howling to the moon themselves."

"However, we seldom bite them," Lucius said gently.

Maybe not so wooden after all, Alexios decided.

Julius Gavros laughed. "It could be a useful reputation to have."

"You see! You're beginning to think like one of us! That's why you've been posted down to Habitancum! Oh I know it's promotion but it's also closer in to civilization." Hilarion picked up his cup and drank. "Ah me, so soon as we get the Commander comfortably into our way of thinking, the powers above send us a new one, and it's all to do again."

"No disrespect to the new Commander intended, Sir." Druim lifted his eyes deliberately to Alexios's face, and spoke for the first time in a long while.

"Who would ever think such a thing?" Hilarion said lazily into the sudden quiet. "Surely not the new Commander? He must be as aware as we, of the honour done us by his posting here." He uncoiled himself slowly from his lounging position, and sat up very straight.

Alexios stiffened, and gave him back look for look. "I am not sure that I understand."

Lucius said quickly, "Nobody ever understands Hilarion when the moon is full." Then to Hilarion himself, "Leave it."

Hilarion did not seem to hear his fellow centenarius. "Who could have dreamed that the Frontier Wolves would ever come up in the world to the point of being commanded by the nephew of the Governor of North Britain?"

Nothing more. But the silence drew out taut as a bowstring. Alexios was sharply aware of the men—even, somewhat owlishly, the Quartermaster—looking on. The thing had turned suddenly to deadly earnest. His mouth felt dry, and he knew that if the outgoing Commander made the least attempt to help him, he was finished. He stared back into the bright narrowed gaze of Centenarius Hilarion, and knew that he must not look away.

"We must hope that the Frontier Wolves prove themselves worthy of the honour done them," he said at last, coolly pleasant. "Will you pass the wine-jug, Centenarius?"

And so the moment passed.

That night in the outer room of the Commander's quarters, where a makeshift bed had been set up for the newcomer, Ducenarius Gavros said, "I'm sorry about what happened in Mess this evening."

"I suppose the whole fort knows," Alexios said, miserably.

"Considering the detailed knowledge of their officers' most private affairs possessed by all self-respecting troops, there can be no doubt of that," Gavros nodded. "That is why we are having a full-dress take-over parade tomorrow morning, and you are going to walk up and down the ranks with me and look every one of them straight in the eye as though you didn't give a broken sandal strap."

Alexios looked back into the face of the older man. It was a face that had been used hard by life and wild weather; and there was wisdom in it.

"The Tribes, too?" He wanted to know to the full what he had to handle.

"Not from the troops, anyway. The Frontier Wolves deal with their own affairs. They may give you a hard time of it themselves, until and unless you earn in their eyes the right to command them—that is the lot of every new Commander. But they'll not let outsiders in on the game."

And he was gone into the inner sleeping chamber, the heavy curtain swinging across behind him.

Left alone, Alexios pulled his leather tunic over his head, then sat down on the makeshift sleeping bench to untie the cross-gartering of his breeks. But after a few moments he let his hands fall idle across his knees, and sat staring at the opposite wall.

"They may make some kind of man of you—if they don't arrange for you to have a fatal accident instead," said Uncle Marius's voice in his memory. It would be humiliating, the last failure, to be murdered by one's own men. Otherwise, he thought, he did not much care. Not as much as he cared about and dreaded what he was going to have to face in the morning anyway.

But in the morning, he walked beside Ducenarius Gavros up and down the ranks of the Third Ordo, Frontier Wolves, drawn up with their mounts on the practice ground outside the fort, and looked every man of them straight in the eye as though he didn't give a broken sandal strap.

He had seen the gate guard and a few of them scattered about the fort when he rode in the evening before. But he never forgot the first full sight of his new command. The British Auxiliaries at Abusina had been a fairly shaggy lot, but they had borne some sort of resemblance to Roman soldiers. These, each standing with an arm through the bridle of his rough-coated pony, seemed to belong to another world. Looking along the lines, Alexios saw men, long and rangy for the most part, clad in greasy and weatherworn leather tunics and cross-gartered breeks, even their iron-bound caps three-parts hidden under the snarling head of the wolfskin cloak each man wore pulled forward over it. Nothing to suggest the Eagles about them at all, save the straightness of the lines themselves, and here and there a belt buckle or a long-service bracelet.

They stood easily, feet a little apart, and looked back at him out of hard-bitten wind-burned faces, rogues' faces, some of them, cautious or reckless, cunning or blank, all of them careful to give nothing away. But in them all, binding them together, something that was different from the oneness of other army units. Maybe it was the oneness of the wolf-pack. Alexios did not know. He only knew that he was shut out from it, and that he felt curiously naked to the thin salt-scented wind off the Bodotria Estuary that set the red woollen fly-whisks swinging from the ponies' bridles and parted their manes and tails and the harsh grey hairs of the wolfskin cloaks, and lifted out the thin vivid sleeve of emerald silk that formed the body of the Ordo's dragon standard.

He gave his shoulders that small betraying jerk, and walked on, up one line and down the next, taking that first long steady look at his new command; while at the same time from behind their carefully unbetraying faces, the Third Ordo, Frontier Scouts, took their first long steady look at their new Commander.

They saw a dark slight young man, with thick black brows that almost met across an arrogant nose, and just above their meeting place faintly raised on the olive skin, the brand of the Raven Degree of Mithras; a grey, haughty stare, a boy's mouth that had not yet firmed into a man's. The Dux's cub. They knew—their old Commander had been right—how and why he came to be there; and what they saw did not look to them promising. But more than one of them had murky patches on their own past records, and for the present they were prepared to withhold judgement ...

It was over at last. The horse-holders brought up the two waiting ponies; and when, following Ducenarius Gavros, Alexios had swung into the saddle, he heard the barked orders of the centenarii, and watched the single well-trained movement as two hundred men set their hands on their ponies' withers and made their own steed-leap. Another order, and they moved off at a hand-canter towards the Praetorian gate. At their head, the standard-bearer raised high the Ordo Dragon on its lance-shaft, and the wind of their going, flowing in through the snarling fantastic mask of bronze and silver wires that formed the head, filled the vivid silken sleeve so that it streamed out behind like an emerald flame, the one point of brilliant colour in all that scene of dark moorland hues.

The practice ground emptied like a cup, left to the thin salt-scented wind and the gulls crying over the shining mud flats left by the ebbtide.

"That was well done," said Julius Gavros quietly, beside him, as they heeled their own mounts into a walk and headed back the same way.

3 | The Hall of Ferradach Dhu

ALEXIOS HAD VAGUELY EXPECTED THAT THE REST OF THE day would be taken up with the office work of the hand-over. But "First things first," said Julius Gavros. "This morning I have shown you and the Ordo to each other, now you come with me to make your salute to Ferradach Dhu."

"Ferradach Dhu?"

"Clan Chieftain of the Votadini in these parts."

"In the town here?" Alexios had glimpsed straight streets and stone walls as he rode in; the corner of a colonnade, a memorial arch rising above the warm huddle of bracken-thatched roofs; enough to suggest more than the turf-walled chaos of tradesmen's booths and wine-shops and the bothies where the garrison kept their women and their hunting dogs, that always sprang up in the lee of any strong-post of Rome.

"Not Ferradach Dhu. The old Eagle holds to his own eyrie."

"Ah—over that way." Alexios jerked a thumb eastward in the direction of the vast wave-break of rock maybe an hour's march away that he had seen yesterday from the road. Certainly it had the look of an eagle's eyrie, brooding there above the moors.

Gavros shook his head, rubbing up the buckle of his swordbelt. "That's the old strong-point of the High King. The War-Capital. There's no one there in time of peace, and the High King rules the Clans of the Votadini from Traprain Law, far over to the south-east."

So just short of noon, with a small escort riding behind them, they clattered out through the West gate, the Dextra gate, and took the steep track plunging to the river that came down from the high moors to join the Bodotria just below the fort.

The wind funnelling up the river gorge made bluish zigzag partings in the wolfskin cloak which Julius Gavros wore, like his men, with its snarling prick-eared head pulled forward over his war-cap. And looking, Alexios saw that it was mounted on the regulation dark green military cloak such as he himself was wearing. Was that one of the things one did? One of the things that made one a Frontier Wolf, officers and men alike?

Gavros glanced round and caught him looking. "There's good sense in it," he said, as though Alexios had spoken aloud. "Good against the north wind; and the head over one's own war-cap helps to break up the outline against a hillside."

"But for all that, I take it it's not army issue," Alexios said.

"The hide of our brothers? No. Every man of the Numerus kills his own wolf—with spear or dagger of course, not the bow. Just the one wolf, and never another except in self defence or dire need of a new cloak. Boar or stag or bear are for hunting, yes, but not our four-footed brothers. It's the custom of the Pack." Gavros's leathery face cracked into a grin. "The Frontier Scouts may be something short on spit and polish, but they have as many customs as the Praetorians, and all of them just as jealously guarded."

Just where the track dipped to the paved ford below the ponies' watering pool, a tall stone stood up, leaning a little, in the wayside grass. Dark, smooth, with somehow the look about it of having passed through fire; the look too of being very old, older than anything else in that countryside. As they trotted by, Gavros leaned from his saddle and lightly touched the smooth worn crest in passing. And Alexios, glancing round for another view of the thing, saw the leader of the escort echo the gesture, and the man behind him …

He looked again at Gavros, but the Ducenarius was staring straight between his pony's ears. Another custom of the Pack, he supposed, and clearly one that you did not ask about. Ah well, there'd be time for finding out about such things later—too much time, maybe. So much time that childish things became important because they helped to fill it up a little. A small cold shiver took him between the shoulders; the kind of shiver out of nowhere that makes men laugh and say that a grey goose is flying over their graves.

They splashed across the ford, and climbed up through the alder and hazel scrub that furred the far side of the river gorge, and headed westward. On their left for a while there was more crop-land, fallow and stubble flickered over by clouds of green plover; on their right the grey waters of the estuary, narrowing as they went, and the sullen darkness of the Caledonian hills beyond; wild country, barbarian country, beyond all frontiers.

Gavros pointed along the track. "This is the road to Credigone—what remains of it; and over beyond, what remains of the old Northern Wall."

"It doesn't seem as though it sees much traffic," Alexios said, looking down at the rutted track and the hill turf that had spread half across the way.

"The Frontier Wolves have not much use for roads." Gavros said, "and the Credigone garrison moved out when the world was young. Nothing but foxes to lair up there now; and the Wall is not much more than a mark on men's minds. It is still a kind of frontier, but for long stretches you would never know it was there at all save for an outcropping bank here and there, with a tangle of hawthorn and bramble in the ditch below it."

In a short while they left the road and turned away southwestward leaving the Bodotria behind them; leaving also, all traces of farmed land. Soon the track they followed dwindled to no more than the faint trace left by feet and hooves following by custom the same line from one point to another. They climbed steadily, the faint track dipping from time to time into small deep valleys choked up with hazel woods, but always lifting again towards the high moors. The black tide of last summer's heather and the white tufted bog-grass brushed about the ponies' legs. Once, three ravens flapped up, laden, from the carcass of a foundered deer, as they passed by. Once, two horsemen showed up for a moment on the crest of a nearby ridge, then dropped out of sight below the skyline. Otherwise nothing moved in the emptiness save for the grey drift of cloud that trailed its own shadows and stray rags of sunshine across the hills. And always, Alexios thought, the desolation breathing between one's shoulder-blades. Even more than at his first sight of the German forests, he felt that here indeed he had come to the uttermost end of the earth. But maybe that was because the German forests had not been without a glimmer of hope between the trees.

"Of course you will understand," said Ducenarius Gavros after a while, "that when on patrol, we do not in the general way of things head straight across country getting ourselves skylined on the crest of every ridge."

Alexios came back to himself. "I imagine it's a question of good manners. This is a courtesy visit."

Gavros looked round at him. "I begin to have hopes of you."

"My thanks," Alexios said gravely. "Why especially Ferradach Dhu? There must be many clan chieftains of the Votadini."

"There are. And you'll meet most of the nearer ones, in one way or another, as time goes by. Ferradach Dhu because Castellum stands on his Clan Territory which runs almost to the foot of the Fortress Rock. It is good to be on friendly terms with the man in whose hunting runs one eats and sleeps."

They rode on some way in silence; and then Alexios asked, "How friendly are the tribes—ah, I know that at one time all this was a full-blown Roman province, but now—" he glanced round him at the desolation, "one wonders."

"The Votadini? How long is a length of picket rope?" Gavros had opened up a little gap between themselves and the following escort, and it came to Alexios that probably this was the kind of talk that passed between incoming and outgoing commanders of irregular troops the length and breadth of the Empire.

"We live very close to the Tribes," Gavros was saying. "It has been like that for more than a hundred years up here. We're bound together by the threat of the Caledoni—the Picts, the Painted People from the North. It's chiefly to keep them from jumping the Old Wall that the Frontier Scouts are here; and to keep an eye open for the Attacotti sea-raiders from Hibernia. And for most of that time the friendship has held well enough, save for the odd cattle raid and a bit of unrest after a bad harvest. There's kinship between us, of course; half our men are locally recruited—younger sons for the most part—and the rest are mostly Dalriads from the north-west over beyond the Wall, close kin to the Attacotti. Odd, that, when you come to think of it."

"Dangerous too, surely, if ever there was trouble," said Alexios. "Wasn't that why we never used to have auxiliaries serving in their own province?"

"Divided loyalties? The Frontier Wolves bring their loyalties with them, and once they have joined the Family, that's it, and if need be they'll fight to the death against their own blood kin. And yet the kinship does remain. Of friendship, I'm not so sure. Friendship doesn't always come into it with brothers. Love or hate, yes, sometimes both together; not always friendship. Do you know?"

"I have no brothers," Alexios said.

"You'll learn, as time goes on. But don't be in a hurry to think you know it all. The Frontier Wolves are not the Third Britannica that you knew at Abusina, and they aren't the Emperor's bodyguard. They take a good deal of knowing. But they're worth it."

"You must hate handing them over to me," Alexios said.

"I'd hate handing them over to anyone. The Lord Mithras knows, I've waited long enough for promotion, but now it has come … Ah well, it's only one step up, from the Third Ordo to the Second; from Castellum to Habitancum. Once I hoped for a bigger step up. I was young then. Now I'm glad I shall still be with the Numerus. Once a Frontier Wolf, always a Frontier Wolf, I reckon."

He turned the subject, which Alexios guessed had got too near to the quick. "The Arcani, now they're a different sheaf of arrows. They're much the same blood as the rest, but they have their own native officers. Druim is the son of a chieftain of the Damnoni, further to the west. They are the eyes and ears of the frontier forces; I expect you've heard that. Not a leaf falls for three days north of the Old Wall, or a man for that matter, that they don't know about it. But sometimes I think that they ride too much alone, and listen to too many strange stories, and dream strange dreams. Dreams are generally dangerous."

As they crested the next ridge, he turned a little in the saddle and pointed. "We arrive."

Before them opened a shallow moorland valley, through which a small swift-running burn looped its way among birch and rowan to the dim blueness of far-off lowlands. And on the steep out-thrust shoulder of the opposite hillside, Alexios saw a huddle of turf-roofed and heather-thatched bothies huddled companionably within a thorn hedge, much like other villages that he had seen on his way north. And in the midst of it, the whale-backed shape that he guessed must be the Chieftain's Hall, rearing itself above the rest; the faint blue waft of hearth-smoke trailing southward over all.

They splashed through the ford, and headed up towards the village. Cattle and brood-mares with their foals still at heel were grazing on the cleared hillsides, and turned their heads to watch them pass, then went on grazing. Within the thorn hedge, women spinning in bothy doorways or grinding the next day's corn, glanced up as they rode by. Here and there a man was going about his own affairs, a bridle in his hand or a riding-rug on his shoulder. From the smithy came the bright ring of hammer on anvil. Ducks and piglets scattered quacking and squealing from under the ponies' hooves, and a handful of children ran in their wake. It seemed a friendly enough place, this Rath of Ferradach Dhu. Also it seemed to be expecting them. Alexios remembered the two horsemen on the ridge. Seemingly the tribes also had their eyes-and-ears.

They dismounted in the Chieftain's forecourt, and leaving their horses to two of the escort, turned to the firelit shadows beyond the entrance of the Hall, which stood open for all comers according to the custom of wild places.

A young warrior sitting cross-legged on the threshold with his spear across his knees, got up and stood aside, and they went in under the heather-thatch and the blue and saffron painted lintel beam.

Ferradach Dhu sat beside the fire on the central hearth, also with a spear across his knees; a beautiful spear with a blade as long and fluidly shaped as a flame, which he was burnishing as man may fondle the head of a favourite hound. A huge man, he must have been once, Alexios thought. The wreck of a huge man now, the skin hanging dry and loose over the big gaunt bones, the crow-black hair that must have given him his name, showing now only a dark streak here and there among the grey, though he was no more than middling old. And he sat sunk in his chair, huddled deep in his magnificent deerskin robe, as though the blazing logs had no power to warm him from the autumn chill. But the eyes sunk far into his gaunt face were full and darkly brilliant as a falcon's and the traces of old fierce laughter still clung about the corners of his mouth.

He sat and watched them a moment in the doorway—then raised a huge bony hand from his spear. "Let you come in to the fire. The sun fades, and the wind strikes colder every fall-of-the-leaf since I took that boar tusk in my flank."

"Ferradach, Lord of Six Hundred Spears," Julius Gavros made a slight bending of the head, "I bring you Ducenarius Alexios Flavius Aquila, who will command at Castellum after me." He spoke, like the Chieftain, in the British tongue, and though it was very different from the same tongue of the south, Alexios was relieved to find that he could understand most of what they said, as he bent his head in turn and followed Gavros to the hearth.

"It is a shadow on my heart that the Old Wolf leaves us," said the Chieftain, as they settled themselves on the skin-covered stools that seemed to have been set ready for them.

"On the Old Wolf's also," said Gavros. "But the Young Wolf will fill my place none so ill, when he has learned the way of it. Give him your help and counsel when he needs it, as you gave it to me when first I came this way."

Ferradach Dhu turned his gaze full on Alexios for the first time.

"He does not look to me to have the making of the Wolf-kind," he said candidly. "Too smooth. Too like the lily boys of the Governor's staff who I saw in my youth when I took the horse draughts for the army south beyond the Wall. Nevertheless, I will do as my brother, the Old Wolf, asks." He turned and called behind him, "Shula, my son's woman, bring here the Guest Cup."

A girl rose from her seat below one of the small high windows where she had been stitching at the chequered lining of a cloak, and disappeared into some inner place, and in a little, returned with a bronze cup which she carried first to Alexios, being the stranger among them.

She spoke carefully in Latin, "Drink, and be welcome."

And Alexios, rising to take the cup from her, answered in the tongue of the tribes, "Good fortune on the house, and on the woman of the house," and drank, and gave it back into her hands.

The Chieftain looked up quickly. "So-o! He knows our tongue and his manners, both—or did you teach him that?"

"Not I." Gavros took the cup and spoke the words of courtesy in his turn. "He speaks it as well as you speak Latin when you choose."

Ferradach Dhu raised shaggy brows at the newcomer. "How comes that about? You have not the look of the tribes in you."

Alexios said with a flicker of laughter, "Maybe I take after the first of my line to come following the Eagles and strike his roots in Britain. He was from Etruria, and the men of those parts are narrow-built and dark. But I do not think he was a lily boy on any governor's staff. I had a British grandmother, and my old nurse came to us through the slave market from Erin; and they both sang me the songs of their own people before ever I knew my father's tongue. The speech of the Votadini sounds something strange to me, as mine must do to you, but time shall mend that, Lord of Six Hundred Spears."

The girl had bought little hard apples, and barleycakes sweating with wild honey; and they sat eating and sharing the great Guest Cup between them; the two older men talking together as familiar friends. Alexios, feeling that he had given enough account of himself for good manners, sat silent, taking in his surroundings. He felt oddly detached from it all, as though he were not part of the scene himself but standing outside it and looking at it with interest like someone studying a wall-painting.

He was looking at the Hall of a Celtic Chief, at first sight almost untouched by Rome. Fine skins and woven hangings, their brilliant colours darkened by smoke, lined the walls behind the benches where the Hearth Companions would gather in the evening when the harper made his songs and the drink horns went round. The roof trees and the great tiebeams overhead were painted with strange interlacing spandrels of colour that seemed to echo the upward-eddying of the hearth smoke. There was a faint stable-smell about the place, and from beyond the hangings at the far end of the Hall came the stamp of a hoof, and the sound of a horse ruckling down its nose. There must be more space beyond there, and used as a stable. A man who had served with the Tenth at Beersheba had once told Alexios that the Desert People often kept their favourite horses in their own tents. Not only the Desert People, it seemed. The Master of the Hall leaned forward, and the beads of a great barbaric necklace of amber and twisted gold showed at the neck folds of his deerskin robe. But the girl, who had gone back to her stitching beneath the window, wore delicate gold drops in her ears such as Alexios's own mother wore, and the window above her head had thick greenish glass in it like the windows of the Commander's quarters back at Castellum. And though the bronze Guest Cup with its circling sun-dance patterns was of the tribes, the bowls in which she had brought the apples and honeycakes were of fine red Samian ware, one with a pattern of struggling gladiators on it, one showing Dionysus strangling the pirate ship with vines growing up the mast while he turned the crew into dolphins. Even the Chieftain's own crosslegged chair stood on finely carved antelope feet. The Hall of Ferradach Dhu, he decided, was a British chieftain's hall and not a Roman villa-house only because the Lord of Six Hundred Spears deliberately chose to hold to the old ways. Probably there were many more of the same kind, up here in the wild lands, where the frontier ebbed and flowed like a tide, and the world of Rome seemed so very far away …

Behind the voices of the two men he caught the sound of horses' hooves from the outside world. Two horses, drawing nearer, coming to a trampling halt, in some stable court, he supposed, at the back of the Hall. A little later voices sounded outside; both young, one light and hard, the other deeper and rough at the edges with anger.

"Risk your own neck if you want to," the deeper voice was saying, "that is no reason to risk the neck of your horse!"

"Why not, then?" demanded the other. "I risk mine; why should he not be risking his?"

"Because he has no choice."

"If he had, he would be choosing as I choose. Horses will always give me what I ask of them."

"Then have a care as to what you ask, little brother. You have come near to killing a good horse before now—"

The hanging at the far end of the Hall was swung aside and two young men came through in full quarrel, bright-eyed and flushed with anger. But they broke off at sight of the two Roman officers by the hearth. Clearly, as with most brothers, quarrelling was a thing one did in private, and not before the outside world.

The girl under the window raised her head as they passed her, and a look like a touch went to and fro between her and the elder brother. Then she went on with her sewing. Ferradach looked up also as they came towards the fire. "Ah, you are here at last, my two fine sons. Did I not send you word, long since, that the Commander and the new Commander of Castellum rode this way?"

"It was the day for backing the red stallion, my father," said the elder brother. "Our hands and heads were full, and the time ran swifter than we knew." He turned to Gavros, "Wolf Commander, we meant no discourtesy."

The younger, speaking no word, sat down on the piled skins beside the hearth, and helped himself to a honeycake.

"Nay now," Gavros said, "I did but come to take my leave of the Chief your father, and bring before him the man who comes after me." He gave a small gesture of the hand towards Alexios, making the introduction again, "Ducenarius Alexios Flavius Aquila."

The younger brother took a long leisurely look at Alexios, and another bite of honeycake. "That's a fine big name, but maybe you'll grow to it in time," he said encouragingly, licking honey off his forefinger.

The Chief smiled, "He speaks our tongue."

There was a moment's surprised pause, and then the elder said, "Then Ducenarius Alexios Flavius Aquila, I will tell you in our tongue, that I am Cunorix, first son of the Chief here, and that this, with his manners forgotten and his mouth full of honeycake, is Connla, my brother."

They looked at each other, the blue hearth smoke, sideways

driven by a gust of wind from the door, fronding about them. Alexios saw that Cunorix was maybe his own age, and Connla a year or so younger. The first son short and strong-boned, with rough hair the russet brown of winter beech leaves, a straight-looking pair of eyes, a mouth like a frog's; a rather ugly young man, but the kind whose shield-shoulder you could rely on against your own in a scrap. The other, taller and slighter, with a mane of blazing copper hair, and skin that showed milky as a girl's in the firelight, a reckless, laughing, wicked face. Life would never be dull in Connla's company, Alexios thought, but relying on his shield-shoulder might be another matter.

Gavros and the Chieftain had returned to their own talk, and the three young men might have had the Hall to themselves.

Connla helped himself to a third honeycake, and said, "Would the new Commander be wanting a good hunting pony?"

"Wanting, yes," Alexios said, "but the new Commander has a light purse at the moment. Ask that again when he has had time to save some pay."

"Aye me, that may be a long wait, I'm thinking."

Alexios stiffened a little. He had already gathered that the pay of the Frontier Wolves was generally in arrears, but that was a matter for the Frontier Wolves.

Cunorix's thick russet brows twitched together, and he cut in quickly, "Meanwhile, if the Commander wishes for a day's hunting, when he has had time to draw breath and find his way about Castellum, it would be a simple thing to bring over a couple of hounds and a spare pony."

"And a wolf-spear," said Connla, nothing abashed, his eyes flickering over the dark green stuff of Alexios's cloak.

"I am thinking that I could come by a wolf-spear for myself," Alexios said. "For the day's hunting, that is another matter, and when the day comes, I will gladly take you up on that offer."

And both in the same instant the soldier and the Chieftain's elder son leaned forward and struck hands like men sealing a bargain. Maybe a bargain that concerned more than a day's hunting.

Alexios did not even notice that in that moment the long smoky Hall had ceased to be remotely interesting like a wall-painting, and had warmed out of its own shadows and become real about him.

But the last memory that Alexios brought away from that day's courtesy visit to Ferradach, Lord of Six Hundred Spears, was an oddly chilling one.

For as he and Gavros rode down through the rath, the escort once more trotting behind them, a tall man in a dark hooded cloak turned to watch them go by. And Alexios, glancing under the hood, met a pair of eyes as brilliant as the Chieftain's own, but with the brilliance of hate. He made a small gesture as though to spit on the ground at his feet, which for swiftness and venom was like the strike of a snake, then turned, swinging the dark folds of his cloak behind him, and strode away.

"And who was that?" Alexios asked, as they rode out between the rough stone gateposts, and across the causeway.

"Morvidd, their holy man," Gavros said, without looking round.

"He doesn't seem to love us."

"The native oak priests have long memories, and few of them have much love for the forces of Rome, even now. Also, a year or two back, I had personal dealings with Morvidd after a bad harvest. He was demanding a human sacrifice, and I—reasoned with him."

"Reasoned?" Alexios said.

"I threatened him in the end with the full wrath of the Legions, and the pulling down of his sacred stones. He cannot have understood how little power I had to carry out any threat, for he went to a great deal of trouble to call down the wrath of his gods and put a death curse on me. But it must be that Mithras is stronger than Morvidd's gods, for I did not drop dead as he bade me, though there *was* a thunderstorm. Therefore," Gavros gave a small crack of laughter, "Morvidd was made to look small in the eyes of Ferradach Dhu and his people. They don't, I judge, give him as many of their best cattle as they used to do. He has suffered in purse and power, and if ever he gets the chance to do us harm, I daresay he will."

"I'll remember that," said Alexios.

A silver-gilt gleam of evening sun had broken through the drifting clouds as they came down to the river ford below Castellum and splashed through; and beside the uphill track, the tall black stone had warmed into unsuspected colour, in the golden dappling of lichen on its weathered flank, and the silken gleam almost like the neck-feathers of a starling, on its poll that had been smoothed through the years by the touch of many hands. Gavros leaned from the saddle in passing and touched it; a light quick touch as though in greeting, as he had done when they set out at noon. And for a moment, Alexios riding behind him almost did the same. Almost but not quite. Gavros had been too long in the wilderness. As for himself, if he was going to rust out the rest of his days in this lost corner of the Empire, the time would come soon enough when he'd be touching bits of black stone with the best of them. But not *yet*! Great God Mithras, not just yet!

4 | *The New Commander*

TWO MORNINGS LATER, HAVING HANDED OVER THE GARRISON and the keys of the pay-chest and as much knowledge of the job as he could in the short time at his disposal, Ducenarius Julius Gavros rode south.

Alexios, standing in the Praetorian gate to watch him away, was unpleasantly aware of panic rising in his belly as the outgoing Commander with his little escort topped the first lift of the moors and disappeared from view on the long road that led by the hearth-cold ruins of Trimontium, by the headquarters at Bremenium to Habitancum and the Wall. From now on, he was responsible for the outpost fort, and for the Third Ordo, Frontier Scouts. Any decisions to be made would be for his making; nobody else in authority nearer than Bremenium, four days' march away.

He turned from the gate, and met the eyes watching him; the eyes of the men on gate guard, the narrow half-amused gaze of Centenarius Hilarion. Surely they must see the dark tide of panic churning within him. He straightened his shoulders with that small tell-tale jerk, and walked straight through them, back to the Commander's office in the Principia, and started checking the muster roll which had no need of checking. It was all he could think of to do, just at the moment.

Over the next few days, the fort itself began to wear less of a stranger's face. The actual lay-out of course was familiar to him from the first, for the lay-out of every station of the Eagles was much the same, whether it was a mud-brick fort on the Nile or a stone one in the German forests, or a turf-and-timber outpost with stone-built gate-towers here on the old northern frontier. At least twice, since it was built by men of the Second Legion in Agricola's day, Castellum had been abandoned to the wild, and then patched up again and re-occupied. The men who had served there when Severus was their Emperor would have blasphemed to see it now, the buildings heather-thatched where tiles had been; not a window with glass in it save for a few in the Principia and the old Commander's house which now lodged all the officers together round its narrow courtyard; old grain-stores pulled down because with only half the garrison the place had been built for, there was no further need for them, and their stones used to block up half the arches of the gates. But the bones of the place were still recognizable for what they always had been. And along with the fort, Alexios grew familiar with the jetties and workshops and dilapidated storesheds which shared with the bath-house the protection of bank and stockade beyond the north gate, and formed a kind of ghost port where the river looped out to join the salt waters of the estuary below the fortress bluff. Soon he could have found his way about Castellum blindfold, as he could have found his way through the pattern of the days that started with Cock-crow sounding from the signal tower, and ended with Late Rounds made by gleam of lantern-light from guard-post to guard-post, from barrack rows to horse-lines through the dark and the wind and often enough the rain; and all the complex routine that lay between. Fatigues and arms drill and stables, patrols out and in, the careful, endless listening to reports and deciding which needed to be sent back to Bremenium and which did not …

But the men of the garrison, the Frontier Wolves, still kept their strangers' faces.

From Hilarion, his Senior Centenarius, he learned a good deal more than Julius Gavros had told him about them, beginning with the fact that the half-mad Emperor Caracalla had taken a fancy to them and called them his wolves, more than a hundred years ago, and they had treasured their name and their reputation ever since.

"We are the scum and the scrapings of the Empire," Hilarion explained one day early on, propping up the doorway of the little office beside the Sacellum. "They tipped out the garbage-bin of the Eagles to make us what we are. Oh yes, I know that for the most part we're drawn from the Votadini and the tribes of the north-west, as Gavros will have told you, but that's not the whole story. They send us up a draft from time to time to add variety to the mixture. Some of them are just hard cases, men who can't take the discipline of the regular army and have made their own units too hot to hold them. Some are thieves—I don't count horse-thieves, that's a gentleman's sport in these parts—but real undesirables, the kind that will pick a comrade's pouch while the drink is in him. Don't worry, you'll not have to deal with them, the Ordo has its own ways of dealing with its own vermin." He saw Alexios's face, and grinned. "Sometimes good comes out of evil, mind you. Once—oh long before my time, or my father's if I'd ever had one—we had half a mutinous company of Syrian archers sent up to us. They brought their bows with them; those short composite bows, good for use on horseback; that's why we're all mounted archers now."

For a sudden moment the silence prickled between them as it had done that first night of all. Then Alexios said, "And now you have me." And pushed aside the papers that he had been working on. "I regret that I am not half a company of mutinous Syrians. It's hard to see what good can come out of evil in this case, isn't it."

"Hard, but not impossible. You may have hidden talents—

You're the best swordsman we've seen on the practice ground in my time anyway."

Hilarion abandoned the doorpost and came to lean his hands on the writing-table. He seldom stood upright when there was anything to lean on—and for a moment there was a flicker of something that might almost be friendliness in his tone. "No need to up with your hackles, Ducenarius Aquila, Sir. You should be very grateful to your noble uncle. If he had pulled a few more strings and got you into a respectable unit you'd have spent the rest of your days trying to live down that little episode on the Danubius. As it is, you're among brothers."

And with a wide half-mock salute, he went about his own affairs.

Listening to his long lazy footsteps growing fainter on the pavement of the cross-hall and the forecourt beyond, Alexios wondered whether his Senior Centenarius was a friend or an enemy, or simply a man who cared nothing either way for anything on earth.

He did not feel in the least as though he were among brothers.

The days went by. In the crop-lands around the fort and the town the autumn ploughing was finished. The river below the fort no longer ran yellow with birch leaves after frost, for the birch trees upstream were bare. The long eight- or ten-day patrols of summertime that had still been in operation when Alexios first arrived, drew in to the short two- or three-day patrols of winter, save for the Arcani, who came and went like shadows, disappearing for long periods deep into the Pictish lands beyond the Northern Wall. And the wild geese were flighting in from the north, filling the windy autumn nights with their hound-pack music. Everybody who could be spared from patrols or garrison duty went hunting. "The corn in the barns and the boar in the forest"; that had always been the way of it on outpost service; and that year there was less corn in the barns than usual, for the harvest had been a poor one. The supply galleys with the winter stores and the pay-chest from Segedunum—in the present state of the roads north of Bremenium, it was easier to supply the fort by sea—were late, and they looked for them anxiously as the days went by.

They arrived at last in a sleet storm; and an hour later, while the stores were being brought ashore under the Quartermaster's keen though bloodshot blue eyes, Alexios was in the Sacellum, confronting the centurion of the marine escort across the open pay-chest.

"It's all there, Sir," the centurion was saying, holding out a pair of tablets. "Will you sign for it?"

"I agree that it is all there, as to this half-year's pay," Alexios said, making no move to take the tablets, "but there's still twenty-seven thousand denarii overdue on the last lot."

"I don't know anything about that, Sir. Here's this half-year's pay for the garrison of Castellum. It was the correct amount when it was handed over to me, and it is the correct amount now."

The sentry on the doorway was swept aside and the Quarter-master stamped in. "Sir—will you look at this." And he thrust a handful of raisins under Alexios's nose.

"Later, Kaeso," Alexios said without looking, "I have more important matters—"

"Nothing is more important than raisins. These are mildewed and there's dirt in them. They have sent us up stale stock."

He was right, Alexios thought, the ridiculous little man was right. Nothing, well few things, were more important than raisins. Along with cheese and barley-bannock and a few strips of dried meat they formed the staple ration of the patrols.

He looked down. "Yes, they're mouldy. What in the black name of Ahriman do you suggest that we do about it?"

"Sir, will you sign this," the marine centurion said wearily.

But the Quartermaster was in full spate. "… some pot-bellied official at the Corstopitum depot! Ever since Constantine went it's been going from bad to worse, until now. Do you reckon this new young pup Constans has ever heard of Britain? The administration is going to the dogs, and who suffers? The soldiers! Always the soldiers! One of these days he'll have a revolt on his hands!"

The marine rounded on him. "You'd best write and tell the Emperor that lot!"

"Quartermaster," Alexios said in a voice which rather unexpectedly cut his splutterings off short, "go and see to the rest of the stores and report their condition to me. *I* shall most assuredly write—not to the Emperor, but at any rate to the depot."

"Not that I imagine it will do the least good," he added, to the marine, when the angry little officer had departed.

The marine shrugged. "The arrears of pay may be made up later or not, whether you write or not. You'll not get fresh stores before spring if you send your demands by one of Jove's thunderbolts. If it is of any interest to you, my pay is in arrears too."

Raging inwardly, Alexios signed for the half-year's pay, and when he had received the Quartermaster's report, for the supplies also. There did not seem much wrong with anything else, except that some woollen breeks-cloth that Julius Gavros had indented for was of poor quality and had had some of the fuller's earth left in it to make it seem thicker and heavier than it was. And he wrote his letter to the Chief Quartermaster at Corstopitum well aware that probably it was not the Chief Quartermaster's fault. But there was no one else that he could write his complaint to; scratching savagely deep into the wax in the tablets, as though he were indeed making his protest to the Emperor himself or to the Senate or to the entire administration of the Provinces of Upper and Lower Britain.

"… My men deserve better treatment than this."

He broke off and looked at the last few words he had written. Had he really begun to feel like that about the Third Ordo, Frontier Wolves? They still wore their strangers' faces: he did not feel that he knew them any better than he had done when he rode in through the Praetorian gate for the first time nearly two months ago. Yet it had seemed natural to write "My men," furious on their behalf. So natural that he did not even think about it until he noticed what he had written.

He finished the letter more deliberately, tied the two wooden leaves of the tablets together and sealed the scarlet thread, and set it aside, the dolphin impress of his signet ring standing out clear and proud on the blob of wax, to be sent off with the returning supply galleys next morning.

The next event of any importance to take place at Castellum was when Cloe, the half-wild cat whose official duty was to keep down the mice in the granary, had three kittens in the Quartermaster's bed.

Kaeso, whose temper had scarcely recovered from the state of the winter stores, flung her out and the kittens after her, and gave orders that they should be drowned. But Cloe was part of the garrison's life, and anyway, the Dalriads among them claimed that to drown kittens was unlucky. So a warm nest was prepared for them at the back of the harness shed, and they were removed there, the optio in charge of the operation getting severely clawed in the process by the ungrateful Cloe, who promptly carried the kittens back one by one half across the fort and in through a broken window at the rear of the officers' quarters, to settle them down again in the Quartermaster's bed. The battle of wills went on for some time, while the garrison laid bets on who would be the victor.

A few days later, wandering around the armourer's smithy while a dint was being beaten out of his belt clasp, Alexios came upon Rufus, his junior trumpeter, huddled in a warm corner of the fuel store with something on which he seemed very intent half-hidden under his wolfskin. He looked up as the Commander appeared, and made to scramble to his feet, pushing the thing further out of sight. But not before Alexios had glimpsed a scrap of golden fur, and a cup of milk slopping darkly onto the ground. "Bide still," he said quickly, "you don't seem to have enough hands for saluting at the moment." And as the boy flushed scarlet, "How long have you been foster-mother to Cloe's kittens?"

"Only one of them, Sir. I am thinking she got tired of carrying all three back from the harness shed, or maybe she was losing count, and she abandoned this one. It was lying out half-drowned in last night's rain."

Alexios looked down at the blind scrap of life, and seemed to see it flickering even as he looked. The young soldier scooped up milk in a horn spoon and tried to trickle it inside the tiny sucking mouth, but none of it got in.

Feeling that he was seeing a side of the Frontier Wolves that was unexpected to say the least of it, Alexios stood and considered the problem.

"It's too young to lap," the boy said frowning. "I can't get it even to take in the spoon."

Alexios went on thinking. He was remembering old Vran the shepherd on the south slopes of the downs at home where they had the lambing pens; Vran dealing with a motherless lamb with a bit of rag wrapped round a scrap of alder pipe and thrust into the neck of a flask. But that would be too big for the kitten. "A bit of soft rag," he said at last, "put it in the cup so that it sops up the milk and get it sucking on the end of that." He stooped and touched the small downy head, then strolled back to the front of the smithy, quite unaware that he had gained at any rate one friend among the Frontier Wolves.

After weeks of gales and sleet and drenching rain, the weather turned clear and frosty; and Midwinter Night was a night of stars, with Orion the Hunter swaggering above the southern ramparts. Ever since dusk, the great fire which the men of the garrison had been stacking for days, had been blazing in the midst of the old waggon park behind the granaries that was now commonly called the Dancing Ground. The cooking pits had been opened and the sizzling baked deermeat brought out, and with the customary extra issue of wine to wash it down, the Frontier Wolves were making merry.

In the lamplit mess of the officers' quarters, Alexios, idly playing dice with his Senior Centenarius, could hear them at it; the throbbing of the deerskin drums, the mouth-music and the rhythmic stamping of feet. It had all grown familiar since the first time he had heard it, for the Frontier Wolves made their wild music and the heady rhythms of their war and hunting dances not only for pleasure in off-duty times, but often in place of the foot-drill and weapon-practice of regular units. That had seemed to him strange at first, but it was the accepted custom; even Hilarion and Lucius joined in sometimes, and certainly the whirling and stamping dances made for speed and skill and control both of a man's self and his weapons as well as any arms drill could do.

Tonight, out there about their great fire behind the granaries the Frontier Wolves were dancing to bring the reborn sun up out of the darkness for another year; and suddenly, in the act of picking up his wine-cup, Alexios was remembering this night of the year at home when he was a boy. Saturnalia. The laughter and the lights in every window and the present-giving; and the fire burning on the high shoulder of the downs behind the house, where the farm-folk were about their own business of bringing the sun up out of the dark.

The sharp rattle of the dice brought his wandering thoughts back to the bare Mess room, with supper over, and himself and Hilarion dicing for a fortune in dried beans—by common consent, the Mess never gambled for money; not with pay always in arrears. Gambling debts in such a small community were something that they could well do without. Save for Druim of the Arcani, who was off about some affair of his own in the town, they had a full gathering tonight. Lucius sitting hitched close to the table, where the light of the lamp fell full on the scroll in his careful hands. Lucius and his Georgics! It was the only book he possessed; the only book in Castellum, come to that. He must know it by heart, but when Alexios had once said that to him, he had said in his quiet, rather serious way that he knew the taste of honeycomb by heart, too, but it still tasted sweet on barley-bannock; and he read it against the time when he left the Eagles and took to growing things himself. The Quartermaster and Anthonius the Medic had drawn back from the table and were huddled close over the brazier, having a low-voiced argument with many finger-stabbings. Kaeso was making heroic efforts to keep sober for the ceremony later that night, and keeping sober after supper always made him argumentative.

They were all waiting, in one way or another, because it was Midwinter Night, just passing the time till midnight. And tomorrow morning Lucius and Anthonius and maybe half-a-dozen of the men would slip away to their own gathering place in the back chamber of the sandal-maker's shop in the town, to celebrate the birth of their own god in a stable. Alexios might have been one of them. His mother had been eager that he should become a Christian when he joined the Eagles; you did not have to be one, even now that Christianity was the official religion of the Empire, but you stood a better chance of promotion to the top if you were. He wondered why he hadn't done as she wished; it would have been sensible. But suddenly, looking at Lucius's face in the lamplight, he knew that he could not feel about Lucius's Saviour laid in a manger as Lucius felt about him; and he had too much respect for other men's gods to pretend to worship them because it was sensible. So he had turned to the old soldiers' Hero-God, to Mithras, the Slayer of the Bull. And soon now, before the Third Watch sounded from the ramparts, he would be gathering up the still heroically sober Quartermaster and two of the optios and another half-dozen men, and heading out through the North gate to the small half-underground temple beyond the bath-house.

And Hilarion? He would not be with either of them. Probably his place, if he had one at all, was behind the granary.

"And it's Midwinter Night for all of us," Alexios thought. "The sun coming up out of the dark ... How odd."

"Your throw," said Hilarion, in the tone of a man who has said the same thing three times already.

Alexios took up the dice cup and threw. A three and a one. "My luck's out tonight," he said.

And Hilarion took back the cup and made the last throw of the game. Two sixes spilled out across the wine-stained table. "Venus! I win. That's another twenty beans you owe me." But even as he reached out to take the small pile which Alexios pushed over to him, he checked, listening. The rhythm of the deerskin drums had changed, grown more urgent, oddly menacing; a rhythm that was strange to Alexios, but not, it seemed, to the other men in the Mess.

"They're dancing the Bull Calves," said Hilarion.

And Lucius nodded, carefully letting Virgil on vine culture roll up on itself and slipping it back into its linen case with the air of one getting ready for action.

"What does that mean?" Alexios swallowed the last mouthful of wine in his cup, and set it down with a small decisive click that unconsciously had the same effect.

"Probably trouble," Hilarion said. "The Bull Calves has private meanings for the Dalriads and the Votadini. That's why they keep clear of that particular dance—when they're sober."

"They can't be very drunk on this pale vinegar the army calls wine."

"They can if they've smuggled in heather beer to drink with it. And it wouldn't be the first time I've known that happen. I do think, Sir, that we had better take a stroll."

Alexios was already on his feet and reaching for his sword that he had hung across the back of his chair.

As he did so, the sounds from the old waggon park swelled louder, the complex rhythm of the drums growing ragged, becoming lost in a sudden ugly tangle of sound that had unmistakably the snarl of trouble in it.

Alexios slipped the sword-strap over his head and settled it across his shoulder, and made for the door, flinging on his cloak as he went; his two centenarii close behind him. After the warm draughty fug of the Mess room with its brazier and faintly smoking lamps, the frosty air was cold and sharp as camphor in his nostrils; and the garboil from the old waggon park grew suddenly louder. They crossed the courtyard, and just as they reached the further colonnade and the street entrance, one of the optios met them, hurrying.

"Sir, there's trouble on the Dancing Ground."

"So I should judge." Alexios did not slacken his long stride as the man turned back beside him. "What's happening?"

"The Dalriads and the Votadini trying to murder each other again, Sir."

As they rounded the corner of the Principia, the Dancing Ground came in view; a reeling and swaying turmoil of flame-reddened figures that beat upon the sight as a drum beats upon the hearing; and the tumult rushed to meet them in a savage wave of sound. Alexios had a fairly shrewd suspicion that if Julius Gavros had still been in command at Castellum, the garrison, even drunk, might not have chosen to wake whatever dark magic lay in the dance of the Bull Calves; and that things had only got to this stage because it was not Julius Gavros but a new and untried Commander who would have to deal with it. But however that might be, the flames of the torches and the Midwinter fire were lighting up a fight that was real enough now; a small but flourishing battle that was already beginning to draw in the onlookers.

Alexios checked his own hand just in time from an automatic movement to make sure that his sword was sitting loose in its sheath. Leave that alone. To use the edge would mean disaster, and to use the flat of the blade would be an insult that would never be forgiven.

"Find me a trumpeter!" he shouted to the optio, and then quickly to Lucius and Hilarion as they closed up beside him, "No! Bide here and be ready to take over if need be. *This is mine!*"

And he walked straight forward into the reeling roaring heart of things.

He shouted, "Break it off! Get back, you fools!" but he could scarcely hear his own voice, let alone make anyone else in that howling mob hear it.

Then someone was thrusting in beside him, and a young voice bellowed in his ear, "Trumpeter here, Sir."

"Sound me the Break Off. Stick close to me and keep on sounding it!" Alexios bellowed back, and ploughed on. About him the press swayed to and fro; he was engulfed in a thrusting turmoil of contorted faces and jabbing fists; the short mule-kick blows of close fighting; a fog of anger that seemed almost visible in the flame-light. A grubbed-up cobblestone flew past his ear, and a random fist caught him on the cheekbone, filling one eye with stars brighter than Orion; a glancing blow, but enough to send him reeling sideways. Between the stars he caught the ugly glint of a knife blade. But the young trumpeter was close at his back; and above him, above the vicious tumult of battle rose the quick bright notes of the hunting-horn that among the Frontier Wolves served the purpose of the Buccina among more regular troops, sounding "Break off! Break off! Break ..." And little by little the familiar sound was taking hold on men trained to obey its orders.

The press was opening and falling back; men sullen and panting but no longer bloodthirsty. The horn ceased its ringing demand, and the uproar sank away to an uneasy silence. One man sat on the ground, with blood trickling darkly from a small deep stab-wound in the shoulder. Another cherished a long shallow gash in his forearm. Alexios found that he was shaking a little, and hoped desperately that it did not show, as he looked from one to another of the men about him. And the men in their turn looked back, taking in the fact that their new Commander stood in their midst with one cheek cut and an eye rapidly filling up and turning black. Maybe some of them were pondering the punishment for striking an officer. Well, it would do them no harm to sweat a little.

Alexios said levelly, "It is in my mind that there has been enough of dancing for this night." He glanced at the wounded men. "Get those two up to the Medic. I will speak with the ring-leaders in the Principia at noon tomorrow. See to it, Optio."

He swung on his heel, and so came face to face with his junior trumpeter who still stood close behind him. "My thanks," he said, and the boy grinned. A whisp of striped fur moved in the hollow of his shoulder between his neck and the folds of his wolfskin, and a pair of golden eyes glared out at the world. The kitten clung on with all its barbs, as its master, wincing slightly, detached it claw by claw. Alexios's brows flicked upwards, and Rufus said apologetically, "I was thinking you were in a hurry, Sir. Hadn't time to put him down where he'd be safe."

"I was in a hurry," Alexios agreed, "I am glad I didn't have to wait while you got free of that thing, it seems to have as many hooks as a cockle burr. Best get back now, it must be close on time to sound for the Third Watch."

By the corner of the granary his centenarii stood waiting for him, Lucius still braced and ready for action, Hilarion draped against the granary wall.

"Sir," said Lucius, gravely, "with respect, the Commander should not get personally involved—"

"But seeing that the dance was in his honour," murmured Hilarion, "surely it would have been discourteous not to join in."

Next day at noon, sitting behind the big writing-table in the office in the Principia where such things were dealt with, Alexios looked from one to another of the four wooden figures drawn up in a row before him, while the four wooden figures stared back at the wall above his head. He did not suppose for a moment that they were the ringleaders; how could you possibly pick ring-leaders out of what had happened last night? The optios would simply have picked two men at random from each side, and the centenarii, poor old Lucius with his thoughts already turned towards the room behind the sandal-maker's shop—would have confirmed the choice. And anyway it didn't much matter.

"Well, and what have you to say for yourselves?" he demanded; and the words sounded stiff and pompous in his own ears.

One of the men stepped forward half a pace; Bericus of the round and guileless face, who stood out as an Emperor's hard bargain even among the Wolves of Castellum. With an air of honest bewilderment, he began, "Sir, if it is about last night, you mean—"

"It is about last night I mean," said Alexios.

"Well Sir, we were dancing the Bull Calves, and that does look very like the real thing to any man who has not seen it before."

"It certainly looked very like the real thing last night," Alexios agreed. He touched his swollen and purpled cheekbone absent-mindedly. "Two men are in the sick block this morning, with knife wounds that look quite remarkably like the real thing, too."

There was a small sharp silence, and the four went on staring at the wall above the Commander's head. "An easy thing it is, for such dancing to get just a feather-weight out of hand," said the Emperor's hard bargain.

"Especially when the dance is the Bull Calves and the dancers are of the Dalriads and the Votadini." Alexios was aware of a slight stiffening in the already stiff figures before him.

"Sir," said another man, "that is an old story and long forgotten."

"So. A cattle raiding story, maybe? Nay then, I do not ask; it is a thing between the Votadini and the Dalriads, and I who am of neither people have no right to know." He let his voice turn musing, as though he were speaking half to himself. This was a new game of skill and suddenly he was beginning to enjoy it. "Yet before he left for Habitancum, the Ducenarius Julius Gavros told me that when a man of the Tribes joined the Frontier Wolves, he brought his loyalties with him so that from that day forward they were to the Wolves and no longer to his old tribe. Therefore," he looked at the last speaker, "it must assuredly be that this—old story is long forgotten." He shifted his gaze deliberately along the row of faces still staring at the wall above his head, and his tone quickened and hardened. "Unless of course the Ducenarius Gavros was mistaken in his trust and pride in the men he commanded."

Again there was a small sharp silence, filled with the crying of the gulls that formed a background to life at Castellum. Someone swallowed harshly, and the four pairs of eyes came down to look him squarely in the face.

"The Ducenarius Gavros was said to be a good judge of men, Sir," said the Emperor's hard bargain.

"I am very sure of it." Alexios began to play with a stylus on the table before him. "If I were not, if I thought for a moment that what happened last night was—what it seemed to be, there would be seven days confined to barracks, *with* latrine fatigues, for the four of you. If it ever seems to happen again, there *will* be seven days confined to barracks for the four of you, and we shall have the sweetest and most shining latrines in all the province of North Britain!" He dropped the stylus with a little clatter, "Which would of course be black injustice. And all because of a misunderstanding on my part; such a misunderstanding as comes from lack of experience. *My* arms drill was only of the regular parade-ground kind. Therefore, to prevent this foolish kind of thing happening another time, you shall provide me with the experience that I lack. You shall teach me, as you have long since taught

Centenarius Hilarion and Centenarius Lucius, to take a part in these weapon-dances of yours—though not, I think in the dance of the Bull Calves."

The gulls swept across the roofs of the fort; and their crying, Alexios thought, had suddenly a hint of ribald laughter in it. The shadow of wings flickered across the patch of thin winter sunshine on the writing-table, seeming to bring the laughter into the bare office room. But the Commander and the evil doers looked at each other without the twitch of a lip or the flicker of an eyelid.

"Sir," said the Emperor's hard bargain, "we shall be honoured."

"Right," said the Commander, and picked up the stylus again. "Charge dismissed."

"Left turn!" barked the optio in charge. *"March!"*

5 | *Wolfskin*

THE DARK THRESHOLD MONTH OF JANUS PASSED ON ITS SLOW way, with nothing save the lengthening daylight to promise that it would ever be spring again, as the still frosty weather of midwinter gave place to snow and sleet and freezing rain that drove before bitter winds from the north-east, and lips were raw and hands chapped to the bone on icy harness. And it seemed that nothing moved in all that snowbound and drenched and frozen countryside but the short winter patrols from Castellum, and their four-footed brothers who howled closer about fort and town and cattlefold through the bitter nights.

But a day came when the wind went round to the south, and there was a new smell in it that could not be quite lost even in the taint that always came up from the tannery sheds in the town when the wind was in that quarter. And there was a faint warmth to the sun that slipped in and out between soft blurred drifts of cloud. It was one of those days that holds a promise of spring as yet far off. And at noon, when Cloe had stalked out to lie blinking in a sheltered corner of number three barrack-row, the optio of the just-returned patrol came to find Alexios who was down in the horse-lines seeing to his mount, Phoenix, who had cut his frog on an iron-hard fang of furze root when out at exercise the day before.

"Sir, word from Cunorix, son of Ferradach Dhu."

Alexios eased the hoof he had been holding gently back onto the hard ground. "It seems well enough," he said to the groom standing by. "Could do with another salving this evening." Then straightening up, he turned to the optio, "So? And what word is that?"

"Cunorix says that the wolves are leaving the winter packs for mating. He says that if the weather holds it will be a fine hunting day tomorrow, and if the Commander would ride hunting let him send word by Govan Heron's-Feather who is in the town now, and he will be at the Western gate with the ponies and hounds by sun-up."

So next morning at sun-up, having handed over to his Senior Centenarius for the day, Alexios went out past the sentries on the Dextra gate, with a pair of borrowed hunting spears over his shoulder, and found Cunorix sitting comfortably with his back to one of the buttresses that on that side of the fort kept the walls from sliding into the river, his arm through the bridles of a couple of rough-coated hunting ponies, two shaggy yellow-eyed wolfhounds lying beside him.

He turned and got to his feet as Alexios drew near, flinging up a hand in greeting. "It will be a good day," he said; and then, glancing at the heavy spears, "and the Commander has chosen his spears well."

"The word was that the wolves were leaving the pack."

"The Commander will have had his hands full with other matters these past months. But now it is in my mind that the time comes for him to be gaining his wolfskin."

"In the Commander's also," said Alexios with a sudden lift of the spirit. In the dark days of winter and all the business of trying to find both himself and his men, he had almost forgotten the hunting trip that the Chieftain's son had spoken of in the Hall of Ferradach Dhu, and the quick handstrike afterwards. Almost, but not quite. It was good to find that the Chieftain's son had not forgotten either.

They mounted the waiting ponies, and with hounds loping on in front, headed down the steep slope to the river crossing, where the black stone that the troops called the Lady stood in the sere winter grass beside the ford. They splashed across it and headed on up the estuary, past the faint track that Alexios had ridden with the old Commander on their courtesy visit to the Lord of Six Hundred Spears, and still on towards the ruins of Credigone and the eastern end of the old Northern Wall. Presently they turned inland, with no track to follow this time, leaving the narrowing estuary with its gulls and its crying and calling shore-birds behind them, and heading up a side glen where alder and hazel crowded the banks of a small fast burn. The burn was coming down in spate, running green with melting snow-water from the high moors, so that they must follow the bank a good way before they could come to a good crossing place; but between the darkly sodden wreck of last year's bracken and the soft grey drift of the sky, the catkins were lengthening on the hazel bushes, making a kind of faint sunlight of their own, and in one especially sheltered place, as the two young men brushed past, the first pollen scattered from the whippy sprays so that they rode through a sudden golden mist. Even here at the world's end, spring was remembering the way back, and for a moment a sense of quickening caught almost painfully at Alexios somewhere below the breastbone.

Last spring he had hunted in the German woods, before his own particular world fell to pieces …

"We can get across here," said Cunorix, just ahead of him.

The burn had widened into a chain of shallows, and they splashed through easily enough, the hounds shaking themselves as they scrambled out on the further bank, and headed up through the steep woods towards the lip of the glen.

The hazel woods fell back, and now they were out into open country; high country that climbed higher yet. Half-melted snow lay puddled in every hollow, and the wind had an edge to it like a scold's tongue, for all that it blew from the south-west. But even up here there was the sense of quickening. The first blossom clung like stray sparks to the dark masses of the furze, and there was the green rooty smell of things growing, and the air full of the lonely bubbling mating-call of curlew that had come up from the estuary as nesting time drew near. It was a day when scent would lie close to the ground but long lasting; a good hunting day.

"Luath has a scent," Cunorix said quietly.

And looking down, Alexios saw the big hound standing suddenly tense, muzzle raised a little and faint tremors running his whole length to the ragged plume-tip of his tail. A moment later, Luffra had it also. The two riders waited, their ponies reined close, careful to make no sound or movement that would draw their attention away. Then with no sound the two great hounds were off, and Alexios and Cunorix, driving their heels into their ponies' flanks, were after them.

It was a long hunting and a hard one, for the quarry whose scent they followed was a big dog-wolf in his prime, old enough to have learned cunning but not yet past the strength and swiftness of his youth. More than once as he twisted and doubled through the wild country, Alexios thought that they had lost him, but always Luath and Luffra picked up his scent again and raced on.

Gradually they were working over to the north-west, and from the ridge crests of the high moorland country they began to glimpse far off a kind of broken shadow-line across the hills, and here and there, grey squared-off shapes that might almost have been outcrops of natural rock.

"He's making for Credigone and the Old Wall," Cunorix

shouted. "It's all wolf country up there." And a moment later flung out an arm, pointing, "There he goes!"

And sighting along the line of the pointing finger, Alexios made out a flicker of movement on the opposite hillside, something that might have been a huge dog, as it broke from cover of a thorn thicket and raced for the next patch of scrub.

Controlling his pony with his knees, Cunorix cupped both hands about his mouth and sent out a long wordless cry; and Luffra, running far ahead, swung right-handwise into a wide curve that made Alexios think of a sheepdog working the flock ...

The hounds were giving tongue now, the deep belling notes caught and flung back by the hills on either side. Alexios drove his heels into his pony's flanks and hurled the willing little beast forward, neck and neck with Cunorix, splashing through pockets of half-melted snow among the black tide of sodden heather, startling the green plover as they went.

Again, desperately, the wolf tried to double on his tracks, but the hounds were too close now on either flank and his speed was too far spent. A shallow glen opened before them, thicketed with hazel and birch and rowan; at its head, half-lost in thorn and brambles, the ruins of what might once have been a signal station behind the Wall.

And there among the rotting timbers and fallen stones, Alexios's wolf turned at bay.

On the outskirts of the tangle the two hounds stood yelling, holding him there but making no attack; for the hounds of men who hunt for food and skins as well as sport are trained to run down and hold the quarry, but not to kill unless they are given the word.

Alexios reined in and dropped from the saddle, flinging the reins to Cunorix's outstretched hand. Both of them knew the custom of the Frontier Wolves; you could ride down the quarry with as many comrades as chose to come with you, but you went in to get your wolfskin cloak alone.

"Good hunting!" Cunorix shouted after him.

Readying his chosen spear in his hand, he ran in, past the yelling hounds, scrambling low through the briar tangle and the fallen stones, his heart racing high in his throat with the swift excitement of the moment. Behind him he heard Cunorix calling off the hounds.

Ahead, in a small clear space backed by a stretch of still-standing wall, his wolf waited for him.

He had tried to leap for a narrow grass-grown ledge high against the face of the wall, maybe the old rampart walk. If he had been fresh he might have managed it, and gone on over the wall top and away, but he had been run long and hard, and he fell back with heaving flanks. As he burst out into the open space, Alexios saw the great brute gather himself and try once more, and again fall back. But he was not done yet; the last desperate courage of the cornered animal was still with him. The crumbling wall at his back, he gathered himself one last time and sprang for the throat of his ancient enemy, the Hunter with the Spear.

Alexios had time to see the hatred in the yellow eyes, the laid back ears and wicked grinning jaws, but above all, the thing behind the eyes that made this *his* wolf; his, and no other wolf in the world. He seemed to see the eyes for a long while, coming towards him slowly as through water, swelling on his sight; and yet he knew that it was only a splinter of time before he felt the shock as his spear took the leaping wolf in the breast. For an instant he smelled the hot breath in his face. The spear was wrenched from his grasp, and he let it go. There was a horrible yowling in his ears; a kicking and struggling on the ground beside him. He ripped his hunting-dagger from his belt and dived in to finish it. Snapping jaws just missed his arm as he drove the point in deep to the heart. The struggling and yowling stopped and the great wolf lay still.

Alexios got up and pulled out the spear, and stood looking at the dead beast, who lay with bared teeth, lips still drawn back in a snarl as though to defy death itself. He had been a beauty, thick-coated, brindled cream and grey, lighter than most of his kind, save for a dark fore-stripe that ran from the snarling muzzle up between the ears. His eyes were still bright and full, golden as yellow Baltic amber, fixed but not yet beginning to glaze. And standing there, Alexios knew the regret that comes in the moment after the kill is made, and the life gone, and all the speed and beauty and danger and courage. He had known all that before, he had killed wolves before; but it had never been quite like this; this was *his* wolf, and no other wolf would ever be *his* wolf again.

Suddenly he knew, a far-down instinctive knowledge that had no words to give it shape, why it was the custom of the Frontier Scouts that each man killed once, for his wolfskin cloak, and except in dire need of a new cloak, never killed wolf again.

Then he heard a sound behind him, and turning, saw Cunorix come out through the thorns and brambles into the small open space.

"That was a clean kill," said Cunorix.

"Not so clean. I should not have had to use this." Alexios stooped and stabbed his knife into the turf to cleanse it.

"Clean enough. There will be but two small rents for mending in the Commander's wolfskin."

And the moment of grief passed from Alexios, giving place to a swift fierce pleasure. He had his wolfskin cloak!

Cunorix kicked aside the hounds who were sniffing hungrily around the carcass. "Off! It is not yet your time!" Then turned to

Alexios again. "He is in fine condition; one that is no stranger to the sheepfolds."

Together they flayed the dead wolf, taking especial care with the muzzle and ears, and left the red carcass to the hounds. Then they went back to where the ponies waited with their bridles over their heads—hunting ponies, like the mounts of the Frontier Wolves, were trained to stand when their bridles were pulled forward, as though they were tied to a hitching-post. Cunorix took the bannock bag from about the neck of one of them, and they knotted up the reins and turned them free to graze.

Just below where the gateway must have been, a tumble of stones brought down by a landslip of some long-past winter, and laced together now by a dense mass of blackthorn made a pocket of shelter from the wind; and there they settled down with the bannocks and a lump of garlic-flavoured curd between them. But before they began to eat, Alexios pulled the wooden stopper from the flask of raw Sabine wine that he had bought with him, and getting up, poured a few drops, red as the wolf's blood, into the rough grass of the lost threshold. He was not sure why he did it. A sacrifice to the shades of the men who had kept the lookout and guarded the signal fire in this place? An offering to the gods—to whatever gods might be interested—for his wolf? (Once, he had seen a fine small altar in the German forests. "*To Pan Sylvanus,*" he had read, carved in the mossy stone, "*In gratitude for the finest boar of his life, Gneus A. Drusillus, Tribune of the Sixth Gaulish Cohort raised this.*") Something of both, maybe.

He turned and squatted down again beside Cunorix, holding out the flask. Cunorix took it and drank. "It was a good hunting," he said, and handed it back.

Eye meeting eye, with no more spoken, Alexios took it back, and swallowed a mouthful of the fiery stuff, and wedged the flask upright between them and they fell to work on the bannock and curds.

Alexios ate one-handed, keeping the other free for his wolf-skin tumbled beside him. It felt harsh and curiously alive under his fingers. (*To Pan Sylvanus, in gratitude for his wolf*...)

Faint blurs of skim-milk blue had begun to show through the soft drifting grey of the sky, and echoing blurs of half sunlight were trailing them across the hills. In the lee of the blackthorn tangle the day was gentle, and when a brief wing of sunlight brushed along the flank of the little glen, Alexios felt the warmth of it on his skin. There was a flittering of small birds among the furze, though the half-thawed snow still lay puddled in hollows of the north-facing slope. The ponies had dropped further downhill, and were grazing along the burnside, snatching at the tussocky grass among the heather. Alexios watched them, listening in the clear air to the contented sound of their cropping. Earlier in the day, they had proved themselves fine, willing-hearted little beasts with a good turn of speed, and now, rested and enjoying them-selves, they were a pleasant sight. Something about the roan, the one that he himself had been riding, caught at his interest, some-thing under the shaggy winter coat and the hillbred toughness of the little beast, the slender legs and the shape of the small well-set head, something that he had seen in the full dark eye when he was knotting up the reins. The best of the army's cavalry horses were part Arab, and it was a look that he knew.

"Does Ferradach Dhu run Arab stallions among his mares?" he asked suddenly.

Cunorix set the flask down again between them. It was almost empty, and they were both on their last bannock. "Not of the pure breed, no; but there is an Arab strain in many of the horse-runs of the Votadini." He swallowed a last crumbling mouthful of curd.

"In the old days, whenever there came a fighting-time between us and the Red Crests, and the Red Crests withdrew to make a 'strategic rearrangement of their frontier defences,' there would be a few good cavalry horses left in our hands."

Alexios grinned, "And when in due course the Red Crests take the war trail and the frontiers are 'strategically rearranged,' yet another time—by such as the Emperor Severus?"

"There are hidden valleys of the high moors, and open places in the great forest with seemingly no track that shows the way into them. And the Tribes have always been skilled at hiding the best of their herds, whether from the Red Crests or from each other." He sighed, half-regretfully. "Ah, but all that is long past. There has been quiet between the Votadini and the Red Crests for a long while now. Soon we young men will forget how to use our spears."

"And so now you must buy your new blood for the horseherds like law-abiding citizens," Alexios said. "It is a sad world!"

"Buy or borrow, or come by as best we may."

"Come by as best you may?"

"Sometimes word comes drifting on the wind, of an especially fine horse in the runs of the Damnoni, or even of the Dalriads …"

"And does that wind never carry word the other way?"

"Now and again. Often enough to keep the young men from forgetting altogether."

"*That* is the kind of thing—among others—that we are here to prevent. I said it was a sad world."

"If it were not so, I could show you a better sport than wolf-hunting." Cunorix cocked a thick russet eyebrow at his companion. "But let you remember this, as I *think* the Lords of the Red Crests remember it, that the horse-drafts for the Frontier Wolves, and for many of the Wall cavalry beside, come from out of our runs. Ask too many questions, keep too bright an eye open on the doings of the Tribes, and you will feel the loss of speed and mettle in your own horse-lines."

Suddenly laughter caught at them both, eye meeting eye; a quiet laughter—men seldom bellow their mirth in the wild places—but quick and potent, linking them together like the handstrike in Ferradach's Hall.

Laughing still, they scrambled to their feet and went to haul the hounds off the flayed carcass. "Hai mai! Leave the ravens their share!" Cunorix said.

They whistled up the grazing ponies, and mounted, Alexios with the raw wolfskin across his pony's withers, and set out for Castellum.

The promise of spring was past and the winter evening closing in as they came down to the paved ford. "It grows late, and the beasts are tired. Let you stable the ponies and eat and sleep with us tonight," Alexios said.

Cunorix shook his head. "Na, the hunting was a good hunting and the day a good day, and we will end it where it began outside the West gate. I have kindred in the town."

And Alexios, who also knew that the day had been a good day (*To Pan Sylvanus, in gratitude for his wolf*—and for more than his wolf …), and had therefore wanted it to go on, knew that he was right.

The watering-place upstream was busy with men and horses. Heads turned as the two riders came down the bank and splashed through; the men nearest to them sketched a salute. Someone spotted what Alexios had folded across his pony's withers, and shouted to a comrade, "Hi! Kuno! The Commander's got his wolf!"

And behind him as he splashed out on the opposite bank

someone shouted back, "So-o! Did you think he was off after squirrel, then, with those fine big borrowed spears?"

And somebody laughed. It was Bericus, the Emperor's hard bargain. "Well, now we shall not be needing to blush for him if the Emperor comes to inspect us!—Back, lop-eared son of all the Furies! Will you drink the pool dry?"

He heard the voices and a ragged cheer behind him. It was all thoroughly disrespectful, but the Frontier Wolves, he had long since discovered, were not strong on respect; not strong at any rate on the outward show of it.

A faint mist was beginning to rise from the ground, wreathing round the dark foot of the Lady where she stood above the ford. And scarcely noticing that he did so, as though it were something that he had done many times before, Alexios leaned sideways and touched the polished crest of the stone in passing.

6 | *The Stone Dancers*

ALEXIOS TOOK HIS WOLFSKIN TO OLD DUATHA IN THE TOWN to be cured and dressed and mounted on his own cloak of the regulation dark green cloth. And spring woke among the shaggy woods along the estuary. The spring barley was sown in the croplands about the fort, and in the sheltered places the first shortstemmed primroses lifted their clean surprised faces; and the swallows came back to their old nests under the eaves of the granaries, just as they had done in his old home in the South Country.

Summer came, and the heather hills simmered in the heat; and Cloe's kitten, now named Typhon for his fiend's temper with all men save Rufus, was almost full grown, with tufts on his ears to prove his proud wildcat ancestry. In the horse-runs of Ferradach Dhu the mares had their foals at heel; and Shula of the golden eardrops began to have a belly that curved out before her like ripe fruit when she walked. The time of the great yearly gathering to Traprain Law came and passed by—the gathering when all the Clan Chieftains and great men of the Tribes came together in council, to settle disputes and make and re-make laws and listen to the voice of the King, with a Government Inspector present to see that the laws of Rome, as well as the laws of the Votadini, were served. Three boys of the Votadini came in to join the Frontier Wolves.

And all the while the life of the fort went on, becoming more and more familiar to its Commander. The patrols came and went; the eight- or ten-day patrols of summertime, each man leaning aside to touch the Lady as he passed; and more than once Alexios went with them, leaving Hilarion in charge of the fort. Eight days out with the lean rangy men who had the look of wild places and long distances about them. He had slept in his fine new wolf-skin cloak among the young heather through the short northern summer nights, ridden soaked to the skin by the mizzle rain of the high moors, known the Fear-beyond-the-Firelight that came to most men the first time they camped within the crowding darkness of the Great Forest that spread like a black fleece over the inland hills of the Frontier country. He had learned from his men how to read and follow a trail; how to melt into the land-scape, making use of every scrap of cover, every trick of wind and light both for himself and his pony; how to travel cross country at speed without ever getting skylined, and other useful skills, including, from Bericus, how to snare wildfowl for the pot.

He had gone hunting more than once with Cunorix alone, or with young Connla as well, or ridden out with them to visit the horses on the summer pastures or watch the two-year-olds being broken in the Makers' Yards. Life had become unexpect-edly good, without his really noticing it.

But the summer was passing by.

A day came, not long before harvest time; on the very edge of autumn, for the harvest, here in the North, Alexios realized, came much later than the harvests of his boyhood in the Down Country. But the heather was still honey-scented and murmurous with bees, and the clump of harebells among the grass at the Lady's foot was still in fragile flower, valiant where the hooves of the patrols went by. And Alexios, with half a day to spare, and riding his own Phoenix as he did when they were not for hunting, had met Cunorix halfway and gone on up with him for a look at the brood mares on the hill run.

He had been tied to the small dark office in the Principia for the best part of a week by one of those sudden rushes of paper-work that come from time to time upon the commanding officers of small units who have no clerks of their own; and the space and sunlit emptiness of the hills seemed very good.

The mares grazed quietly in the sheltered upland valley, under the watchful eye of Finnan the herdsman, who sat with his back to a sun-warmed rock, his small sturdy pony grazing nearby. Cunorix whistled lazily, and a mare of the soft mouse-colour much prized among Tribes and Frontier Wolves alike, raised her head, then as he whistled again, came cantering gently up the slope to take the lick of salt from his out-held palm.

Alexios put out a quiet hand and drew it down her muzzle, fondling her crest, pleased that she did not fling away as she had done the first time they met, but bent her head as though in plea-sure, ruckling softly down her nose.

"Shadow—see, already we be friends, you and I."

"She is used to much petting. She has been my father's favou-rite since the day that she was foaled," Cunorix said. "It is hard for him that he cannot ride up to the summer pastures any more."

There was a little silence. In the few times that he had been to the rath it had seemed to Alexios that the old sick Chieftain was growing weaker; sitting yet closer to the fire even in the summer days.

"He should not have gone to the Gathering," he said.

"That we all know," Cunorix said harshly, "I could have gone for him, I who am his eldest son. But he is the stubborn one; he would go, even though it must be in a litter."

Again there was the little silence between them, only the faint soughing of air through the long grass. Then Cunorix spoke again, more lightly, "Aye, well, soon the time comes for the mares to be brought down to shelter. Then she will eat from her manger at the back of the Hall again, and they will both be glad of each other's nearness."

Alexios looked round at him with a half smile, "And soon, if the gods be good, there comes something else to make him glad."

"Very soon now." Cunorix still fondled the mare's neck, while she nuzzled against his breast with delicately working lips, "My son will be born before this moon is out. Maybe the gladness of that will give him strength again."

"And what if it is a girl child?"

"I have made the proper sacrifices, and the old women who know about these things have told Shula that it will be a son."

Even as he spoke, a faint rhythmic quiver of sound disturbed the upland quiet; the beat of hooves on the hard end-of-summer turf; and looking that way Alexios saw a horseman top the skyline and come plunging down into the long curve of the valley. The mares and their foals scattered, snorting in panic as he swept by; long red hair streamed behind him like the tail of a torch.

"That's Connla," Cunorix said, "and by more than his fiery crest. No one else would ride through the brood herd as though the Wild Hunt were after him."

The herdsman had drawn his legs under him and risen from his dozing-rock. "It will be that the old Chief goes beyond the sunset."

Alexios half expected Cunorix to be astride his own pony next moment and off to meet the wild rider. But there was no movement beside him except that Shadow flung round and went cantering off back to the scattered herd. And when he looked round, Cunorix was standing very still, with the look of a man braced to receive the shock of a breaking wave or landslip or an enemy hurling against him. But all those were things that could be run from or fought against. This was something else. "Finnan is right," he thought, "and Cunorix knows it."

Connla was upon them, reining back in full gallop, his pony spattering froth from its muzzle. "It is our father!" He gasped it out before his feet touched the ground.

For a moment longer the elder brother held his braced stillness. "He seemed stronger this morning."

"So much stronger that he would have out the weapon kist and check over his war-gear. And then he called for his sword, and stood up as though to test that the weight and balance were as he remembered, and began to take great sweeping strokes about him as though he stood in the midst of battle. But the sword fell from his grasp, and he fell forward into the fire—"

"He was burned?"

"Na. His body and that great cloak of his smothered the flames, and we hauled him clear in three heartbeats." Alexios noticed for the first time a long angry burn on the boy's forearm. "But now he lies still, like one already gone out of his body; and Sinnoch the Healer says he is for the West, beyond the sunset."

Cunorix had turned to his own horse, and was in the saddle by that time. He checked for a moment to look down at Alexios. "The sun and the moon on your path," he said, as though it would be a long time before they saw each other again, then drove his heel into the horse's flank, and was away at full flying gallop, with Connla after him.

That night in the officers' Mess at Castellum, Alexios in the midst of making himself a new birding bow, heard a long-drawn booming horn-call a long way off. He looked up from the work in his hands, and saw Hilarion check in the act of moving a piece on the drafts board between himself and the Quartermaster, and Lucius's nose come out of his beloved Georgics.

The long, haunting note died away, and then as they listened, was taken up by some horn further to the south, like an answer or an echo.

"Ferradach Dhu?" Alexios said: but he did not really need the answer.

The Quartermaster, who had been there longer than any of them, nodded. "The old Chief goes beyond the sunset, and they're passing on the news. Listen—there speaks Rath Colgrim, and there the Glen of the Alderwoods." Faint as the ghosts of echoes, the horns were sounding away and away over the lowland hills.

"So now Cunorix is the Chieftain," Alexios said with a sense of loss that he did not care to look at too closely.

Hilarion set the drafts piece down on the board with a small sharp click. "Not for three days. The Tribesmen believe that for three days the spirit does not set out on its journey. And so for the three Death Days the clan lacks a chieftain. Then they hold a great feast to set the old Chief on his way and the new one in his place—but you'll see when the time comes."

"I?" Alexios said, surprised.

"Even among the wolf pack, the courtesies must be maintained. The fort Commander must attend both the Burial Feast and the Chief-making. Lucius and I and the rest of us, save for a small escort who have to stay more than half sober to see you don't get knifed or disgrace the Empire and bring you safe back again, shall miss all that. Aye me, it's an unfair world."

"Not so unfair when you come to think of it." Lucius gently rolled the long scroll up on itself. "We shall also miss the after-morning's headache."

Below in the town, the women had begun to keen.

The three Death Days passed; and on the third, with a ten-man escort, Alexios duly represented the Frontier Wolves and the

Empire at the feast that was at once funeral feast for the old Chief and Making-Feast for his son.

The rath was packed and spilling over with the men of the Clan, and also with the stray-comers, horse-dealers and silversmiths and wandering harpers who always swarmed to such occasions as to a midsummer gathering. But in place of the usual cheerful hubbub, there was a heavy waiting quiet. Even the eating and drinking when the evening cauldrons of pig-meat stew were brought out, was done for the most part in silence; and from the inner court came the sound of the women keening.

The day had been grey and heavy, threatening rain that never came; but towards sunset the sky began to break up; and when they carried the old Chieftain from his Hall, the West was barred with watery gold.

Wrapped to the chin in his great deerskin cloak, his necklace of raw yellow amber pulled out to lie upon his breast, his sons and four others of his nearest kinsmen carried him shoulder high on a hurdle. Ahead of him walked the Priest-kind, led by Morvidd with his black hood laid back, and a garland of oak and yew upon his head. Before him also, and behind and on either side, men bearing torches that burned murky red and gave off little brightness in the fading daylight. And all the men of the Clan falling in behind him, as they bore him out through the gateway of the rath.

Alexios and his Wolves walked in the honourable places allotted to them immediately behind the household warriors. He caught the resiny smell of the torches trailing back to him along the quiet evening air, and heard the muted throbbing of the drums. At his back he heard the marching feet of his welldrilled ten; a foursquare sound that was somehow alien among all the rest; and beyond that, the formless movement of the Clan following after, and the bleating and lowing of beasts for sacrifice.

And behind all else, the keening of the women, growing fainter as they left the rath and headed south-east.

Alexios knew where they were going.

About four miles up-river from Castellum lay the Long Moss, a wide stretch of level country, inland marsh, and loch and winding waterways running a good three hours' march from east to west. He had crossed it the day of his first coming to the fort, by the ridge of higher ground that carried the inland road from Trimontium. And in the past few months he had circled its sodden fringes more than once with the patrols. An empty sky-reflecting land alive with the crying and calling of wildfowl whose voices seemed to be the voice of its own loneliness. Once, in the clear light of a summer morning, he had seen far off something that looked like a group of great figures; figures turned to stone and checked for ever in some circling dance. Only a circle of standing-stones on one of the islets of firm ground that were scattered here and there amid the marshy waste. But his optio had told him that it was the Death Place of the Chiefs of the Votadini; all the Chiefs of the Votadini from the High King himself to the Lords of a Hundred Spears. No one went there in the ordinary way of things, said the optio, not even the Frontier Wolves. Only the Spirit Folk, and the marsh birds flying over. And afterwards, not thinking that Alexios noticed, he had taken a piece of his evening bannock from the leather bag at his saddle-bow, and crumbled it and let it fall behind him, as though he did not know what his fingers were doing.

The pale gleam of westering sunlight had blazed up into a sunset that set all the West on fire when they came to the edge of the marsh country; and the standing water caught and gave back the mingled reflections of flaming sky and ragged-burning torches, as they still moved on by some unseen track that sniped this way and that, following the firmer ground. At last it seemed that they had reached the end of all solid land. A low broad bar of sour grass and alder scrub stretched to right and left of them; ahead lay only water, reed-patterned, dappled with sky reflections and the evening movement of the air. And across the water, already shadow-bloomed, the great stones that he had seen before circled in their frozen dance.

The foremost torchbearers had come to a halt, the formless brushing of many feet fell silent, and the drums ceased their low rhythmic muttering. Now they were bringing up the beasts for sacrifice. Only sheep and cattle, Alexios saw with relief; seemingly the Chiefs of the Votadini did not take favourite hounds and horses with them, only food for the journey. He would have been sick at heart to see Shadow in that small wild-eyed knot of driven beasts.

The head of the procession was moving off again.

Alexios heard the optio's voice low and warning in his ear. "This is as far as we go, Sir."

He nodded. Only the dead Chief and his priests, his kindred and household warriors and the beasts for sacrifice would go on from here. He knew that instinctively; but his escort were making doubly sure, feeling their responsibility for him as he felt his for them; and he knew that instinctively also. The knowledge brought with it a fleeting sense of warmth; and he could do with warmth just then, despite the milky heaviness of the evening.

The leading torchbearers were well out into the shallows now; the men who bore the old Chief's body were moving steadily down through the alder scrub and into the water after them. Then the household warriors, and the driven cattle showering up brightness from the dim golden water as they went.

The blazing West was fading, and as the fires died, the loch water grew shadowy, and the flames of the torches began to bite. Watching them go, men and torches and lowing cattle, and the one lying still in their midst, Alexios saw that they were not streaming straight across, but following the same kind of sniping course that they had followed since they came into the Long Moss. The water came midway up the men's thighs in places, never higher; and from the reed beds and the look of the surface, he guessed that it would not be much deeper on either side. It must be that along that hidden sniping causeway there was firm ground; and elsewhere? Who could say? Maybe the kind of hungry bottom that sucked men down into its own dark heart. A little chill seemed to come up off the water, and despite himself Alexios shivered under his wolfskin cloak. Then the heavy warmth came back, and he told himself not to be a fool.

The torches had reached the further side. The red glare of them was moving to and fro among the tall stones of the Sacred Circle. No sound came back across the water. Even the lowing of the cattle was lost. The old Chief and his attendants had passed from one world into another; and presently from that other world the new Chief would return to them. Meanwhile there was nothing to do but wait.

Those who might follow no further spread out along the alder ridge and settled down to their waiting.

As though he had eyes in the back of his head, Alexios was aware of his men squatting motionless behind him, each man with his sword laid across his knees, and settled himself carefully into the same position.

Presently, with a musical throbbing of wings, three swans flew over, with the last of the sunset tipping their flight pinions with fire. Almost all the gold was gone from the west, now fading to rose, to ash grey; the evening star hung moth-pale in the clearing sky. Far over towards the east, a faint wet murmur told where the familiar river that came out to the estuary below Castellum, gathered its waters among the lochans of the Long Moss and plunged down over rocky falls into the gorge that it had cut for itself. A faint mist began to rise from the surface of the loch, and the torches among the standing-stones were lost in it. The crying and calling of the wildfowl began to fall silent.

Alexios was getting cramp. The long waiting began to nibble like mice at his nerve ends. He longed to move, find an easier position, get up and walk about. But to do that would be gross discourtesy to the Clan—Cunorix's Clan—and shame to his own men. He called up in his mind all that he had learned in nearly a year, of the ways in which a man in hiding on the scouting trail could sit hour after hour unmoving; and shut his teeth and sat on, his sword across his knees.

Once, long after dark, when the mist rolled back a little, a ruddy smear of light spread for a while across the water, and then was lost again. The Death Pyre of Ferradach Dhu.

The darkness was turning towards dawn, and the sky once again full of the haunting voices of marsh-birds, when they saw the torches coming back. Faint stains of light growing out of the mist, gathering strength and a fiercer brightness as they drew near. And their brightness caught and flung back in answering shards of broken light from the churned shallows as the dark figures came wading in towards the shore. The Dark Time, the Waiting Time during which the Clan was without a Chieftain, was over. The whole Men's Side were on their feet now, but the silence still held them, as they stood, every face turned towards the figure who walked in the midst of the torches that made a golden smoke about his head.

A magnificent deerskin mantle lifted and swung out behind

him on the water, and the torchlight caught the great necklace of twisted gold and raw yellow amber about his neck. He was coming up out of the shallows now, wet and shining and flame-golden. Morvidd and the Priest-kind walked at either side of him, Connla, heading his household warriors, strode close behind. The drops of loch water scattered from him like sparks as he came up through the alder trees. He was the Chief, back from beyond the sunset, and the weariness of the journey was upon him, tangible as the fine new deerskin robe and the yellow amber of the Chiefhood at his throat.

Alexios, standing within arm's length of him, watched him come, taller, surely, than he had been, unless that was only that his head was held so high, and looking into his eyes that never moved to right or left, wondered what had happened to him in the Death Place of the Chieftains, and felt a little chill that was more than the mist and the coming dawn.

The long waiting silence had fallen from the Clan, and they were greeting him with shout upon deep triumphant shout of welcome, each man bringing his spear or sword blade crashing down across his shield in salute, until the marsh-birds burst up and scattered in alarm, filling all the misty darkness with their cries and the beating of startled wings.

And then Cunorix the Chieftain had passed by, and his household warriors after him, and Alexios and his ten Frontier Wolves, were turning in behind them; and at their back all the Men's Side of the Clan. The torches were losing power as the first grey light of dawn began to water the dark. And the Death Place was behind them, and ahead, the waiting rath, where the women would have stopped keening, and the cooking pits would soon be opened. And they began to sing the song of bringing home the new Chief.

7 | *Making-Feast for a New Chieftain*

IT WAS FULL DAWN WHEN THEY CAME BACK TO THE RATH. THEY had left the mist behind them over the Marsh Country; and the torches were quenched and the first gold of the rising sun lay level across the threshold of the Chieftain's Hall. And on the threshold Cunorix stood, beginning to look out of his own eyes again, one foot shod and the other bare and planted on the red oxhide spread there. And one by one, Connla and the chief men of the Clan came up to lay each man the flat of his right hand on the flat of the great spear that the new Chieftain carried, and take upon him the oath that was as old as the Tribes, and the Tribes that were before the Tribes. "If we break faith with thee, may the green earth gape and swallow us, may the grey seas break in and overwhelm us, may the sky of stars fall and crush us out of life for ever."

The cooking pits were already opened, and great joints of cattle and pig and deermeat were being lifted smoking from their beds of hot stones, while the women and the slaves brought out huge bowls of bannocks and curds and honey-in-the-comb, and deep jars of heather beer and the fermented mares' milk that went to men's heads like fever. And looking among the women, Alexios suddenly thought it strange that he could not see Shula the Chieftain's woman anywhere. No woman had gone with them when they went to set the old Chieftain on his way; but surely now … He glanced past Cunorix into the shadows beyond the open doorway of the Hall. But there was no sign of her that way. Maybe her coming was a part of some later ceremony.

The last of the warriors had sworn his faith, and Alexios realized that it was his turn now; and Cunorix was looking at him, waiting. This would need care. He could not swear faith like the Clan warriors, and he could not hold back from some form of greeting and acceptance to the new Chieftain who was his friend. Had been his friend. But he felt so far off from Cunorix now. "The sun and the moon on your path," Cunorix had said that last time they parted, as though one or other of them were going far away. He found himself walking forward, on the edge of raising his hand in the Roman salute, the formal Latin words of greeting and congratulation already in his mouth. And then Cunorix's right hand came away from its two-handed hold on his great spear, and they struck palm to palm like men sealing a bargain, much as they had done in that Hall close on a year ago.

"Good hunting to you on the new trail," Alexios said.

The face of the ugly young man before him lit into a smile. "Let you give me time to get the feel of this new thing, as I gave it to you, last winter, and I am thinking that we will have good hunting on the old trails again, also," Cunorix said.

It could have been only largesse, one man promising to another who asked, though the asking was without words. And then the sense of loss that had been with Alexios for three days would have become complete and for all time. But suddenly he knew that it was an asking as well as a promising; that the loss had been for Cunorix as well as for himself; and the morning sun was warm between his shoulder-blades and the smell from the cooking pits made him hungry so that the soft warm water came into his mouth, and life was good.

And in that moment, above all the sounds of the morning, from somewhere beyond the Hall, in the direction of the Women's Quarters, came the bleating cry of a newborn baby.

So Alexios knew why Shula of the golden eardrops had not come out with the other women to take her place at the Chief-making. An old life had gone out from the Chieftain's Hall, a new life had come into it.

Cunorix heard the cry. Alexios saw him hear it, though he made no movement, only stood waiting, as it seemed suddenly that the whole crowded rathe was waiting. Then something moved in the shadows of the Great Hall. It drew nearer, and the bleating with it; and someone laughed and someone else took up the laughter; and an old woman hobbled out into the sunlight, carrying a bundle wrapped in a spotted fawn-skin. From all over the broad fore-court Men's Side and Women's Side alike were gathering in.

"What have you there, Old Mother?" a big man shouted.

And another answered him, "It's a lamb. Cannot you hear it bleat?"

"No lamb, as well as you know, oh makers of foolish jests." The old woman shrilled back at them. And to Cunorix she shouted, "Shula the Chieftainess begs forgiveness of her lord, that she cannot be with him at this rising of the Sun, for she has been about women's work this night, and is weary. But see, she sends him his son in her place."

The bundle kicked and bawled as she held it out, and Cunorix suddenly flinging his great spear aside, took it from her. The creature's eyes were screwed up against the morning light. It was furious at being torn from the warm darkness of its mother's body, its face crumpled and scarlet as a bruised poppy bud. It was so newly born, they had not even washed it yet, and there was blood on its forehead and the birth smell about it that Alexios remembered from the lambing pens of his boyhood.

Cunorix had it between his hands. He looked at it a moment with something between awe and amusement. "So small, and a warrior already!" he said, and held it up into the morning sunlight high over his head and the heads of the crowding Clan, and gave a great triumphant shout, "See, oh my brothers! See, all ye of the Clan of Dumnorix the son of Ferradach Dhu! As my father the old Chieftain had sons to follow after him, so now I also have a son to take the Chief's collar from my neck and the spear from my hand when I am old and tired and full of sleep!"

But Alexios who had drawn back into the throng, thought, looking at him, "He does not believe that he will ever be old, not at this moment!"

And all about him the Men's Side were shouting and tossing up their spears to the squalling bundle. The last shadow of the night that was over fell away behind them, and the day roared up like a bonfire when somebody throws barley spirit on the flames.

Alexios had thought, in the first place, to return to Castellum as soon as the new Chief was made, but the Quartermaster had shaken his bald head. "One night for the old Chief, and one for the new. You will give offence to many if you do not wait for the feasting."

The Quartermaster had been long enough on the Frontier for his word to carry weight, and Hilarion was perfectly capable of taking over the command for two days, probably more capable than he was himself, Alexios thought. And so he stayed on through the feasting, squatting in his place of honour at the Chieftain's own fire, the High Fire, with Cunorix and his kinsfolk and chief warriors, eating more than he wanted of sizzling boar meat and barleycakes and honey, drinking as little as might be of the wine and heather beer that the slaves and women carried round.

All day the feasting went on, while from time to time the young braves would leave the fires and turn to racing or wrestling or javelin throwing one against another by way of a change, and then return to eat and drink again. Alexios wished that he could have joined them, instead of sitting here representing the Empire, listening to the talk of old warriors and the long involved story-songs of the harpers while the shadows crept from west to east. Och well, Cunorix must be wishing just as sorely, to be away to the Women's Quarters to his woman and new son. Alexios tried to look as though he were spellbound by the harp-song, and took another honey-cake that he did not want from the dish that suddenly appeared before him.

At last the shadows began to lengthen through the crowded rath. Much wine and beer and fermented mares' milk had been drunk, and men's eyes were growing brighter and their tongues looser. There began to be wild bursts of laughter, and here and there the swift snarling flare-up of a quarrel as men grew fierce and merry with the drink within them. The main business of eating was over for a while, though the drinking would go on through the night; and there began to be a general breaking up and shifting between the groups round the fires.

And suddenly Connla who had disappeared for a while, was back and calling, "Commander! Oh Commander of Castellum!" And looking round, Alexios saw him standing there, eyes narrowed and laughing into the last of the sunlight, and holding up a calf's head with the hide still on it that must have been left over from the slaughtering for the feast.

He got to his feet, feeling for the moment rather sick. And Connla cried, "Tain Bo! Cattle Raid!" as though in some kind of challenge, and still laughing, flung the calf's head on the ground between them.

There was a sudden crowding in of young warriors all about them. Whatever the thing was, clearly it was to their liking. "Cattle Raid! Cattle Raid! Let's get the ponies and set up the gate posts!"

"Not so fast!" Connla said. "The Commander has not yet taken up the challenge."

They all looked at Alexios expectantly.

"Tell me what it is, this challenge," he said, slowly, "and then I will choose whether to take it up or leave it lying."

Connla stood rocking on his heels and grinning. "Never look so on your guard! We have no thought to take you moon-riding into Dumnonian territory! See now; it is no more than this, that we set a pair of hazel saplings for a gateway at either end of the level ground by the burn, and you call out your team and I mine, each man with his horse and spear; and whichever team is first to carry the 'bull,'" he stirred the calf's head with his foot, "seven times through its own gateway has the winning of the game, and can claim from the Chief—"

"A jar of fine Greek wine to wash off the blood," said Cunorix who had left his skin-spread stool and come to join the throng.

"Nay now, my brother the Chieftain, what blood—unless it be the calf's? Here is a game so simple that a bairn could play it—"

"Or a Roman?" said Alexios, his eye brightening to the challenge. And there was a burst of laughter from the men around him.

"Even a Red-Crest Roman, oh Commander of Castellum." Connla stirred the calf's head with his foot again.

Alexios felt a sudden movement, a pressure of men behind him, and looked round quickly, to find his escort optio close at his shoulder, and the rest of the Frontier Wolves pushing in through the crowd. From the look on their faces, he judged that it wouldn't be the first time most of them had played this game.

He turned back to Connla, "How many for a team?"

The other shrugged. "Any number that seems good."

"I can call out ten," said Alexios.

And so a short while later, the valley floor already in shade though the last run-honey sunlight of the late summer evening still lay across the hills, Alexios with a borrowed spear in his hand was astride Phoenix and facing Connla across a rough circle made up of the two teams. At either end of the level ground the hazel saplings had been set up, with coloured rags tied to the tops of them. Midges danced in the heavy air among the rowans and alders of the burnside, and the ponies stamped and fidgeted, swishing their tails against the stinging clouds. Then somebody flung the calf's head into the centre of the circle, and the teams plunged forward, becoming a dense struggling ruck of men and ponies, from which one of Connla's warriors broke free with the calf's head on the point of his spear and made for the home gateway with the rest yelling at his heels. And the game was on.

If you could call it a game.

Looking back on it afterwards, Alexios had only the haziest memories of something more like a savagely joyful running fight that streamed to and fro between the pairs of gateposts; a free-for-all in which it seemed that nothing was barred except the deliberate and obvious use of the spear-point on a horse or rider of the opposing team.

To and fro, now clotting into a struggle, now skeining out into a chase. At first it seemed that Connla's team would have a shamingly easy win, as they got the "bull" back through their own gateway three times in quick succession; but the Frontier Wolves were getting the feel of the thing, and little by little their score crept up and the game began to go their way. At least, Alexios thought it did. He was not quite sure. He was not quite sure of anything. It was enough to struggle for each capture of the "bull," to try to head off the enemy, to guard against the bumping and boring of other riders, one eye always on the home gateway. He thought both teams were running level now. Still not sure; but anyway there were plenty of onlookers to keep the count ...

The light was suddenly different; a red fierce light with smoky shadows that made it harder still to know what was happening or see where the "bull" had got to; and he realized that the sun had gone long since, and men had come charging down from the rath in the gathering dusk, with torches to light the play. The calf's head was almost stripped of skin and flesh now, battered and hideous, and becoming almost impossible to pick up on the spear-point. A joyful cry went up from the crowd; another gateway for the tribesmen; another, and then another for the Frontier Wolves. It seemed to Alexios that the torchlight was in his own head, and the drum of hooves and the shouting all became a part of himself—or he became a part of it. The optio went past him in a smother of spun clods, the ragged and bloody skull on the end of his spear, and shouted as he went past, "Seventh gateway, Sir!" Then he was lost in a milling knot of horsemen. But next instant, out of the midst of the ruck his spear went up and flung the "bull" free, arcing over the heads of men and horses in the direction of the Wolves' gateway.

Alexios swooped upon it, flinging off his nearest adversary with Phoenix's shoulder, and managed to get his spear-point through the empty eye-socket. The gateway seemed a long way off, and there were a lot of enemy horsemen between him and it. He drove his heels into his pony's flanks and headed for them, travelling like a bolt from a catapult. The first man swung to block him and he leaned sideways, controlling Phoenix with his knees, the flat of his hand finding the other's face, tipping him backwards over his pony's crupper, and he was past; three others scattering before him and wrenching their ponies round to crowd him from either side. Close behind him he heard the yell of the Frontier Wolves. But Connla, the foremost of his opponents racing beside him, was half out of his saddle, arms flung round his body to drag him from his mount. Alexios fought him off as best he could with only one hand to spare. They were so close as they struggled, that the other's red hair, bright and ragged as the torches massed about the gateway, whipped across his face and got into his mouth until he spat it out. Behind them there seemed to be a running battle going on, ahead, rushing towards them, the gateposts with their bright crests of coloured rags and the crowding torches. He crouched forward onto Phoenix's neck, urging the game little horse on with voice and heel and gripping knees, but he seemed to be dragging forward with him the whole weight of Connla and Connla's pony like a swimmer battling against some kind of merciless undertow. And he was slipping—slipping—at the last instant he managed to bring up his spear and fling the ragged skull free from the end of it. Then his last grip gave, and as the gory thing spun up and over towards the massed torches of the gateway, he went down among the horses' hooves, with Connla sprawling on top of him.

There were a few moments of utter chaos; torchlight and darkness spinning over each other, and trampling hooves, and a great roaring like a forest gale. And then the world shook itself and settled the right way up. Groaning a little, for most of the wind had been knocked out of him, Alexios drew his knees under his belly and slowly got up. The "bull" lay fair and square within the Wolves' gateway, and the forest roaring had become the cheerful voice of the crowd, who by that time cared little enough who won the game, so long as it was a good fierce one with a little blood to show for it. Connla also was getting to his feet, panting and shaking the fiery hair out of his eyes. They looked at each other and grinned, cherishing their bruises.

"Did I not say that a child could play it, or a Red-Crest Roman?" said Connla.

Someone had caught their ponies, and they remounted and rode up from the level ground beside the burn with their arms across each other's shoulders, and the mingled teams following on behind, both loudly singing their own praises; and the onlookers with their torches streaming after them and on either side.

They did not return to the Chief's fire, but when Alexios had claimed the victor's jar of wine, bore it off in triumph to one of the lesser fires, to which they made their claim by propping up the unlovely remains of the calf's head now decked with coloured rags and ribbons from the Wolves' gatepost on a spear beside it.

It seemed to be the custom, at least according to Connla, that victors and vanquished in a game of Cattle Raid should share the prize between them. That seemed to Alexios a very good arrangement, for the slender necked Greek amphora was a good size and would not be their first drinking of the day, though the fast and furious game had helped to get rid of some of what had gone before. And he had no wish that the Commander of Castellum and his escort should return to the fort tomorrow morning lying across their ponies' backs like a string of leaking wineskins.

They knocked the head off the amphora as the quickest and simplest way of getting at the wine inside. Some of them had gathered up whatever they could find to drink from: a bowl of sycamore wood, a black pottery cup, a magnificent bull's horn bound with silver which somebody would be raising a tempest for when they found it gone—others drank from the amphora itself, until their friends took it away from them. Overhead, the smoke of the fire wafted across a sky of stars as soft as honeysuckle; the dancing flames seemed to Alexios the brightest that he had ever seen, fringed and feathered and quite extraordinarily beautiful, and slightly out of focus.

But still it seemed that Connla found something lacking. He rose and disappeared into the darkness full of moving shadows that lay between the fires, and almost before they realized that he had gone, was back, thrusting before him a shambling figure. "What is wine without harp-song to spread the wings of the spirit? See, I have captured us a harper."

There was a ragged outcry of approval all round the fire. Shouts of "A song! A song!" as men tossed up their wine-cups in greeting. And the harper stood swaying a little on his heels, and looked down at them; a small hairy man with unexpectedly the eyes of a dreamer in his narrow fox face.

"But first, a drink," said Connla, pushing the small man down into the space between himself and Alexios, who held out to him his own re-filled cup.

The harper took it, and held it up to the remains of the calf's head propped drunkenly on its spear beside the fire. "I drink to the Lord of the Feast!" He took a long gulping drink, then gave it back. "It is not every day that a man may taste such wine as that!"

"Then let the song be all the better for it!" someone shouted, and was echoed all round the fire. "The song! Give us the song, then!"

The harper had slipped the embroidered harp-bag from his shoulder, and taken out the small finely shaped instrument of black bog-oak strung with horsehair. Sitting with his head bent over it as a woman bends her head over the child in her arms, he began to tune the five strings, paying no heed to the voices baying all about him. Only when the thing was done to his complete satisfaction, he looked up. "So. Shall I sing of war? Or love? Or hunting?"

"We have heard over many songs of love and war and hunting. Old songs, old tales that all men know before the telling. Make us a new song!" Connla demanded.

But someone on the far side of the fire laughed. "Surely, let him make us a new song, if his wits are not too drowned in mares' milk!"

The harper looked round at them with immense dignity. "There are those who sing most sweetly when the drink is in them. I will not be singing you a new song, not because I cannot, I Nuada the Weaver of Tales, but because I do not choose. Yet I will give you a song that is new to you, as it was new to me when first I heard it, not half a moon since, in a High King's Hall."

And settling his harp into the hollow of his shoulder, he began, drawing his hand over the strings, lightly at first and almost hesitantly, as a little wandering wind, then more and more strongly until one expected to see sparks fly from beneath his fingers as from a weapon on a sharpening-stone, then dying to a haunting throb that was like the sound of a swan's wings in flight. And as the voice of the harp changed, so the voice of the harper changed, passing from singing to story-telling and back again, after the way of his kind.

Certainly, Alexios thought, sitting with the half-empty cup on his knee, the small foxy man was among those who sang most sweetly when the drink was in them. The drink was in himself, a little, too, and he heard vaguely, through a pleasant haze. Then after a while raised his head, suddenly alert, to listen.

This was a song that he knew. Half knew, anyway. One of the tales that his nurse had told him when he was small, among all those other songs and tales of her own land. The story of how Cuchlain came by the Black Seinglind and the Grey of Macha, the two horses of his chariot team. He had not recognized it at once, because he had known only the simple childish version told by a woman to a bairn, while this, though confused in places, with incidents left out or misremembered, was the true bard-telling, rich and fierce and darkly splendid; a telling for warriors in a High King's Hall.

And as he listened, something began to stir at the back of

Alexio's mind, not a warning, not yet strong enough for that, but a sense of something vaguely out of place and needing to be inquired into. A story new-come out of Hibernia in these days when the possibility of raids from across the Western Sea was one of the dangers that he and his kind were here to guard against … He was being a fool, he told himself, making an armed man out of a shadow. Harpers picked up songs wherever they went; and if the man were a spy of the Attacotti the last thing he would do, however much the drink was in him, would be to make the songs of his own people here among the Votadini. Nevertheless, when the song was finished, and the men round the fire had done shouting its praises and tossing gifts to the harper, and the talk had turned to other things, Alexios felt within his tunic and brought out a gold half-solidus which he could ill-afford, and dropped it into the empty cup which he still held, and gave it to Nuada the Weaver of Tales.

"That was a noble song, my friend, and worthy of gifts of hunting-dogs and golden arm-rings. Let you take this, since I have neither dog nor arm-ring about me."

"It was indeed a noble song," agreed the harper, and received the coin gravely, stowing it in his folded crimson waist-cloth.

"And this High King's Hall in which you heard it—I am thinking that would be the Hall of the High King of Erin himself?" Alexios gave the land its native name.

"Nay, but another as great. Not half a moon since, I was in the chief place of King Bruide, Lord of the Caledones, the Painted People."

Something tightened in Alexio's belly, then he let his caught breath go quietly, and made a great show of sprawling into an easier position, as one ready to listen to another story.

"Great doings there were, at the court of King Bruide," said the harper reflectively, "and many strangers there; men from over the Western Sea, carrying the Green Branch and come to talk of a princess's marriage."

Again Alexios felt that small cold tightening of the belly. Men from over the Western Sea, carrying the Green Branch. An embassy from the Attacotti to the Painted People. A marriage alliance—or might that be just a cover for something else …?

"Great lords, they were, and brought their own harper with them."

"And it was he who taught you the song of Cuchlain's chariot horses?" Alexios said, with seemingly only half-interest. That was odd, too, for surely such an embassy would not want to send out word of their coming on the four winds.

The small foxy man laughed. He had a hard head and was not very drunk; no harper could afford that until after the harp-song was done, lest his skill became entangled, but he was drunk enough to be reckless. "A harper's songs are his treasures and his stock-in-trade that he does not share with all comers. Many a one will not so much as take his harp from its bag when another of the brotherhood is by."

"But this one was more generous?" Alexios said idly.

"As to that, I did not put his generosity to the test. Na, na, being minded to gather anything that might be there for the gathering, I made pretence to be very drunk; sleepy-drunk beyond remembering anything that I heard, and lay snoring and twitching almost at the man's feet. And so—behold, I have a new song for the singing!" He leaned closer, "Aye, and there were other things I learned, beside the song …"

Alexios glanced at the man's sly vainglorious face. Almost he said, "And what things were they; these other things beside the song?" But the midst of a feasting crowd was not the time or place to be asking such a question. That would have to wait. He said only, "So—that was a trick worth ten!" and laughed.

But in the same instant he saw the answering laughter and all traces of the drink drain out of Nuada's face, leaving it suddenly stone-cold sober; and saw also that the harper was no longer looking at him, but up at someone standing behind his shoulder.

He glanced around quickly. A tall cloaked figure stood there on the edge of the sinking firelight. He could not make out the face in the shadow of the hood, but he scarcely needed to, the shape and the menace in the angle of the bent head was enough, even before a burst of flames as a half-burned log collapsed into the red heart of the fire woke the coldly venomous brilliance of the eyes under the hood. Eyes that there was no mistaking. Morvidd the oak priest seemed only to have checked a moment in passing; and having checked, moved on, leaving a chill on the air where he had passed.

The harper tried to laugh again. "Nay now, you should never believe aught that my kind is telling you. We are overused to the weaving of stories. And I—I have plied my craft in Erin before now." But the laughter had not enough breath to it, and his hands were shaking as he stowed his harp back in its bag. Then, scrambling to his feet he was gone, lurching away into the dark.

Alexios shot a quick glance at Connla; but with head tipped back and a frown of deep concentration, the Chieftain's brother was shaking the very last drops from the wine jar down his throat. Clearly he had seen nothing. If indeed there had been anything to see.

But in his heart, Alexios knew that he had not been imagining things. And for the second time, the memory that he brought away most vividly from the Chieftain's Rath was of the brilliant eyes of Morvidd the Priest in the black shadow of his hood.

A small memory, but a chill one.

8 | *Thunder Brewing*

As soon as he got back to Castellum next morning, Alexios let it be unofficially known that he would be glad to have a word with a certain harper who had been at the Chief-making feast, but would probably have gone his way by now. Then he sent for Druim of the Arcani and asked him if his men had heard anything of envoys from Hibernia coming to the High King of the Caledoni under the Green Branch; or of a gathering in the North to discuss plans for a marriage between the two peoples.

"Why should my men know of a thing so far beyond our hunting runs?" Druim asked.

"I have heard it said that not a leaf falls from the tree for three days' march beyond the Old Wall, that the eyes-and-ears of the Frontier do not hear it," Alexios said.

The other shook his head. "If a leaf had fallen from a Green Branch, and my men had heard it, assuredly the Commander would have been informed."

But there was something in his spy-master's open blue gaze that Alexios did not completely trust.

And next day three men who had been part of his escort at the Chief-making, reported finding the harper over towards the Long Moss.

"Face down in a soft patch, very dead," said one of them speaking for the rest. "We left him where he was, in case anyone came to see how he died, and missed him."

"You think—he didn't just lose his way?" Alexios said, feeling sick. "He was probably drunk."

"It was meant to look like that. But there was a little mark on his neck—if you knew where to look."

"And you are sure it was the same man?"

"We all saw him at the feast, Sir. And his harp was still in its bag between his shoulders; and this—in the folds of his waist-cloth." The man set down a gold half-solidus with a little click on the office table.

Alexios talked the thing over with Lucius and Hilarion, put the Frontier Wolves on double alert, and gave Druim orders to send some of his men up beyond the Old Wall. He was still not sure about trusting the Arcani, remembering with uneasy clearness Julius Gavros's opinion that they rode too much alone and listened to too many strange stories and dreamed dreams that could be dangerous. But he did not see that there was anything much he could do but assume that they were loyal. If they were, they might still pick up something. If they were not, and there *was* something brewing in the North, they would be off to join it when the time came, anyway.

Then he made out a detailed report and sent it to Breme-nium, though he very much doubted if it would serve any useful purpose, with Praepositus Calventius, the old Commander of the Numerus, a sick man, only holding on long after he should have been relieved, for his successor to take over.

"Why in the name of Ahriman the Black One couldn't they have promoted Gavros Praepositus and found somebody else for Habitancum?" Alexios demanded of his Senior Centenarius that evening as they stood together on the southern rampart, looking out over the thatched roofs of the town to the crop-lands beyond. "If there is going to be trouble we could do with an old Frontier

Wolf at Headquarters, and not a sick one, nor some new man who knows nothing of the Frontier and nothing of *us*."

"Spoken like a true Frontier Wolf yourself," said Hilarion beside him, his tone glinting with laughter, "and you not yet a year with the Family."

Alexios grinned, "Not so far short, though. It was none so long past harvest when I came—and look at the crop-lands now."

Leaning elbows side by side, they looked. In another three days it would be time to start cutting on the southern slopes. Alexios watched the barley whiten under a long warm sigh of wind from the south. Well, it promised to be a good harvest this year, anyway. That lightened his anxiety a little. Six years' service on the Frontiers had taught him that it was generally after a lean harvest that troubles came.

But Hilarion had begun sniffing the warm wind like a hound.

"Smelling Picts?" said Alexios. "Or is it the tanning sheds?"

"Wrong direction for Picts. No, I was thinking it's turning a bit thundery."

The thunder came in the night, with wind and hissing rain; and by next day's spent and sodden dawn, the croplands that had been sleek with promise in the evening light were rough and staring like the coat of a sick hound, pock-marked with threadbare patches where the ripe barley had been beaten flat to the earth.

In the days that followed, between the returning storms, garrison and tribesmen laboured side by side to get in what could be saved of the harvest. But much of the grain blackened before it dried enough to be cut and carried, and in the end the granaries made a poor showing that year as they had done the year before.

And the shadow of another lean harvest had had no time to lift before the government tax-gatherers were at Traprain Law, their underlings scattering through the Frontier raths and villages according to the yearly custom. For a while the Frontier Wolves were kept busy acting as escorts for the tax officials, a job which they did not relish. But it was over at last, and the Commander of Castellum heaved a sigh of relief. "Well at least nobody seems to have been knifed."

"I am thinking of some of those pot-bellied officials must have come fairly near to it," Lucius said, picking an early-fallen birch leaf out of his pony's mane. They were riding back from exercise in the time of long shadows. "The government might have chosen a better time for this new tax on broken horses."

"Do you think that's all it is?" Alexios asked after a moment.

"All what is?"

"I don't know. A feeling like thunder brewing in the back of my neck."

"The Votadini are resentful, of course," Lucius said slowly. "Wouldn't you be, if breeding and breaking horses was your way of life? But if there's trouble brewing—real trouble—"

"It's more likely to come down from the North or across from the West," Alexios said.

The Junior Centenarius cocked an eye at him. "Still brooding on that harper's story?"

"Not really, no. The Arcani report nothing out of the ordinary stirring beyond the Wall. Only …"

"Only?"

"*Only* I've got a feeling like thunder brewing in the back of my neck."

"And that's not the kind of thing you can put in an official report," Lucius said soberly; and then, turning the thing into a jest since there was not much else that you could do with it, "Heart up, Sir, it's probably the weather."

And laughing, they struck their heels into their ponies' flanks and took the last stretch back to the Sinister gate at full gallop.

The weeks passed, with still no sign of anything amiss beyond the Frontier; and life seemed to settle into its usual pattern again, as the dust sank behind the tax-gatherer's heels. After the storms that had wrecked the harvest, the autumn came in soft and gently; an open autumn of soft blustery winds and rain, and long spells of quiet gleaming days stretching far on into the time when they should have given place to winter. The swallows lingered about the eaves of Castellum as though unwilling to fly south, and long after they were at last gone, the honeysuckle was still in flower in the small walled wilderness behind the officers' quarters that had once been a garden; and the pessimists and weatherwise wagged their heads and talked about Paying for it Later.

Anyway it was getting late now for any kind of trouble from overseas—unless, said a small chill whisper somewhere deep within Alexios, the long mild autumn was to give anyone ideas for a gambler's surprise attack at the last possible moment when the garrison were already off-guard … Alexios kept the long summer-time patrols going weeks after the short two- or three-day patrols of winter would normally have come in, and there was a good deal of grumbling at Castellum in consequence. Even his two centenarii looked at him, Lucius with slightly puzzled surprise, Hilarion with amusement. But they had not seen the face of Nuada the Weaver of Tales when he saw Morvidd standing beside him.

The thing *could* still come.

What actually did come, a short while before midwinter, was word from the new Praepositus who had at last taken over command at Bremenium.

The message arrived late in the evening, brought by a weary galloper. And when he had opened the cloth packet and broken the sealed thread that held the tablets together and read what was scratched in careful clerk-hand on the wax within, Alexios broke the news to his officers gathered with him in the smoky Mess room. "We have all that we need to make us happy! Our new Commander is coming on a three-day visit of inspection!"

Everybody stopped whatever they were doing.

"When?" said Centenarius Lucius, looking up from Virgil on bee-keeping.

"He doesn't say. He's for Traprain Law first; I suppose it depends on how long the King keeps him there."

"But at *this* time of year!" said the Quartermaster, with disgust.

"It's an open season, roads still quite passable," Lucius pointed out reasonably. "And I'm thinking he'd have to dip his dragon to the Lord of the Votadini as soon as possible."

Hilarion leaned wearily back against the wall. "That will mean he's the keen type. All the virtues; not to be put off by the chance of a little wind and rain. That kind's always the worst."

"Take heart," Alexios told him, "the weather is bound to break soon. He may founder on the way up here."

"He'll want fresh meat, they always want fresh meat," said the Quartermaster fretfully.

"We'll send out a hunting party, Kaeso dear."

"What are we going to do with him for three days?" Lucius asked with slightly worried interest.

"He's coming to inspect us," Alexios said, closing the pair of tablets and dropping them on the table. "And inspect us he shall, Typhon included—and the fort, even to the old owl's nest in the armoury. Pray the heating in the bath-house works better than it usually does. And I suppose we'll have to put on some sort of manoeuvres or a display of weapon-dancing. You'd better get the optios busy on that."

It all sounded fairly pointless, and the troops would hate it, but it was the kind of thing one had to do on such occasions. He picked up the tablets again, and began thoughtfully to turn them over and over between his hands. "And it might be none so bad a thing to invite Cunorix and a few of his household warriors to come over here."

"What precisely for?" Hilarion asked.

"I don't know, yet—eat—grumble about the new horse tax—make contact, anyway."

Hilarion wagged his head gently, without troubling to lift it from the wall. "How *did* the Empire manage before it had you, Sir?"

Five days later Praepositus Glaucus Montanus arrived, clattering in through the Praetorian gate on a magnificent golden bay stallion, with his escort behind him.

And from that moment, the trouble started. The Praepositus did not understand the Tribes and clearly did not want to; and therefore, though they were his command, he did not understand the Frontier Wolves either. In his company, Alexios realized how much he himself had had to learn in the first year. But at least he had been willing to learn; Praepositus Montanus was not. He was an embittered man who had hoped for better things of the army than a command of Frontier Scouts at the back end of the Empire; but since that was what he had got, he would make them over into something more like troops he knew or break his neck and theirs in the attempt. An hour in his company was enough to tell Alexios that much.

And the Frontier Wolves would not take kindly to being made over.

When, on the very first evening, after watching the ponies taken down for watering, Montanus gave orders that the heathen custom of touching the black stone beside the ford was to cease, they were outraged and insulted. Also, they were afraid. The Lady would be angry, and there would be trouble for the horses, and for the men who rode them. But chiefly they were outraged that a cherished custom of the Ordo should be spat on. They showed nothing, but Alexios, who was well-tuned to his men by now, felt their mood and longed for the three days to be over.

On the morning of the first day, Praepositus Montanus inspected the fort and the Third Ordo, Frontier Scouts. He said little, but his rather full dark eyes touched on all things, especially Typhon perched on the junior trumpeter's shoulder, with a marked lack of enthusiasm.

And soon after the light noon meal had been eaten, Cunorix arrived, with Connla and a handful of his household warriors. Cunorix riding one of his best horses, and clad in all the splendour of a Celtic Chieftain from the huge brooch of enamelled bronze that held his cloak of red and saffron plaid at the shoulder, to the tip of the magnificent inlaid spearhead, which he carried reversed, according to the ancient custom, to show that he came in peace. His warriors behind him almost as fiery-fine as himself.

"I'm dazzled!" Alexios said, when the courtesy-greetings were over and the Guest Cup passed round; and he got a moment's chance of a word alone with his friend as they headed for the practice ground to watch the display of rough-riding which the Ordo had made ready for the Praepositus's entertainment. "Surely we have mistaken the time of year, and the sun stands at midsummer!"

Cunorix's big mouth curled suddenly almost from ear to ear. "Wolf Commander, are we not here to help you do honour in all ways to *your* Commander?" But his gaze followed where Glaucus Montanus rode just ahead, holding his golden bay on a short rein to make him prance and fidget. "Oh you beautiful!" he said very softly in the vernacular, "Oh you begetter of fine and fiery sons!"

"Horse or rider?" Alexios asked, equally softly, and there was a spirit of laughter from Connla beside him, while Cunorix murmured something about the rider which Praepositus Glaucus Montanus would not have cared to hear.

Alexios touched his heel to Phoenix's flank, and pushed forward to his Commander's side as they came out from the narrows of the half blocked up Sinister gate and saw the Ordo ready mounted and waiting for them in the open space beyond. All round the edge of the practice ground were the people of the town who had crowded up to watch the show, with the sellers of honey-cake and cheap wine busy among them as though it were a fair.

And the show was certainly worth the watching, Alexios thought, when he and his guests had taken up their position, and to the shining notes of the hunting-horn, the troops came flying by, skeining out like wild geese after the standard-bearer. He saw Typhon clinging to the shoulder of the junior trumpeter, his ears laid back and his bushy tail streaming out behind him as though in echo of the green silk tail of the Ordo dragon as it whipped out on the wind of their going. Certainly, he judged, the men were enjoying themselves, once the heart lifted in them and the thing warmed up. No one could do the crazy things that they were doing with such swing and dash unless they were also delighting in what they did; riding backwards, exchanging horses at full gallop, flinging off every trick of the rough-rider; while the ponies, linked to their riders by an inner communication, delighted also, you could see it in the way they tossed up their heads as they wheeled and turned to the signalling yelp of the hunting-horns, and the hand and heel of the men on their backs. And under all the seeming lightness of heart and almost-foolery,

Alexios sensed the concentration that must not be allowed to waver for an instant.

A pony streaked towards him, the rider half-out of the saddle, clinging tensely along the flank of his mount; then as they swept past, he gathered himself and swung down under the creature's belly among the flying hooves, and up again on the far side, and as he swung back into the saddle, Alexios saw that it was Bericus the Emperor's hard bargain. The crowd roared its approval, headed by a wild high hunting yell from Connla.

But as time wore by the Commander of Castellum became more and more aware that neither of his chief guests was giving their full attention to the riders who swept and swirled in front of them. The Praepositus because he did not consider such a back-woods display worthy of his full attention, and Cunorix because, though he was taking care not to show it to the world, he had seen the Praepositus's bay stallion with the eye of love, and also with the eye of a horse-breeder.

And the first of these things annoyed the Commander of Number Three Ordo for his men's sake, but the second touched him with a light chill finger, foreboding trouble ahead.

That evening they gathered for supper at a table set up in the cross-hall of the Principia, since there was not space for so many in the ordinary Mess room of the officers' quarters. Four braziers, burning wild cherry logs above the charcoal, gave off a fragrant smoke that hung among the rafters overhead where the light from the lamps on the table could scarcely reach.

The cookhouse orderlies had bestirred themselves to produce such a meal as Alexios never remembered to have eaten in Castellum before; and he exchanged glances of congratulation with the little round red Quartermaster, as they ate their way from hard-boiled duck-eggs through deermeat baked with moorland herbs to little crisp honey-cakes and the last of the dried figs.

With the serious eating over, and the thin Government-issue wine going round, the talk which had ranged wide over Frontier matters, had turned as Alexios had known that it would, to horses and to the new trained horse tax.

"It is an unjust tax," Cunorix said flatly.

"All taxes seem unjust to those who pay them," said the Praepositus affably. "Why this one above the rest?"

"For this reason: we breed and break horses for the Government—we have done that since first the Red Crests came—and we have done it at an agreed price. Now says the Government, 'For every horse you breed and break you shall pay us so much.' Therefore is the old price pulled down below what was agreed. Yet how if we say, 'So be it, then we can no longer sell to the Red Crests, but must look for better paying markets elsewhere?'"

"I imagine the Government would make an order that this could not be," Montanus said without much interest, taking another fig from the dish before him.

"I also. Therefore do I say it is an unjust tax."

"Say it to the tax-officers then." The Praepositus sounded slightly bored.

Cunorix grinned. "Do you think that I have not? Na, na, I do but grumble as one man may do to another over supper, when both have an eye for a horse to make common ground between them. It is a long time since I saw a better horse than the one the Praepositus rode this afternoon."

("Now it's coming," Alexios thought, listening with one ear while he continued to talk hunting with a warrior of the Chieftain's household.)

"As to that, I doubt very much whether you have seen his equal," said Montanus.

"Oh yes, but seldom, I grant you."

"Among your rough-coated hill ponies?"

"I have seen beyond my own horse-runs. But even there, let the Praepositus never think that there is neither fire nor beauty to be found among our northern herds; or that we of the Votadini take no pains with our blood-lines. I have a mare, part Arab, the beloved of my father the old Chieftain's heart, before he died—"

"I have no need to buy a pony, and if I had, this is surely neither the time nor place for horse-coping," said the Praepositus, with all traces of his affability quite gone. The two men looked at each other in a sudden silence, as the talk around the table fell away, and face after face turned to watch them.

Cunorix's eyes seemed to grow larger, gathering the brightness of the lamplight into them. He said very gently, "That is as well, since the mare is not for sale. As to the time and place, I can but hope that the Commander of Castellum will forgive me—I would have waited until tomorrow and come to you with all formality, but it has been told to me that you will be here only the one more day, and therefore there is no time for the proper courtesies."

"If I knew what you were talking about—" began the Praepositus.

"Nay, but you do not. Therefore listen a little. The thing is very simple. The mare is ripe to breed—late, yes, but the autumn has been a long and gentle one, and we have kept her as my father used to do, under our own roof. A foal begun now would be born at a bad time of year, but there would be food and warm shelter for him and his mother."

There was a pause, during which Montanus's good-looking fleshy face turned a greyish red. "The foal? What foal? Do you imagine that I would lend out a good horse for the breeding of scrub ponies?"

"No scrub pony," Cunorix said, still gently, "did I not say she was part Arab?"

Alexios, watching, knew what the gentleness cost him, and judged by that how surely he must want the bay stallion for the fathering of Shadow's foal.

"You said, yes, but what proof have I?" The Praepositus laughed harshly. "Nay, do not trouble. If you could show me her blood-line direct from Pegasus himself, can you think of any reason why I should agree to this extraordinary request?" His flush deepened still further. "Do you suggest *paying* for it?"

"I had not thought that the Praepositus would wish to be paid. Rather it was in my mind to offer a hunting pony or a pair of hounds as a gift in gratitude. Yet lest the Praepositus should think that also a kind of payment, let him remember only that it was a request made in all courtesy, and a tribute to the beauty and mettle of his horse."

Slowly, the colour of Montanus's face was returning to normal. He bent his head somewhat stiffly in acknowledgement. "There is no more that need be said. If I was overquick to see offence where none was meant, remember that I am strange to Frontier ways and Frontier manners." But there was no warmth in his tone, and it was clear what he thought of Frontier ways and Frontier manners.

Thankfully, Alexios heard the horn sounding from the rampart for the Second Watch of the night. Hilarion, who was duty officer, lounged to his feet and took up his sword which he had slung from the back of his camp chair, saluted the Praepositus, and strolled out. Behind him, the men around the table passed the wine and began idly to talk again of this thing and that. "It's over," Alexios thought, "it's over, and not too much harm done. Thanks be to the Lord Mithras, Connla didn't see fit to join in!"

But the thought made him glance at Connla, all the same, and what he glimpsed for an instant in the face of the Chief's younger brother, a silken brightness, a kind of dancing devil behind the eyes, made him wonder uneasily if the thing was over, after all.

Next day the Praepositus announced that he wished to spend the morning in the Principia office, looking over the paperwork of the fort. Alexios, hurriedly going over in his mind the state of payrolls and duty rotas and armament and store lists, thought that everything was more or less in order, and that anyway they would be having the same problems about faulty supplies and arrears of pay at Headquarters. Also it would give him a chance to make sure that his Commanding Officer had seen the report that he had sent in after the death of the Weaver of Tales. But when he brought up the subject, Praepositus Montanus heard him out but seemed not at all impressed.

"That was upward of four months ago, and there have been no further developments? No more reports brought back by the Arcani?"

"No, Sir."

"Then I think that it can be safely written off as mere wind-blown rumour. All Frontier folk are fine tellers of tales."

"The man died," Alexios said.

"He was drunk and missed his way in bog country."

Alexios said nothing; and sitting at the office table, Montanus turned to look at him. "What *is* it, then?"

And Alexios could not say, as he had said to Lucius, "A feeling like thunder brewing in the back of my neck," so he said nothing.

"You see?" The Praepositus pushed away the papers that had been in front of him. His tone was suddenly kindly but tinged with scorn. "I'd be careful about this kind of thing if I were you;

sending in too many scare reports. Your record won't stand it, Ducenarius. Are we finished here?"

Alexios carefully unclenched his hands. "Yes, Sir, quite finished."

That evening, the last of the official visit, Number Three Ordo entertained their new Praepositus to a display of weapon dancing. They had carried out the heavy chair from the Commander's quarters, and set it just within the entrance to the old waggon shelter, with bundles of hay piled at either side for Alexios and his officers to sit on. And from his place beside the Praepositus, Alexios looked out across the glow of the brazier set before the entrance, and saw the empty space of the Dancing Ground ringed round with torches, and the shadows that moved in the darkness between, and heard the first waking murmur of the drums.

From the shadows on the far side two rows of men stepped forward, each man carrying a pair of native dirks, and advanced to the centre of the open space. They nearly always started with Dirk-Drill, it was a kind of warming up; and a good deal more like drill in the Legion's sense of the word than anything that was likely to come after. Alexios watched them spread out until each man could just cross dirk-tips with the man next to him, and take their stand, feet a little apart, ready and waiting. The drowsing drums woke suddenly and coughed into the night. The blades swung up and over, catching the torchlight, sank, and swung out to touch tips each with the blade next to it—Alexios heard the light kiss of metal on metal—then rose again in perfect time to the rhythm of the drums. A slow rhythm at first, growing faster and faster, beaten out by swift hard fingers and the side and flat of the hand, until the blades whirled almost faster than the eye could follow; until at last, to a final roar of the drums, each man flung his dirks spinning up into the air and caught them again by the blade as they came still spinning down. And *that* was not in any drill book.

Nor was anything else that came after, that night.

The Ordo were doing themselves and their Commander proud, and their Commander watching with a swordsman's eye, knew it, and felt a warm rush of pride towards them as he watched the shifting patterns of war and hunting dances perfectly carried out, and heard the staccato belly-cries of the dancers, and saw the weapons catch the torchlight and cut the darkness with their speed-flash. And the weapons were not blunted. When two men stepped out before the rest, and laid their crossed swords on the ground and wove their intricate web of steps through and round and over, a false step could have cost the man who made it a foot; and when the lines of yelling spearmen pranced to and fro, a moment's mistiming could have been somebody's death.

The dancing was drawing to a close, only the "Wolf Spears" with which they always ended, to come now. The Dancing Ground was empty again, waiting in the torchlight. Alexios was aware of a new creeping cold; a rawness in the air, a kind of curling golden smoke around the torches. There was a mist coming up from the estuary. He was aware also, as the chosen dancers stepped forward, of his senior optio standing before him, holding two spears, his own and another. The man grinned, "Sir?" and gave a small upward flick to the spare weapon.

Alexios did hesitate for an instant. The Frontier Wolves had taught him well in the year since the incident of the Bull Calves, but he had a very clear idea what the Praepositus would think of his Ordo Commander joining in the barbarian weapon-dances of their men.

Then he got up and flung off his cloak, and stepped out past the brazier, neatly catching the spear which the grinning optio tossed to him, and took his place in the forming circle.

The deerskin drums woke again, and he moved forward,

stamping with his right foot, then his left, then pivoted, crouching low with bent knees.

The beaten ground gave back a rhythmic pulsing beneath his stamping heels, as of a heartbeat somewhere very far down. The swift throb of the drums was waking in him, as it always did, ancient blood-memories that at other times he did not know he possessed, drawing him into a oneness with his fellow dancers, so that while the dance lasted they were all part of each other ... But the dance was coming to its whirling climax; the voice of the drums rose to a booming howl then fell sharply silent. And the dancers turned, and swept with levelled spears straight for the place where the new Praepositus sat. At the last instant they checked, raising the long-drawn mournful wolf-cry, and tossed up their spears in salute.

And it was over.

Alexios handed his spear to another man and returned to the pile of hay on which he had been sitting. He was breathing quickly, the sweat trickling under his leather tunic. The rhythm of the dance still seemed pulsing through him as he flung on his cloak once more, against the chill of the thickening mist.

"An interesting display," said Glaucus Montanus, but nothing showed in his face save a somewhat chilly boredom.

"Thank you, Sir." Alexios turned and flung up his hand in thanks and dismissal to his men.

From the direction of the Praetorian gate, now that the drums and the stamping heels were silent, he could hear voices upraised in song and laughter. A bunch of revellers returning from an off-duty evening in the town, and exchanging the customary insults with the gate guard.

He supposed that would be something else for the Praepositus to disapprove of. Well, thanks be to the Lord of Light, tomorrow morning the visit of inspection would be over.

9 | The Praepositus's Horse

NEXT MORNING, WITH THE COLD RIVER MIST SWIRLING BETWEEN the buildings and turning Castellum into a ghost fort, Glaucus Montanus ate his morning bread and cheese and raisins huddled in his cloak beside the glowing brazier that filled the Commander's quarters with smoke and a little warmth. He had summoned the fort Commander to join him, and was engaged in telling him exactly what he did not approve of in the handling of the fort and Number Three Ordo. There was a good deal he did not approve of, and he dealt with it in detail, so it took some time. To Alexios, sitting with his bread and cheese untouched before him, it seemed that it was going on for ever. From outside, muffled in the mist that seemed to blur sound as well as sight, came the familiar sounds of the ponies being taken down to the drinking-place. He wondered if the men were obeying orders and not touching the Lady as they passed. If the mist got much thicker, the Praepositus wouldn't leave at all today. The clatter of hooves died into the distance.

The Praepositus had got as far as last night's dancing. "Am I to understand that here at Castellum it is the custom for the Commanding Officer to join in these barbarian war-dances with the men?"

"All the officers, sometimes," Alexios said, determinedly starting on his bread and cheese, "not always, but sometimes—on special occasions."

"On special occasions? Such as when the Commander of the Numerus is here? It is considered an edifying spectacle?"

"It isn't considered anything, Sir." Alexios felt his hackles rising. "It's just something that happens. It wasn't even planned for last night."

"I should not let it happen again, if I were you." Montanus bit into the last of the dried figs that had been brought out in his honour. "That kind of thing is not the best way to keep your men's respect."

Alexios wanted to say, "When you have served a year with the Wolves, come and tell me what keeps and what loses the men's respect." He wanted to add, "That is to say, if they haven't dropped you head foremost in a peat bog before then."

But before he could say anything, footsteps came along the colonnade, and there was an urgent mutter of voices outside. The door opened and one of the optios appeared, grey mist swirling like smoke behind him, his wolfskin headed with a bloom of wet. "Sir," he said, "Sir, the Praepositus's horse—"

Montanus sat forward with a jerk, "What about my horse?"

The optio looked quickly from Alexios to his senior officer and back again; then spoke as it were to the air between them. "Sir, I have to report that the Praepositus's horse has been stolen."

The Praepositus let out a roar, "Stolen? What in Satan's name do you mean stolen?"

Alexios cut in quickly, getting to his feet. "What happened, Optio?"

"We took the ponies down to water and exercise as usual, Sir, the Praepositus's groom had the Praepositus's bay. Everything just as usual till we were clear of the fort, and then," the man shook his head as though he simply could not believe what he had seen, "he just galloped off into the mist."

"No question of the horse bolting with him?"

"Och, no, Sir. He heeled him into a gallop—and the mist took him. We gave chase of course, but in this murk we lost them. Half a patrol is still out after him, but—"

"But you let him slip through your fingers," Glaucus Montanus snapped. "God! If I ever get my hands on that groom of mine, I'll make him weep that he was ever spawned!"

"Sir," said the optio woodenly, "his hood fell back—one of the men says he had red hair. The Praepositus's groom is dark."

There was a sharp silence. It seemed as though the cold still-ness of the river fog had seeped into the Commander's quarters. From outside, the sounds of the fort came muffled. A pine knot in the brazier went off with a small sharp crack and a spitting of sparks.

"Optio," Alexios said, "will you ask Centenarius Hilarion to meet me in the Principia office." He was already wearing his leather tunic; he slipped his sword-belt over his head, and reached for his wolfskin cloak where it lay across the end of a bench.

"Red hair—then if it wasn't the groom, who the Devil—" he heard Praepositus Montanus's angry voice behind him.

"I don't know," he said, "that's what we have to find out. Will you wait here for me, Sir. I'll be back …"

And he plunged out into the mist, flinging on his cloak as he went.

In the office, Centenarius Hilarion joined him, and they stood for an instant looking at each other.

"Cunorix?" Hilarion said.

Alexios shook his head. "I do not think he'd be such a fool; and his hair's not red."

"Connla, then."

"How will he have got in?" For once, Hilarion was not prop-ping up the furniture.

"How will whoever it was have got in? Probably with that

bunch back from town leave last night." Alexios thought for a moment. "Send a patrol over to Cunorix's Rath—with a trumpeter under the Green Branch—to ask if the Praepositus's horse has strayed in that direction."

"Sir," said the Centenarius Hilarion.

"And have a thorough search made of the fort and the town for that wretched groom or his body—try the women's huts."

There was a flash of grim laughter in Hilarion's face. "I know the kind of places to look." He saluted and turned about.

A few moments later, Alexios was back in his own quarters and once more facing his raging commanding officer.

"It must have been one of those accursed tribesmen." The Praepositus made it sound like an accusation against Alexios himself. "And he must have been in the fort all night!" He was pacing up and down, flinging his words over his shoulders. "If I do not get my horse back, I shall hold you personally responsible as the Commanding Officer here. I shall send in a report that discipline is slack and the security at Castellum leaves a great deal to be desired."

"You will get your horse back, Sir," Alexios said, with more optimism than he felt. "Also we are mounting a search for your groom."

Montanus made an impatient gesture, as though brushing the groom aside, then checked, and turned his head at the sound of hooves trotting down towards the West gate.

"I have sent a patrol with a herald to inquire at a certain village if the Tribune's horse has strayed that way."

"*Strayed!*"

"Strayed," said Alexios quietly.

Montanus's face turned ugly. "You are supposed to keep the peace in this part of the Frontier; hold the Tribes quiet, but it seems that you are scarcely fitted for the work. Maybe you are afraid of these North British, as I seem to have heard that you were of the Danubius tribes!"

That was the second time. And this time it was a deliberate insult. Alexios drew a quick, shaking breath, and let it out very carefully. "As you have pointed out to me, Sir, Castellum and Number Three Ordo are my command. Unless you wish to relieve me of it, I make the Commander's decisions here. Hold me to account for them *afterwards* if they prove wrong."

And then he heard what he had said.

Soon after, the groom was discovered, perfectly unharmed save for an aching head and the loss of all his clothes, sitting on the steps of the half-ruined temple to Castor and Pollux in the middle of the town, and staring owlishly in front of him. Dragged up to the fort, muffled in a blanket, and standing rather shakily before Ducenarius Aquila, he admitted that he had given himself leave last night and gone off with the rest into the town. He had gone to the women's huts. There was a girl, a pretty girl. No, he had no idea which hut, in the darkness and murk; and they had all gone to a wine shop first—that was where he had first seen the girl. She had taken him home and given him more wine, and the next thing he had known, he had been sitting on the temple steps with no clothes on.

Looking at his greening face, Alexios knew that there would be nothing more to be got out of him. "Take him away," he said, "he's going to be sick. When that's over, pour something hot down him, or we'll have him on our hands with the lung-fever."

At about the same time in the Rath of Cunorix, Connla clad in the groom's missing cloak and breeks, was facing his very angry brother. Connla laughing, and with every flaming hair of his head seeming to be living a life of its own quite unquenched by the smoking wet.

"The Chieftain said he wished to breed from the horse. I only did the thing to please the Chieftain my brother."

Standing on the threshold of his Hall, Cunorix looked back at him with no trace of answering laughter. "Did you so, little brother? It is in my mind that you did it because the Praepositus refused and you do not like the Praepositus, and also because you thought it would be fine sport."

Connla swaggered a little, his hands on his hips and the laughter dancing like summer lightning behind his eyes. Several of the tribe who chanced to be about their business nearby had drawn closer; among them two or three girls from their looms or their grinding querns, and among the girls one who was red-headed as himself, Teleri the swordsmith's daughter.

"It is true that I do not love the Praepositus. And it *was* fine sport. Did our father himself not say that horse-raiding was a fine sport and kept the young warriors in trim for the war-trail?"

"Horse-raiding between us and the Damnoni or the Caledoni is one thing," Cunorix said. "To steal a horse from a fort of the Roman kind in the night is another, especially from a fort commanded by a friend."

Connla shrugged. "The Ducenarius Aquila is a Roman as well as a friend. Let him keep his horses if he can."

"But it is the Praepositus's horse, and the Ducenarius who will suffer for it. Is there not one thought in your head?"

"Do not you for ever treat me as though I were a bairn!" Connla flared.

"Then do not you for ever behave as though you were one! Where have you left the horse?"

"In a safe place," Connla said; and then meeting his brother's slightly widened gaze, added sullenly, "In the old branding corral."

"Then go now and fetch him in," said Cunorix.

They stood and looked at each other, the battle of their wills making almost visible sparks in the air between them. Then into the silence came the sound of running feet. Faces turned towards the gate-gap in the hawthorn hedge. The mist was beginning to thin out and grow ragged, and out of it appeared Gault, one of the young warriors of the Clan and a close friend of Connla's. He came on and up to join the little group about the Hall threshold, and spoke to Cunorix, but exchanged a grin with the Chief's younger brother. "There is a band of Wolves coming this way."

"One of their patrols?" asked Cunorix.

The boy shook his head, out of breath a little, but not much, with his running. "Not an ordinary patrol. They are heading straight for the rath, and their leader is carrying the Green Branch."

"How far behind you?"

"Hard on my tail," said the boy. "Listen."

In the silence they heard the green plover crying, and then the faintest quiver of sound that strengthened to the light beat of hooves: ponies coming up from the ford at a trot. No patrol ever rode like that.

Out of the thinning mist appeared the silvered shapes of the troop. They checked in the gateway, as good manners demanded, then as the warriors who had gone down to meet them stood aside, came on, to the faint jingle of accoutrements and creak of damp saddle leather. In the midst of the Chieftain's forecourt they reined in, and the troop leader, he with a sprig of broom in his hand—green branches were not easy to come by in the North in winter—swung down from his pony.

"The sun and moon on your path, Lord of Six Hundred Spears," he said in formal greeting.

"And on yours," Cunorix returned. "What is it that brings a patrol of the Frontier Wolves within my gates?"

"The Praepositus Glaucus Montanus has lost his horse," the grim flicker of a smile touched the troop leader's mouth, "and we are come to inquire whether by chance he has wandered this way."

Cunorix gave him back look for look, while the ponies fidgeted. "Yes," he said clearly and deliberately. "My brother Connla found him wandering and recognized him."

Connla opened his mouth, then shut it again. One of the ponies ruckled down its nose. "So, that is well," said the troop leader. "Now if you will have him brought out to us, we will be on our way back."

"It will take a small while," Cunorix said. "My brother found him up at the Glen head, and since he was already bringing in two lead horses he could handle no more, and left him up there in the old branding corral." And to Connla he said, "Go now, and fetch him."

Connla stood a long moment quite unmoving. He had gone an odd pearly white, his eyes suddenly very dark, fixed on his brother's. Then he flung around and strode away.

Behind him the rath went about its usual affairs. "Come," said Cunorix to the troop leader, "you must drink the Guest Cup while we wait." And the two men went together into the Hall, while the rest of the Frontier Wolves dismounted and squatted down to wait, each man with his arm through his pony's bridle. Someone produced a pair of knuckledusters, two more began to play Flash the Fingers. The mist was clearing quickly now, a gleam of thin winter sunshine finding its way through. A few children and dogs gathered to stand and stare. From just beyond the entrance to the stable court, the tall, dark-cloaked figure that had stood there looking on from the first, still stood unmoving.

Presently, for the second time that day, the Rath of Cunorix heard the sound of nearing hooves, but this time it was one horse only, and being ridden at a furious gallop. Cunorix and the troop leader came out from the Hall, and suddenly from houseplace doorways and dark entrances of smithy and stables and store-sheds, men and women appeared, drawn by the fierce drum of nearing hooves. And up from the ford and through the gate-gap swept the Tribune's bay stallion with Connla already half-out of the high military saddle. Before the Hall threshold he brought the animal up, rearing and plunging to a halt; blood flecked the white foam that spattered from its muzzle—the Tribune rode with a wolf-bit but did not misuse it—the poor brute's eyes were wild and its flanks streaked with sweat.

The troop leader stepped forward quickly to take the bridle and draw a consoling hand down the shivering neck. "Was it needful to ride him so hard?" he said to Connla who confronted him grinning, still with that odd pearly whiteness in his face.

"I was not wishing to keep the Praepositus waiting," he said.

"Very good of you," the leader said with heavy sarcasm; then jerking his chin to the number two rider of the troop, "Here, take him in charge. Go easy with him, you can see the state he's in and his mouth's been cut to ribbons."

He took no care to keep his voice down, let anyone hear who wanted to. But he and Cunorix took leave of each other with the ritual courtesy which the Green Branch demanded. Then he barked an order, and the whole troop swung into their saddles, and with the Praepositus's bay horse among them, went clattering out through the gate-gap and down towards the ford.

The swordsmith's red-haired daughter who had come out again with a knot of other girls to watch gave a crow of high mocking laughter. Connla swung round on her, but what she saw in his face made her laugh the more. "So much for your horse-raiding, my bonnie lad!" she said, and turned with a flick of her saffron skirts, and walked away.

The tall watching shadow in the entrance to the stable court made a small hissing sound of satisfaction, almost like the dry whisper of a snake moving over dead leaves, and turned his hooded head to watch her go.

If the red-haired girl had not laughed, much of what happened after might never have happened at all.

Before evening, the Praepositus's horse was safely back in the Castellum stables, and the life of the fort had returned to normal—or as near as it could get to normal before the Tribune took his delayed departure next morning.

But in a herdsman's summer bothy in a fold of the high moors, three men sat huddled in their cloaks with no fire on the little stone hearth to warm them or betray their presence to a passing hunter.

"It is a full-moon-crazy plan," one of them said. "But I am thinking it might work, for all that."

"Of course it will work! It is the fine plan!" said Connla's voice out of another of the huddled shapes.

"First we must find another mare in season, and it's over late in the year. Pity it is that we cannot use Shadow herself."

Connla gave a crack of laughter. "That would be a jest for the gods!" And added regretfully, "No, Cunorix goes to whisper love talk in her ear every night; and besides, we'll not likely be able to get her back. It will have to be a little scrub mare. The Praepositus's bay will fancy her just as well."

"If there's one to be found. What if there is none?"

"Then we'll use fire arrows and stampede them that way. But first we will go to Finnan Horse-herd. If there's another horsy mare to be found in the runs, he'll know. I sometimes think

Epona the Mother of Foals whispers all the secrets of the herd in that one's ear at night."

Next day dawned wet and squally, the stillness of the mist given way to blustery rain, and the men taking their horses down to the watering-place cursed and huddled deep into their wolfskins; not that they really cared about the weather, they were too well used to it; but cursing it was almost as much a custom as touching the Lady as one rode past. In the dusk of the winter morning the alder scrub along the bank took on strange shapes, and the horses seemed on edge, sniffing the wind and dancing.

The Praepositus's tall bay in particular was almost out of hand, and his rider cursed, "Misbegotten son of a lop-eared mother! What call for all this fretting and fuming?" The Praepositus's groom was confined to barracks, and the Frontier Wolf in charge of him, whose own pony would have to wait until this pampered brute had been seen to, felt thoroughly hard done by.

The last troop had gone down to the watering pool, their riders slipping from their backs, and among the wiry hill ponies the red stallion dipped his head to drink. The clear brown water riffled round his muzzle, the sky-reflecting ripples spreading out from the bank to meet and mingle in a criss-cross web of brightness from a score of other thirsty muzzles.

And then it happened. First one and then another of the ponies lifted their heads to look round. There was a shrill whinny, answered from upstream, and out from the alder scrub trotted a small rough-coated mare who flung up her head at sight of the troop-ponies, and came bucketing down the bank to join them. Instantly there was chaos at the watering pool, the ponies milling this way and that as the mare in their midst stood tossing her head, waiting as her nature told her, for the stallion fighting, and the Lord of the Herd to take her. The stallions bit at each other's crests, one upped with his heels and caught another squarely in the ribs.

"She's in season!" the optio shouted. "Who in Typhon's name let her loose—"

The man had plunged into the mêlée, trying to sort things out; the red stallion neighed like a trumpet and made straight for the rough little mare, heedless of the efforts of the Scout in charge of him to hold him back.

Then it seemed to the Scout that a small thunderbolt took him in the back of the neck. Lightning shot inwards through his head from the point of impact, and he pitched forward into ringing darkness.

Up at the fort, the optio was once again reporting the loss of his horse to the Praepositus who seemed to have passed through yesterday's fury to something quieter and more dangerous. "They let a mare in season in among the troop while we were watering them. Of course the ponies went mad, and in the general garboil, they—some tribesmen—knocked the man in charge of him out with a chop below the ear and got away with the horse, Sir. Him and a couple more of his friends that were hiding in the scrub upstream. It was all pretty quick, Sir, couldn't rightly see what happened. A couple of troops are off after them, and without the mist they'll not get far."

"For the sake of the troops concerned, I sincerely hope not," said Montanus in a tone that was softly vicious.

"The country will help them. It's their country," Alexios heard himself saying. He felt sick and furious and helpless. He and his men were being made to look fools before this high-nosed new-come Commander, and something within him knew that this was a situation that could very easily get out of hand. When he saw Connla again ...

The optio's eye was on him. "With respect, Sir, for a good many of us, it's ours too."

The hunt was streaming out across the hills of the border country; the three wild riders far ahead, the pursuit strung out like a skein of wild geese, streaming grimly after.

The Frontier Wolves, too, felt that they were being made to look fools. The thing that had started out as little more than a rough jest had gone beyond that now and was turning ugly. They settled down in their saddles and rode, knowing that the chase was like to be a long one. They forded the river further up, and swinging right-handwise made for the broken scrubby valleys of the high moors westward. Doubling and twisting, the quarry tried to throw them off the trail; once they almost succeeded, but just as the Scouts were swinging southward to come between them and the fringes of the Forest Country, a stray gleam of winter sunlight picked out a flying speck of fox-red, far up the opposite hillside; and one of the men shouted, pointing, "There they go! They've doubled back—"

And the hunt was off again, streaming northward.

Hills and valleys, high moors dark with the sodden wreck of last year's heather; broken country choked up with tangles of hazel and rowan along the steep burnsides. Both hunters and hunted knew every foot of that countryside drawing up towards the Old Wall; knew the run of the valleys, the wooded patches where one could break through from one valley into another without getting skylined. Streaming along the hillsides, splashing burns and boggy places the hunt went on.

Until suddenly, as suddenly as Alexios's wolf-hunt had ended close on a year ago, and with scarcely any warning, the end came.

It came in the upland valley below the ruins of the old signal tower where the Commander of the Third Ordo had killed his wolf. And it came because the bay stallion, racing ahead, for all his fire and speed and courage, had not been born and bred to the northern hills, and weary as he was, his willing though bewildered heart near to bursting, slipped in crossing the burn where the autumn rains had pulled down the bank, and came crashing down. And Connla, flung clear, caught his head on a twisted alder root and knocked the senses half out of it.

The other two swung back to him; one hauled him half across his own pony's withers, but the dark skein of the hunt was upon them, and below the ruined walls of the signal post, just as Alexios's wolf had done, they turned at bay.

The wintry light glinted on the dirk blades. There was a sharp vicious scrap among the fallen stones and bramble scrub, and when it was over, and the hushing of the wet wind closed over the ugly snarl of fighting, two of the Frontier Wolves and one of the tribesmen lay dead, the third tribesman had escaped, and Connla, his teeth bared and eyes narrowed like a noosed animal, was standing with his hands lashed behind his back, in the midst of his captors.

A little downstream, the beautiful bay stallion was screaming and struggling to get up, with threshing forelegs and a broken back.

"Someone see to that poor brute," the optio said.

One of the Frontier Wolves—it was Bericus—drew his knife and went down the streamside; and among the alders the terrified threshing ceased.

"Right," said the optio. "Bring him along."

They flung Connla up onto his dead friend's pony, and laid the dead Scouts across the backs of their own mounts. "What about him?" someone asked, jerking a thumb at the sprawling body of the young brave.

"Leave him to our brothers the ravens," said the optio.

Men were swinging back into the saddle. Someone took the dirk from the dead tribesman's hand and cleaned it by stabbing it into the turf before adding it, with Connla's, to his own belt.

Bericus came back up the streamside with a sullen, sick look to his mouth and the bay stallion's gear and saddle over his shoulder.

They closed round the captive. Connla had begun to struggle in his bonds, shouting "Let me go! Let me go! My brother will make you weep blood that ever you laid hands on me—"

Someone struck him on the mouth and wrenched the pony's head round. The first cold winter rain was sweeping in from the estuary as they headed back towards Castellum.

Among the stones of the ruined signal post, the grass of nearly a year had grown in over the small black scar of a cooking-fire, and no trace now remained of the day that Alexios and Cunorix had made it, and the shared day's hunting that had been a good day and shot through with laughter.

10 | *Fire Along the Frontier*

THE FRONTIER PEACE HAD BEEN BROKEN. TWO SOLDIERS HAD been killed and so had the Praepositus's favourite horse.

Now in the Sacellum of the fort, the Praepositus and Ducenarius Aquila faced each other. The lamp had been lit on the table, for outside the wet and windy daylight was fading fast, and in the upward light the snarling silver dragon-mask of the Ordo standard seemed to hover forward on its spearshaft, its shadow, and the shadows of the two men flung far up the rough plastered walls behind them.

Only a few moments before, Connla also had stood there under guard, listening to his sentence decreed by the Tribune. He had stood there with that wicked laughter of his like summer lightning all about him. Only once he had licked his dry lower lip, as though maybe the thing was not so funny, after all. That had been so short a time ago that it seemed to Alexios that he could still hear the footsteps of guard and captive in the colonnade outside.

"In the Name of Light, Sir!" Alexios was saying, "Horse-raiding—horse stealing—they're a rough sport, a—a game of skill, to the tribesmen."

"I do not need that you should explain the tribesmen of North Britain to me," said the Praepositus.

"With respect, Sir, I think you do." (With respect, with respect …) "The whole thing was more than half in jest—only the jest went wrong."

"It went wrong indeed. Therefore I intend to make an example of the jester, that no one may make the same kind of jest again." Montanus raised his voice as Alexios tried to cut in. "These people forget who is master all too quickly. They need to be taught the lesson afresh from time to time."

"I doubt you'll teach it them by putting the Chief's brother up as a live target for javelin practice!"

"It is a usual enough form of execution—and quicker than the old style crucifixion used to be, if your heart is so tender toward these people—I presume your men *are* trained to cast a javelin at a target?"

"When they can see it," Alexios said desperately. "But the light is almost gone."

"Have torches brought out onto the place you call the Dancing Ground. That will give them light enough."

"Not in this wind, and with the rain driving. At least, Sir, wait till morning."

Montanus leaned forward across the table. His face was a narrow-eyed reddish mask in the lamplight, and his shadow ran up to engulf half the Sacellum behind him. "And give your friends the chance to rescue him?"

Alexios was silent. He was thinking more that it might give the Praepositus's temper time to cool; but that was a slim chance, and he knew it. It was a cool anger already, which was what made it so deadly. It was beyond mercy or reason.

"No, Sir, I ask only to wait for better light, that the work may be done cleanly and quickly; my men are not butchers."

"No? I did not know that the Frontier Wolves had a great reputation for squeamishness. Will you give the necessary orders now, Ducenarius Aquila?" A pause. "Or would you prefer me to take over the command and see to the matter myself?"

Again Alexios was silent, and into the silence came the sharp spatter of sleet against the window, and somewhere far off the cry of a wolf on the hunting trail. That could be his way out. He could refuse. Hand over his command. That would mean the end of whatever career was still left to him; the execution would still go on, but he would keep his hands clean of it. Only suddenly he knew that keeping his hands clean wasn't the important thing. The important thing was that he should do what he could—the only thing he could—for Connla.

"Well?" said the Praepositus.

"I will give the necessary orders, Sir," Alexios said stiffly. "I request that it shall be set down in the day-book that before doing so, I made an official protest against this execution, which I am prepared to stand by, before any future Court of Inquiry."

"Your request is noted," said the Praepositus.

Alexios spoke to the sentry at the door, and a few moments later, Centenarius Hilarion stood in the doorway. In a dead-level voice Alexios gave him the necessary orders to assemble the men for javelin practice; to have the Dancing Ground as well lit as possible by torches; to have the captive brought out.

"Sir," said Hilarion, his voice as dead-level as Alexios's own, and saluted and went out.

"I am going to my quarters," Glaucus Montanus said when he was gone. "Send me word when all is ready."

Alexios remained alone in the Sacellum, staring down at the table before him. He felt sick. His mouth was dry and the palms of his hands wet, and his heart had taken on a slow, heavy, drubbing beat that seemed to shake his whole body. He tried not to think. He knew what he had to do, and beyond that, thinking would not help either himself or Connla. He tried to make his mind a blank; but things from the outside world kept breaking through into the blankness of it. The squally spatter of sleet on the window, somewhere far off the howl of the wolf, answered by another, near at hand the bark of orders and the quick confused tramp of booted feet coming up from the barrack rows; a flicker of torchlight going past the window.

The duty optio appeared in the doorway. "All's ready, Sir."

Alexios carefully unclenched his hands and straightened his shoulders. "Right. I'm coming, Optio. Tell the Praepositus." He went out from the lamplit Sacellum and through the cross-hall into the squally murk of the winter's dusk, and headed for the red flare of torches in the open space behind the granaries. Suddenly he felt quite calm, his heartbeat had returned to normal and he was no longer sweaty-palmed. Only nothing seemed quite real.

Along the near side of the Dancing Ground the men were gathered with their javelins. On the far side stood Connla, bound to the post that normally held up the straw-filled roughly man-shaped target for javelin practice. He had fought like a wild thing for his freedom when he was taken, but now he stood completely still, his head up, his bright hair blazing in the torchlight, like another torch, seemingly withdrawn from all that was about him as though none of it concerned him any more.

Alexios was aware of the Praepositus coming up beside him; Centenarius Hilarion reporting that all was ready, saying in a quick undertone, "You should have got drunk first—shall I take over, Sir?"

Alexios shook his head, "Thank you, Centenarius, no." He started walking forward across the Dancing Ground, saying something for anyone who happened to be listening, about making sure that the prisoner's bonds were secure.

The light of the torches jumped and streamed in the wind so that sometimes the bound figure almost disappeared, sometimes sprang out into fierce relief against the tiger-striped shadows behind. The emptiness of the Dancing Ground stretched for miles like some spreading plain in a nightmare, and it seemed to take a very long time to cross it, with so many eyes on him; the eyes of his men standing with their javelins, the eyes of the Praepositus that he could feel behind him, Connla's eyes watching him come …

He was in front of Connla now. He had stopped walking.

"Have you come to save me from this target practice?" Connla asked, with a last flash of the old wicked laughter somewhere behind his face.

"There's only one way I can do that," Alexios said.

"Fool! Do you think I do not know? Two inches in the right place is enough, they teach you, don't they? Make it three, to be on the safe side."

"Are you ready?" Alexios said.

Their eyes held each other's. They had never been friends in the way that Alexios and Cunorix had been friends, but in that moment they were nearer to each other than they had ever been before.

"I am ready," Connla said.

Alexios's hand had already gone to his military dagger. His eyes held Connla's, willing him not to look down, not to see the flash of the blade in the torch-flare.

The thing was done and over almost before he knew it.

Connla gave a small wet cough and sagged in his bonds. His eyes remained for one instant fixed on Alexios's face, but they were empty, only for an instant a kind of surprise showed through, then nothing. His fiery head fell forward.

Alexios pulled out the dagger. The feeling of being in a dream had left him and he felt stripped and naked and sharply aware. He heard a sharp intake of breath here and there among his watching men, and turned and strode back to where the Praepositus stood looking on with a frown deep bitten between his brows, from the entrance of the old waggon shelter, and stopped in front of him and saluted.

"You can have what's left for your javelin practice," he said between shut teeth. And then, returning to the formal. "And now, Sir, I request that I resign my command here."

"Your request will be dealt with in due time and at the proper level," Praepositus Montanus said. "Meanwhile, as a temporary measure, Ducenarius Aquila, you will retire to your quarters and remain in detention there until further notice."

The voice was not much raised, but pitched to reach the nearer men on the torchlit Dancing Ground; and Alexios heard the sudden faint stir among them, and felt behind him the solid wall of hostility building up on his behalf. It was his duty to obey quickly, before it could gather more strength. But something was happening down at the Praetorian gate. Someone coming? A messenger?

"Optio, go and find the meaning of that," Montanus said.

The men around the Dancing Ground shuffled their feet; heads turned; the little group in the entrance to the old waggon shelter seemed caught into waiting stillness like a bee caught in amber.

The optio was back so quickly that it was clear he must have met the cause of the stir halfway. Behind him came two Frontier Wolves supporting between them a ragged and bloodstained ghost; and as they came into the leaping torchlight, Alexios recognized the third figure for one of the Arcani.

The man staggered clear of their support, and stood swaying on his feet. His face was already a dead man's face, and new blood oozed out from below his ribs to make a shining track over the old clotted blood which fouled what was left of the rough herdsman's jerkin he wore.

"The Caledoni—" he croaked. "Heading down for the Old

Wall—way over beyond—Credigone—there's—word of a landing of the Attacotti—a joining of spears—"

"Where? How many?" the Praepositus demanded.

But the man had staggered against the waggon-shed wall and was already sliding down it, leaving a thick red smear on the stones behind him.

"How many, man?" the Praepositus shouted.

Druim the spy-master had thrust through to the fore, and was kneeling beside his man. He looked up straight at the Praepositus with that level open stare of his quite unchanged. "No good, Sir, he's dead."

"And no need to ask what happened," Alexios said beside him also. "How he got back to us only Mithras knows!"

The Praepositus's eyes came round to him. "Still here, Ducenarius?"

Alexios straightened up and saluted, then turned and went quickly back past the Principia and across the courtyard of the officers' quarters to the down-at-heel room he had taken over five days ago when he turned out of his own quarters for the new Praepositus.

Behind him he heard Montanus's voice, and then Hilarion's raised in a quick crackle of orders, and the sound of feet as the men on the Dancing Ground broke ranks and scattered to carry them out. He shut the door behind him and stood leaning against it.

He felt coldly sick and his hands were shaking. When he looked down at them the light of the small lamp in its wall niche which always burned night-long in the Commander's quarters, showed him his dagger that he was still holding, juicy with Connla's blood. He pulled off his neck-cloth, and sitting down on the edge of the narrow sleeping-cot, began to clean it. It seemed the obvious thing to do.

Presently the door opened and someone came in bearing a platter of bannock and meat, and a cup of wine. "Supper, Sir," he said, and set them down on the clothes' chest, then went out.

Alexios went on rubbing and rubbing at his dagger blade that was long since clean.

The lamp flickered and leapt up when the sleety wind gusted against the broken window-glass. From outside he could hear feet, voices, the ordered sounds of the fort clearing for action. Footsteps came along the colonnade, and someone spoke to the sentry on the door. It opened and Hilarion came in.

Alexios laid down the dagger on the cot beside him. "Should you be here?"

"No orders against communicating with the prisoner," Hilarion said, and sat down on the clothes' chest beside the untouched food.

For a moment there was silence between them, and then Alexios said in sudden desperation, "Hilarion, did I miss something? Was there anything else that I could have done?"

"Done?"

"About Connla."

"Nothing except call a mutiny." Hilarion gave him back look for look, with a face more sober than Alexios had ever seen it before. "And even if you felt like getting yourself beheaded and one in ten of the rest of us stoned to death, it's scarcely the moment for that now."

"Not if the word that poor devil brought in was true."

"Oh, it's true all right. A pity he died before he could give us a few more details, but there's no doubt of its truth. Things have been happening while you've been in here. The Arcani have deserted—just faded out like the shadows that they are. It must have been a nasty shock for Druim when his man got back."

Alexios stared at him, while the implication of his words sank in. "One of them was loyal," he said after a moment. And then, "Well, that puts it beyond doubt; we're in for the worst kind of trouble. Hilarion—what has been happening since Montanus took over—what's the state of things in the fort?"

"Don't worry as to that," Hilarion told him. "Montanus is a soldier, whatever else he isn't. All things that should have been done have been done. He has sent off a couple of gallopers to report to Bremenium and pass it on to Habitancum and the Wall. And he's doubled the guard and posted lookout men up in the old signal tower; not that there'll be anything to see in the dark and this foul weather—except maybe the Cran-tara playing at spirit-lights across the moors."

The Cran-tara, the hazel branch dipped in goat's blood at one end and the other turned into a blazing torch, carried through the tribal lands to call the warriors to a war-hosting! And now it would not be a hosting against the Caledoni and the Attacotti, Alexios thought. Not a chance of the old bond holding between the Vota-dini—Cunorix's Clan of the Votadini anyway—and the Frontier Wolves—not after Connla's death; and the Arcani would have made sure that word of that was well and truly out by this time.

No need to say any of that to Hilarion, who knew it all as well as he did himself. Instead, he said, "We still have one patrol out."

"And there's nothing we can do about them. But they'll get the warning of trouble as quickly as anybody else—and they're the Frontier Wolves, not a bunch of raw sucklings to run blindly into a trap."

Outside the horn sounded for the Third Watch of the night, and Hilarion lounged to his feet. With the guard doubled, he would be on duty again.

When the door closed behind the Senior Centenarius, Alexios

pulled his wolfskin cloak more closely round him. It was very cold in the old quarters with the wind wailing in through the broken window-pane. But he had no thought of getting under the striped native rugs on the cot. Part of him was aware of the cold, and the footsteps of the sentry pacing to and fro in the colonnade outside, and beyond that, the tense waiting quiet of the fort standing by under arms. Part of him was back at Abusina nearly a year and a half ago ... Scarcely thinking what he did, he took up his dagger and slid it back into its sheath, and getting up, began to walk to and fro. Four paces one way, four paces back again. The walk of a man in prison, or a wolf in a cage. He had walked like that in his sleeping cell in Regina, waiting for the Inquiry. The lamp was getting low in oil; the flame jumping, long and ragged, making batwing shadows; finally going out. The darkness rushed in on him, and still he walked in the dark; four paces one way, four paces the other, sometimes checking and flinging himself down on his cot, but always springing up again and returning to his caged pacing, listening for any sound from the outside world. It was not likely that the attack would come before first light. The Votadini never fought in the dark if it could be avoided, lest with no sun to guide them, the dead should not be able to find their way to the Western Land; but it would come; sooner or later it would come, and here he was, pent up, while outside his men stood ready for it, another man commanding them.

Four paces from the door to the window, four paces from the window to the door.

The night crawled by, and the Third Watch became the Fourth, and the Fourth ended with Cock-crow sounding its jaunty burst of notes from the rampart; and presently, the darkness in the room began to grow thinner as though a little grey water was seeping into it.

And with the first light, the first attack came.

Alexios heard the sharp clear alarm-notes of the horn, shouted orders, the surge of sound from the ramparts. This was it, then. He stopped pacing. He stood quite still before the high window. Out of the habit of his training, his hands were going over harness buckles, making sure that sword and dagger sat freely in their sheaths. He dragged open the window, and the sound of shouted orders and the distant clash of weapons came in on the grey sleety wind.

He stood rigid, his hands clenched on either side of the window-frame. He never knew how long he stood there. Outside, between him and the surf-roar of the fighting, he heard the steps of the sentry in the colonnade. He could simply open the door in the blind instant after the man had passed and take him from behind. He did not think that anyone of his Wolves would try to stop him but that would be better for the man than just walking past him—and then he would be out. But if he did that, he would create a diversion and raise divided loyalties, and his little hard-pressed fort could not afford such luxuries at the moment.

The daylight was coming fast under a low racing cloud-roof, and he thought the noise was lessening, as though the attack was drawing off. He heard feet in the colonnade, coming at a stride that was almost a run. Lucius's voice this time, speaking to the sentry. The door opened and the Junior Centenarius stood there, breathing hard, with a smear of blood on one cheekbone.

"Sir," he said formally, "will you come and take over your command?"

"Praepositus Montanus?" Alexios said, turning from the window.

"Praepositus Montanus is dead."

11 | *"We're Pulling Out"*

FOR A MOMENT ALEXIOS WAS BACK IN THE NORTH SHOOTING turret at Abusina. ("Centurion Crito"—"What of Centurion Crito?"—"He's dead, Sir.")

"Oh God of the Legions!" he thought, "Not again!"

Aloud, he said, "I'm coming." He caught up his iron-bound cap and put it on, hurriedly knotting the thongs, hitching at his sword-belt as he passed Lucius to the open doorway. The sentry stood aside, and looking after them, shrugged and went off to join his comrades.

"What is the situation?" Alexios was demanding, as he made for the south rampart and the sinking sounds of the attack.

"It looks like about six hundred of them," Lucius said. "We have inflicted heavy losses on them and they're drawing back for the moment. But there'll be more—a lot more I reckon. The Caledoni must be over the Wall in some strength—there have been Pictish arrows coming over the ramparts since the rain slackened off."

The reserves were massing in the clear space below the ramparts, the wounded were being brought down.

"The Votadini?"

"Mostly the Votadini at present—couldn't expect anything else, Sir, after what's happened."

They came to the rampart stair, and Alexios took the steps two at a time with Lucius at his heels.

The Senior Centenarius turned from the breastwork and saluted. "They're pulling off, Sir."

Alexios nodded, looking down over the timber coping, and saw a dark mass of figures falling back out of bowshot. One figure a little behind the rest, pitched headlong, screaming like a hare, with a parting arrow from the ramparts quivering in his back. There were dead and wounded men in the ditch and all across the open ground between the fort and the first buildings of the town; dead and wounded sprawling grotesquely along the rampart walk, hampering the feet of the living defenders. Two men stumbled past, carrying a third close-wrapped in an officer's dark green cloak, stark dead men's feet in fine bronze studded boots sticking out at one end, the feathered crest of the Praepositus's helmet sticking out at the other. Alexios scarcely wasted a glance at it. He looked right and left along the ramparts, seeing men standing leaning on their weapons, here one cradling a wounded arm, there one sitting with his back to the breastwork and staring down with a kind of numb surprise at the Pictish arrowshaft sticking out of his belly. And they were so thinly strung out; two hundred men—a few more counting the First Ordo Wolves who had formed Montanus's escort—to hold a fort that had been meant for five hundred. Not even the full two hundred now, come to think of it, and fewer still by the time the next attack was over. And the Caledoni swarming down from the north to join spears with the Attacotti, the men of the White Shields from across the Western Sea? And the Votadini who yesterday had been their friends? Curse Connla! Curse Praepositus Montanus!

There would be time to get the wounded under cover and the dead cleared from the rampart walks, to bring up more arrows and javelins from the armoury and get a morning ration of bread and curds to the troops and maybe do something about watering the horses. Not much more. He heard his own voice giving the needful orders. Then on the point of departing about the score of other matters that must be seen to by the fort Commander at such a time, he checked for a few moments longer beside his Senior Centenarius, looking down into the roof-huddle of the town, "Any idea what has happened down there?"

Hilarion shook his head. "The place was buzzing like a hive about to swarm in the earlier part of last night. Then it went quiet. My guess would be that it was empty, in one way or another, before our war-painted friends arrived."

Still looking down at the huddle of roofs, Alexios was thankful that unlike most "Long-stay" troops, the Frontier Wolves seldom bothered to take wives. They went down to the women's huts in the town when the mood took them; but there would be no wives or families, however unofficial, down there to tangle the situation more than it was tangled already.

Something like a hornet sang towards him, and with a small vicious "tock" a Pictish arrow landed and stood quivering in the timber coping between himself and his Senior Centenarius.

"But it's not empty now," added Hilarion, ducking behind the breastwork, but with no change of tone.

"Seemingly not. They've probably left one of their marksmen behind every wall." Alexios pulled out the arrow, which had not penetrated deeply. "Well, this was loosed at fairly extreme range, and our bows have the range of theirs. Keep a few of our best archers here to pick off anyone who tries to get nearer." He tossed the arrow back over the breastwork; it would not fit the Scouts' composite bows anyway. "Let me know the instant the main force breaks cover again."

And he dived back down the rampart stair and went off to see about his score of other matters.

Presently the horn sounded again from the look-out tower, the harsh bright notes of the Alarm scattered on the squally wind, and the respite was over.

Out from a passing sleet-scurry the tribesmen came swarming; and standing in the shooting turret beside the Praetorian gate, Alexios watched them come; the Caledoni half-naked for battle under their sad-coloured cloaks, grotesque in their warpaint, running low from wall to wall up through the deserted town; the Votadini pouring in from the flanks. Only on the western side the river gorge would make it hard to mount a strong attack. Thanks be to the Lord of the Legions for the river gorge; that meant only two sides to bear the full force of the attack; three if they managed to break through the stockade covering the bath-house and the old shipyard quarter beyond the Northern gate. "Start loosing at extreme range," Alexios had ordered. The sleet-scurry was passing and had not been enough to wet the bowstrings. And in the shooting turrets the best marksmen among the Frontier Wolves stood loosing steadily through the embrasures into the thick of the rush.

The main thrust seemed to be against the Praetorian gate this time, and among the spearmen ran others carrying bundles of brushwood to pile against the gate timbers, others with torches that streamed behind them as they ran, and above their heads flew the arrows of the hidden Pictish bowmen to give them cover.

"Get a fire party ready," Alexios shouted to the optio behind him. "Bucket chain." And to the archers in the gatetower, "Keep them back from the gates, and pick off any you can of the Caledoni covering them."

The tribesmen were flinging brushwood bundles into the ditch to swarm over. They carried long notched poles for scaling the ramparts. The attack was roaring in from all sides, but still it seemed the main thrust was against the Praetorian gate; and in the forefront of it, Alexios saw a short strong figure with russet hair flying from under a war-cap, a glint of amber among the neck-folds of a red and saffron plaid, a long sword-blade catching the light of the torches. There was nothing much to set the Chieftain apart from the rest of his warriors, except the intangible something by which one man recognizes another, friend or enemy, in the distance or the almost-dark.

As though he felt Alexios's eyes on him, Cunorix looked up, and for a single heartbeat of time their gaze met. Then a bowstring twanged beside Alexios's ear; the shaft passed through Cunorix's hair as he sprang forward and took the man behind him in the throat. The bowman cursed softly. Next instant the young Chieftain was beneath the gate arch, where no arrow could reach him.

There was an acrid smell of burning, and a crackle of flame shot up in the archway, and the fire party went into action. All along the breastwork the fight was reeling to and fro, the war-cries of Frontier Wolves and Votadini mingling with the hideous wild-cat yowling of the men from the north. The smoke thickened and began to mingle with a fresh sleet squall sweeping across the fort so that the far side was all but lost in the murk. And out of the murk the warning call of the horn sounded again, and fresh forked tongues of flames were leaping up from the direction of the bath-house beyond the north walls.

Alexios was down from the shooting turret and halfway across the fort when Bericus met him. "Sir, word from Centenarius Lucius; the stockade is near to its going."

He waved up the reserves on the Dancing Ground, and raced on with them for the North gate. The space beyond seemed fringed with fire; slim hungry tongues of flame licking up from the stockade in a score of places, and against the glare, the figures of tribesmen and Frontier Wolves struggling for the defences. Lucius's face, blackened now as well as bloody, was suddenly in front of Alexios, saying with his usual slightly wooden calm as he saw the reserves, "Now we'll be able to do something about the fires—couldn't spare any men before, you see Sir."

They fought the fires with water from the bath-house supply; at least there was plenty of water on the northern slope of the hill; fetching it in their war-caps or anything else that came to hand, beating out the flames with their wolfskins dripping from the plunge-bath. They fought the tribesmen with their spears and swords and bare hands and with the last weapon of the wolf-kind—Alexios saw one man with his teeth sunk in a tribesman's throat, and never forgot the sight. He never forgot, either, the grating of blade on bone as he pulled his own sword out from the rib-cage of a boy he had known and drunk mares' milk with, or the painted giant whirling an axe with heron's feathers on its shaft, and Bericus' surprised grunt as he went down beside him with his head split open …

At last, like a wave spending itself, the force of the attack wavered and curled over on itself and began to stream away. The shouting and the clash of weapons died, and in the silence between the gusting of the wind, the only sound was the stamping and neighing of terrified and angry ponies from the horse-lines, and the heavy gasping of men leaning on their weapons to get their breath back. "That was a hot fight well fought, my wolflings!" Alexios called to them.

But standing with Lucius in the bath-house doorway, he said, "Pull them back into the main fort."

"You mean—abandon this quarter?"

"Yes," Alexios said.

"If we do that it will mean losing the water, and there's only the one well in the main fort."

"One will have to serve. If we don't pull back, it will mean losing the men."

They looked at each other, knowing the real decision that was being taken in that moment.

Then Lucius said, "Sir," and saluted and turned away to carry out the order.

So the men were pulled back from the old bath-house quarter, carrying their dead and wounded with them, and the half-blocked North gate was closed and made fast. And Alexios, having given orders for the tally of dead and wounded to be brought to him, went to the Sacellum and got out the muster rolls and duty rotas and pay lists; and put more charcoal on the brazier and watched the glow under the white ash brighten.

Not that he could imagine such things being much use to the Painted People or even to the Votadini; and the things that mattered, the reports of comings and goings on the western coast or up the northern glens, of tribal unrests and men who talked sedition were not kept written down in the fort but sent straight back to Headquarters. But standing orders were standing orders, here or at Abusina; no papers to fall into enemy hands, and there might not be a chance to see to the matter later on.

As at Abusina ... But there was no chance of a relief force this time. The scattered ordos of the Frontier Scouts, as Julius Gavros had said that first evening of all, were in no position to back each other up in time of trouble, and the Wall was six days' march away, even if one did not have to fight one's way through.

Funny, he thought, after nearly a year and a half of trying to get clear of Abusina, to have come round full circle and be back exactly where you had started.

Not so funny really, a jest in very poor taste.

("Stop thinking about yourself, Ducenarius Alexios Flavius Aquila, it's not just you and the choice you have to make; it's the two hundred or so men out there you've got to make it for!")

He pushed back his shoulders with the small jerk that he was unaware of, but that would have been familiar to anyone who knew him, and turned to the door and the orderly waiting outside.

"Ask Centenarius Hilarion and Centenarius Lucius and the Quartermaster to join me here as soon as they are at liberty. Anthonius too, if he will spare me a few moments from his wounded, when he can."

"Sir." The man went off.

A short while later the two centenarii entered the Sacellum almost together, and found the Commander sitting at the table, leaning on his elbows and staring at the stack of papers before him.

He looked up as they entered. "All quiet?"

"For the moment." Hilarion drew a forearm across his scorched and filthy face.

"I'm sorry to have dragged you here; I know you have enough on your hands."

Alexios drew a long shuddering breath and got to his feet, pushing himself up from the table with his spread hands as though the decision he had made had drained all the strength out of him. Vaguely he was aware of the Quartermaster's red rumpled face in the doorway.

"You will agree, I think, that there is no chance of relief getting through to us, despite the Praepositus's gallopers," he heard his own voice saying.

"None whatever," said Hilarion cheerfully.

"And there is certainly none of being able to hold Castellum for more than a couple of days. Even with the bath-house quarter lopped off, we have too few troops to man the long stretch of defences, and we shall have fewer with every attack that we beat off, while the Tribes can call on all the fresh men they need—

and on the supplies of the country round, including water." He spoke slowly, like one who has thought some complicated matter out with great care and wants to keep it all in order. "We're well enough for stores and weaponry, but not water. One well would serve for the men but not for the horses." He crossed glances with Lucius. "I had not forgotten that when I gave orders to pull back into the main fort. The loss of the bath-house spring wasn't worth the lives of the men that it would have cost to hold it—and it wouldn't have made all that much difference in the end, anyway." He broke off and stood looking at their three waiting faces. "Hilarion, Lucius, Quartermaster, am I missing something? Is there any useful purpose that we can serve by holding out and dying here at Castellum?"

"None, if you rule out heroics," said Hilarion lightly after a moment.

The Quartermaster snorted, though what the snort meant it would be hard to guess. Lucius said nothing at all.

"Then let us rule out heroics—or save them for another time. The men have been fighting like heroes; but the Frontier Wolves are at their best and most dangerous in open country, not behind walls. Our mobility and field-craft should give us a good chance of getting back to Headquarters. So …" Alexios's mouth felt very dry. It was the right decision this time, he knew it; but it took almost more courage than he possessed to force out the words. "We shall pull out at first dark tonight."

There was silence, and a sharp spatter of sleet against the window. It was almost dark enough to need a lamp, though it was not yet noon.

Another figure was in the doorway, bloody as though he had come straight from a butcher's shop. "What about the wounded, Sir?" asked Anthonius.

Alexios looked at him for a moment, not quite understanding.

It was Lucius who answered, touching the dagger in his belt. "Among their own kind it's the custom to—make sure they don't fall alive into enemy hands."

"Not that way," Alexios said. "We'll take the wounded with us—sling them across their ponies' backs if need be; any way we can."

"It will probably kill some of them," Anthonius said, clearly anxious that the Commander should understand all the facts.

"But at least they'll have a chance."

The Medic's long-nosed weary face creaked into a shadow of a smile. He exchanged glances with Lucius. They had brought the matter up in all seriousness, and would have seen to the carrying out of the order; but both were glad that it was not being given.

"Make your own preparations for their transport," Alexios said. "But keep me in touch."

When the Medic had gone, Hilarion returned to the point they had reached when he arrived. "*So*—we're pulling out at first dark. How, Sir? We're pretty well ringed about, and they'll make their watch-fires all around us after dark."

"They can't on the river side," Alexios said. "The scarp is too steep; nor right down to the estuary shore. Both those ways might be possible."

He picked up the first of the muster rolls, crumpling it into a ball for easier burning, and dropped it into the brazier. "Right. Pass the word round. We had better get the senior optios in here and work out plans in detail in, say, an hour from now, if we haven't got another attack on our hands at that time."

He added another crumpled papyrus to the brazier as they went out. Too slow. He'd have to do as he had had to do at Abusina, put them on the floor and fire the lot.

He was just heaving the table aside to leave a clear space when Centenarius Lucius appeared once more in the doorway. "Sir, will you add this to the pyre."

And Alexios saw that he was holding out the familiar scroll that seemed almost a part of himself; his beloved Georgics. "Going to have to travel light on this trip," he said simply. "I don't really need it, anyway, you're always telling me I know it off by heart."

Their eyes met as Alexios reached out and took it from him; and without a word he turned and strode away.

Alexios stood for a moment looking at the treasure in his hands, then let it unroll, tore off the wooden scroll-ends and added it to the pile on the floor. Then he took a flaming stick from the brazier.

He had just finished, and the Sacellum was full of the acrid smell of burned papyrus, a stinging fog that wafted across the snarling mask of the Ordo dragon against the back wall, when the Alert sounded once more.

The first notes of an Alert, that broke off short, leaving the last three notes unsounded …

In the brief respite that followed the next attack, the Commander and his centenarii and the four senior optios were gathered in the Sacellum; seven wolf shapes squatting on their haunches. They had brushed aside the flakes of burned papyrus, and on the cleared patch of floor in their midst, Alexios was drawing with a charred stick.

"We take the whole force out by the Dextra gate and down to the ford." Six pairs of eyes followed intently the tip of the stick moving over the map that he had drawn. "There, we detach ten men for a decoy party, under Optio Vedrix," he glanced at a small foxy-looking man who nodded in reply. "You will make downstream and work round under the coastwise bluffs. It will be low water in the estuary, when? Sometime about the start of the Second Watch? Take the ponies round through the shallows until you judge it safe to come ashore, follow the coast towards the old naval station; then strike inland round the back of the Fortress Rock, and head south, leaving a good trail behind you, down as though to join the Trimontium road. That way you'll be out of the Clan hunting runs and into the Votadini Royal Territory."

The optio nodded again. "Just what Cunorix would expect us to do—the whole lot of us, I mean, this being largely a Clan matter."

"Yes, well, make it look as much as you can as though you *are* the whole lot of us. Then get lost, about—here, and head southwest to meet up with the main force somewhere—hereabouts."

"And the main force, meanwhile?" Hilarion asked.

Alexios's charred stick returned to the place where he had marked Castellum. "The main force crosses by the ford, straight into the heart of the Clan's hunting runs, and heads south along the river gorge."

Hilarion whistled softly and musically. "Which they *won't* be expecting!"

"We can but pray to all the gods the Ordo prays to, that they won't," Alexios said grimly, the point of his stick moving on.

"Sir," Lucius put in, "in four miles, going that way, we'll have the Long Moss straight across our line of march."

Alexios sat back and looked round at them. This was the dangerous bit, he knew, the bit that depended not so much on the lay of the land but on his men's hearts, things about them that he simply did not know. "I had not forgotten. And in the heart of the Long Moss there stands the Death Place of the Chiefs of the Votadini. There is a way through from this side to the Place—you and

I travelled most of it together, Optio Garwin, when we followed the old Chief and brought back the new one, last summer. And there must be ways from the far side as well. Have we anyone in the Ordo who knows them?"

A third man, who was of the Clan himself, looked up from the marks on the floor. "I do, Sir. Two or three of the men as well—I've taken a horse through that way from time to time, before I turned law-abiding and became a soldier of Rome. But my mother had the blood of the Little Dark People in her, the Old People of the Forest; she had the ancient knowledge, and set upon me the marks for protection."

"And lacking these marks for protection?" Alexios said. "Will the troops take that way?"

Silence. And again the sleet-spatter sounded very loud on the window.

Then Optio Garwin suggested, "How if we keep to the east bank of the river, and pick up the causeway road to Trimontium?"

"That is a possible way," Alexios said, "and we will take it if need be, but the tribesmen will be the sooner on our tails, because that way will be closer to what they expect."

"I have often heard it said," Hilarion murmured silkily, apparently talking to himself, "that the Frontier Wolves are a godless pack. If a man has no gods, what is there to be afraid of?"

The fourth optio, an older man, who had not spoken before, said, "Sir, let us keep both roads in mind for a while. It is in my heart that the men will take your way, but it would be an ill thing to bring them to the point, and find that they will not. Let you leave it to us for a while, and take the plan on from here," he leaned forward and touched a point on the rough map, "where I think, in any case, both roads become one."

"So be it, Optio Brychanus," Alexios said. "I leave it to you; but make haste with the finding-out ... From here, then, it is simple, we go thus—and thus, to meet with the decoy force somewhere here, west of Trimontium, from where it is only two days' march to Bremenium—unless of course they come too close on our heels ..."

Presently, from the vernacular in which they had been speaking most of the time, he snapped back into the Latin tongue. "We have still two hours' daylight to get through. Get the horses fed and watered as soon as maybe, the men at dusk. The rest I have told you. Do not take too long about that matter of the two roads."

When dusk came, the fort was still in Roman hands; but the defenders had taken heavy losses, dead and wounded, since dawn, and their fighting strength was down to less than two-thirds.

With the darkness, the sleety squalls of the day had settled into a foul night of winter rain driven before a howling northeast wind, and under its cover the last preparations for pulling out were going forward. They had collected their dead into one of the store-sheds and covered them with all that they had time to move of the grain and stores that they would not be taking with them, and pulled the roof down over all. Alexios would have liked to fire the building; he would have liked to fire the whole fort, but to do that, besides giving early warning of their retreat, would look as though they were not coming back one day; and the tribesmen would know that and gain heart, while his own men, knowing also, would lose it. They had fouled or destroyed in one way or another, almost everything about the place that could be of use to the tribes, and that must serve.

Food had been given out at dusk, and three days' iron rations for himself and his mount issued to each man. The ponies had been fed and watered, their hooves muffled with strips of bed-rugs that they might make no sound on the track down to the ford;

muzzle straps attached to their headgear lest a stray whinny at the scent of the tribesmen's horses should betray them. Weapons had been checked, quivers filled and spare bowstrings issued ...

Now all was ready; and under the booming wind it was as though the fort drew a long waiting breath. And the men keeping the last moment's watch on the ramparts stared out towards the wind-torn enemy watch-fires that ringed them on three sides, and saw no sign of movement anywhere.

Soon it would be low tide in the estuary.

In the Sacellum the smell of burned papyrus and melted wax still lingered. The lamp burned on the now empty table, and in its guttering light the floor still showed traces of the rough map; and Alexios paused for a moment in what he was doing and rubbed them out with his foot.

("It is as the centenarius said," Optio Brychanus had reported "the Frontier Wolves are a godless lot. They will take the trail that leads by the Chieftains' Death Stones, though they say that there will surely be a payment demanded." "Payment?" Alexios had said. "A life." The optio had been quite matter-of-fact about it. "They say the Guardians of the Place will demand the life of one in payment for the rest to pass by. But it will cost more lives than one to get back to Headquarters, anyway; and they say the Commander's way gives them the best chance.")

Alexios gave a final rub to the smeared and blackened patch of floor, and returned to the work of his hands.

He had taken down the Ordo dragon and laid it on the table, and was hammering the snarling fantastic head flat, with the heavy iron-shod butt of his own spear-shaft. That should have been for the standard-bearer to do. But the standard-bearer was dead, and so it was for the Commander to get the unit's standard back to Headquarters. He gave the thing a final blow, and flung the spear-shaft aside. The fierce head that used to rear up in beauty, drinking the wind when the troops went by at the gallop, was a grotesquely flattened mask of bronze and silver wires, as he looked down at it. But it was the Ordo dragon still. He took it up and began to bind the bright wind-sleeve like a silken scarf about his waist, starting at the tail-tip and tucking the flattened head into its own folds last of all.

He cast one last look round the narrow chamber, stripped and bare, and leaving the lamp burning, went out through the cross-hall into the winter darkness.

On the Dancing Ground and in the alleyway that led to the Dextra gate, the Ordo was ready and waiting, each man beside his mount. And Alexios saw the dark shapeless outlines of the laden baggage-ponies, and those with wounded men slumped across their backs. Centenarius Hilarion appeared out of the night. "Sir, the scouts have reported back all clear—also they have met up with our missing patrol—left them a couple of miles upriver."

"One thing less to worry about then." Alexios drew a small quick breath of relief. He had done quite a lot of worrying about his missing patrol in the past few hours. "Is all ready?"

"All's ready, Sir."

"Right. Then get to horse. Lead off, Centenarius."

The Dextra gate, well greased in advance, opened without sound onto the windy darkness of the night beyond. And men and horses slipped forward like a long skein of ghosts, one after another through the gate and down the steep track to the ford, the men of the decoy party leading the way.

Alexios, riding with the Fore Guard on that first stretch, pulled Phoenix aside at the edge of the ford, beside the dark still shape of the Lady, muttered a quick "Good luck to you—for all our sakes" to Optio Vedrix, and saw the ten shadows peel off from the rest and melt into the stormy darkness, down towards the bend of the river and the open estuary shore.

For what seemed a long time, he sat his fidgeting pony to watch the rest go by. Twenty men to the Fore Guard; then the Main Guard, upward of a hundred, riding two by two. The rag-tag company of the wounded and the baggage-ponies. The Rear Guard of twenty-five. The Third Ordo, Frontier Wolves, pulling out in good order. He wondered what kind of order they would be in when they reached Headquarters. How many of them would reach Headquarters at all. Well, if anyone could make it, the Frontier Wolves could.

One after another, the shadows passed, slowly gentling their ponies down into the water, pulling out to disappear in rainy darkness on the far side. At least the storm gods were giving them the cover they needed, seeming to spread dark wings over them, and the boom of the wind through the alder woods to cover any sound from the ford.

Alexios waited, every sense straining for some sound that might tell of trouble for the decoy party—but none came. Once a pony squealed as his feet went from under him in the swift running water, and his rider gathered him, cursing softly. But there was no rush of spearmen down the streamside.

And then clear from the fort behind them, scattered and half-lost on the wind, he heard the steady notes of the horn sounding for the Second Watch of the night. A few moments more, and Conan the senior trumpeter would come down from the Dextra gate, and the last living man would be out of Castellum. Alexios remembered with a sudden ache at the heart, the Alert that had broken off so sharply a few hours ago. Young Rufus with a Pictish arrow in his throat, lying among the rest of the dead under the pulled-down roof of the old store-shed; and with him the limp bundle of bloody fur that had been Typhon. They had done every-thing together from that first day behind the armourer's shop, and they had not been parted in their dying.

There was a faint movement on the steep track, and Conan ranged up alongside. "That should be keeping them happy, at any rate until the Third Watch falls due," he said, quickly and quietly. They set their ponies to the ford.

Alexios, reaching aside by long custom to touch the Lady in passing, felt the stone rain-wet and heart-cold and curiously empty, and knew, though he instantly denied the knowledge in himself, that Rome would not come back.

12 | The Rath of Skolawn

Once clear of the alder scrub that furred the slopes of the river gorge, Alexios heeled his pony forward and took his place at the head of the Main Guard as, with a couple of their best trackers out ahead, they swung south of the old Credigone road. And so, with the river on their left, they melted into the heart of the Clan hunting runs; into the broken country that lay between them and the Long Moss. Bremenium was four days away, maybe more, and the immediate thing was to get as far south as might be before daylight.

The wind was behind them now, on their left shoulders; thanks be to the Lord of the Legions, the flurrying sleet that had mingled all day with the bitter rain squalls had not yet turned to snow, though Alexios, huddling his chin down into the thick hairy folds of his wolfskin, was unpleasantly sure that that was coming in the next day or so.

Sometimes the night was dark as the inside of a wolf's belly, sometimes when the skies hurrying overhead broke a little, a faint lessening of the darkness would show them the crouched shapes of thorn trees or even the outline of a hill shoulder against the low-scudding cloud mass. About midway between the fort and the start of the Long Moss, they picked up the missing patrol waiting for them at the ford of a shallow side burn coming down to join the river, added them to the Main Guard with no more than a few muttered words out of the stormy darkness, and pushed on. Presently there began to be the cold rooty smell of bog country ahead; and here and there the faint broken gleam of water.

A figure from the Fore Guard dropped back to Alexios's side. "Here we are, Sir. Best call a halt for the moment."

Alexios gave a long low-pitched whistle. His remaining trumpeter was beside him, but this was no time to be broadcasting one's presence across the dark hills. Ahead of him, from Hilarion with the Fore Guard, and all down the long line of shadows behind, he heard the call echoed and passed on. It might have been a string of marsh birds whistling to each other. The column halted. All down the line the Frontier Wolves were swinging down from the saddle. A man leading his pony slipped by Alexios into the lead, a patch of lime daubed thickly white between the shoulders of his wolfskin.

Looking at it, Alexios thought, "Mithras! It doesn't show up as well as I thought it would! What if we lose sight of it? What if the safe-way shifts with the weather? What if the ground gets softer with the winter?"

"The trackers report the way firm and clear, Sir," said the man beside him.

"Firm enough for a hundred and fifty men and horses?"

"Firm enough for Hannibal's elephants, if we take it well spread out."

A short while later, they were on the move again, the men walking beside their ponies to spread the load, the long files broken up into short irregular skeins each following one with a lime-daub between his shoulders. Try to take too long a string behind one leader on such a bog-trail, and unless you could leave markers at every turning point, in the nature of things each man would turn off a fraction before he came to the place where the man ahead of him had turned, and soon the men towards the rear would be turning off badly short and into real trouble.

Alexios, walking beside Phoenix, remembered the still summer night when he had come that way, following the old Chief to his Death Place, the Clansmen sniping this way and that along the firmer ground between the winding waterways and sky-reflecting pools. The flaming torches and the mourning throb of the drums, and the lingering late northern sunset casting its golden cloud-streamers across the sky. He supposed they were on the same track now. He must suppose it; must trust to the men with the lime-daubs between their shoulders. "When they join the Family, they bring their loyalties with them," Gavros had said, but he felt how it might be with him, new loyalties pulling against old, if he knew the secret and sacred ways and was being asked to betray them to men of other tribes who did not.

Presently, below the boom of the wind he caught somewhere far over to the left, the hoarse familiar winter song, so unlike its summer crooning, of the river that ran out by Castellum to the estuary; and a while later they came to the long ridge of land, its thorns and alders bare and writhing in the wind, where they had checked to see the old Chief go away from them, and waited all through the short summer night, for the young Chief to return.

Ahead, mealy-pale where the wind ruffled it as another squall came scudding by, stretched the shallow water, blurring away to a further shore that was only a formless darkness half blotted out by the driving rain.

This time there was no pause. Ahead of him Alexios saw the men and horses of the Fore Guard move steadily down into the water. "Easy now," he said to Phoenix. "Easy now, it is no more than a ford ... that's my old hero." The icy water was swirling to his knees, to mid thigh. Looking back, he saw the long skein of dark figures following. Looking forward, he saw the man imme-diately ahead, with the lime-daub showing faintly between the shoulders of his wolfskin. The wind blew Phoenix's wet mane across his face. In a little they changed course, and then changed course again. The water boiled into icy turmoil around the legs of men and horses. The cold seemed eating from his legs up into his very heart. He wondered how it was with the wounded, straggling far behind among the baggage train. He was piercingly aware of the terror of the hungry bog on either side.

It seemed an endless crossing, though memory of that silky summer night told him that it was probably no more than eight or ten bowshots. There began to be a pull under the surface of the water; a steady pull over towards where the river must be. And then he felt the hidden safe-way rising under his feet. Reeds crowded to meet them, sere winter reeds parting to let them through, and ahead, sound and feeling more than sight, told him that the Fore Guard were pulling clear of the water, up through the alder scrub onto firm ground. A few moments more, and he and Phoenix were plunging together up the slope, with the first of the Main Guard close behind them.

And a short way ahead, the great standing-stones reared up, shapes of utter blackness against the lesser blackness of the winter's night. Alexios felt them more than saw them; felt the Thing that the place had gathered to itself, tangible as the breath of some vast brooding being; this place that was the Death Place of the Chiefs of the Votadini and did not belong to the world of the living. Even the wind had a different note here; it harped against the great stones with a strange cold harping that seemed almost to have the tone of unhuman voices. And yet under the storm-voices of the wind and the rain, there was a great stillness.

The Van Guard had swung left hand and was skirting the standing stones. The Main Guard followed. "I'll catch up with you in a while," Alexios said to Optio Garwin beside him. And leading Phoenix aside, he stood with his arm over the pony's neck to watch the rest go by. He knew that having brought them to this place, he could not leave until the last of his men were clear of it.

He watched section after section loom out of the murk and disappear into it again like a legion of ghosts. Horribly like a legion of ghosts. The wounded came by, those who could walk lurching along blind and deaf to everything but the need to get themselves forward, here and there one supporting another; those who could not walk slumped in their saddles or lying along their horses' necks, a few carried between unwounded men. He heard the slipping and scrambling that was the first of the baggage ponies coming up from the water. Soon now, there would be only the Rear Guard to come. Hilarion and the Fore Guard would be out into the winding ways of the Marsh Country again by now; the crossing of the Long Moss was half made, and nothing had gone wrong.

But in that moment there came the beating of great wings from among the alders on the islet's northern shore, and the harsh "Krank!" of a startled heron. A pony squealed in terror, and a man cried out. Back at their landing place a sudden small tumult had broken out; a scared threshing and floundering of ponies, men's voices cursing. Alexios dropped the reins forward over Phoenix's head and ran back. Through the wind-lashed branches of the alder trees he could see the thresh of men and ponies in the shallows; and frightened beasts under slipping packs were being hauled up the bank, by men struggling to get the way cleared for the Rear Guard following after.

"What has happened?" he demanded of the nearest man.

"Heron—startled the pack ponies, Sir—two of them tried to bolt. It's pretty treacherous footing."

The ponies came crashing up through the alder scrub, and

Alexios, pushing forward, met two men carrying up a third between them. Clear of the alder tangle they laid their burden down, and Alexios found himself squatting beside the dark shape that was coldly sodden under his exploring torch. Drowned? But he couldn't be, not in that shallow water, he thought stupidly. The helmet thongs had been burst and the helmet was gone, and the neck felt odd—twisted. Wolf-dark. Couldn't see—"Who is it?"

"Quartermaster, Sir. Trying to stop one of the packs slipping. Got kicked on the head."

"Light! Get me a glim here," Alexios said. "Somebody go up yonder and send back the Medic. Tell Optio Garwin there's nothing to turn back for. Tell him to keep the Main Guard going. *Keep going* at all costs; we'll catch up …"

Somebody had produced a tinder-box and strike-a-light from its pouch of oiled linen and got a spark going, and was crouching close, shielding the tiny glim under his cloak; and by the faint glow Alexios saw the Quartermaster's balding head twisted at an unnatural angle.

"His neck's broken. The hoof must have caught him here under the jaw," said Anthonius's voice, and he realized that the Medic was kneeling beside him, hands moving steadily and surely over the damage.

Within a spear's length of them the hooves and feet of the Rear Guard were trampling up from the water. But among the little group under the storm-lashed alder branches, where the tinder-box still cast a faint glow over the dead face and living faces that stooped over it, there seemed a curious hush.

"The lads said there'd be a payment demanded," said Centenarius Lucius's voice above them.

"And the payment has been made," Alexios said, speaking to Lucius and to himself and to every man within hearing. He looked down into Kaeso's watery slightly puzzled blue eyes in the crumpled face that had lost it usual red; the old chap had been annoyingly drunk most nights, and his constant niggling about his stores had been a burden to them all. But he had been the chosen one; the one who paid the toll for the rest of them to pass that way.

There was a sudden ache in Alexios's throat. He swallowed it and got up. "Put him across his pony."

"We're taking him with us, Sir?" the optio said.

"We're certainly not leaving him here."

The men of the baggage train were checking the bindings of the packs. One pony, lacking his load, stood head down and shivering. Alexios drew a consoling hand down his neck. "No fault of yours, old warrior." Then to the optio, "His pack is gone?"

"Yes, Sir, burst open and swept away."

"What was it?"

"Meal, Sir."

Alexios checked, his hand still on the pony's drooping neck. "Well, we've good strong belts for tightening." There was still the three days' iron rations at each man's saddlebow; and the Frontier Wolves were trained, like their ponies, to keep going on what would mean starvation to any other troops, in time of need. They could worry about all that later. The immediate thing was to push on.

Things were being sorted out, the pack train was moving forward again with its added burden of one dead man. Anthonius had already hurried ahead after his wounded. Someone brought Alexios his pony, and he fell into place for the moment beside Lucius at the head of the Rear Guard.

Soon they had left the Death Place of the Chieftains behind them, and were out in the open Long Moss once more.

On the second part of the crossing there was no more unbroken water, for the islet which had seemed from the north to be set in the midst of its shallow loch, was in truth on the southern edge of it, and beyond lay another maze of firm ground and winding waterways and lochans, reeds bending in the wind, streaming long-fingered alder tangle. Then the alder began to give place to hazel and rowan, and Alexios realized with almost sick relief that they were pulling up out of the Long Moss, with solid land ahead of them once more.

In the lee of a thorn thicket they checked to look to the wounded and check the pack ropes again, and wring as much water out of themselves as they could, then remounted, the men with the lime daubs between their shoulders returning now to their normal places in the column, and pushed on again. There was no sign of the hunt on their trail as yet, but they must be many miles further south by dawn. And anyway, better to push on than stop here too long soaking and frozen and unable to light a fire.

There were a few grumbles of protest, but not many. Alexios, back in his old place with the Main Guard, said quick and low-voiced to Optio Brychanus beside him, "Optio, am I pushing them too hard?"

"Anything short of foundering them isn't too hard at this stage, Sir," said the man. "Later we may have to slacken speed for the sake of the wounded."

Presently they came out onto the old half-lost track that ran direct to Castra Cunetio. For a few miles that would give them quicker travelling and be easier for the wounded. But after a while it began to carry them too far westward, and they left it and struck away in a more south-easterly direction, while the hills grew more wooded around them.

At daylight, well into the eastern thrust of the great forest that lay like a fleece over all the heart-land of the old province, they made a halt at last, to feed the men and see to the wounded. Mercifully the rain squalls had slackened off, and in the clearing where they had checked, there was a certain amount of shelter from the wind that boomed through the bare trees overhead. Beeches and oaks for the most part here, that flung gaunt imploring arms across the hurrying sheeps-wool sky, but two or three of the dark pines, outriders of the true forest further west, had crowded to the clearing's edge, and made a sheltered place where the ground was drier than elsewhere; and there they had laid the wounded on the brown mat of pine needles; and Anthonius had got his medical case from the back of the pony who carried it, and was busy among them. Alexios, having seen the ponies grazing under guard—there was grass here, and the iron-ration corn could wait a while—and the men busy with their slim rations and the cleaning and drying out of their weapons, went over to see how it was with them.

In the patch of shelter they lay or sat, one man with his bandaged head in his hands, one man propped on an elbow looking down at the bloody remains of his sword hand, another with a knee smashed by a spear. Anthonius was bending over one who lay very flat, easing away the blood-clotted dressing from a stab wound in the belly. The man turned his head as Alexios checked beside him, and looked up with clouded eyes, "Water—"

"Soon," Alexios began. "A couple of lads are bringing some up from the stream—" and broke off, as the Medic also looked up with a small shake of the head.

"They won't give—so thirsty—Sir, you tell them—water for Christ's sake," the man said.

"Can't, Sir, not with a belly wound. Wipe out his mouth with a wet rag, no more."

"I'm sorry," Alexios said, and turned and walked away feeling the man's eyes following him.

Close by, a couple of men had cut down straight whippy beech saplings and were lopping off the branches and lashing spare cloaks and bale-sacking across them to make travoises, towed pony stretchers, for the most sorely wounded. On the far side of the clearing a burial party were finishing digging out a shallow grave.

Alexios and his two centenarii stood by as they lifted the Quartermaster's body into it and laid the earth back over. And Alexios spoke the few words for one of his own faith. "Lord of Light, Lord of the Ages, slayer of the Bull, here we lay all that can die of Kaeso Quintillius, of the Third Ordo of Frontier Wolves, Thy son. Receive back into Thy strong hands all of him that cannot die. The Sun rises and the Sun sets, and always the Sun rises again." And when the turfs had been replaced over the small lonely mound, he knelt and made on it the Sign.

"Poor old Kaeso," Hilarion said. "He never seemed to have much of a life apart from his store-sheds. And then to lose what he had in trying to save a bag of meal. Sometimes the gods make mean little jests."

"It is not the meal that matters," Lucius said softly, "he paid the toll for the rest of us to pass."

"And you a Christian!"

They were all on edge; and Alexios cut in quickly and somewhat at random, glancing towards where the pack ponies were already being reloaded, "A bag of meal that was worth more to us just now than the Ordo pay-chest, anyway." Two men were loading up the small iron-bound chest at that moment, and he added, "Even if it wasn't almost empty."

Hilarion's voice took on its lazy, mocking note. "What fools we are, all of us, that we go round getting ourselves killed for an Empire that doesn't even keep our pay up to date!"

Only a short while later, just as they were about to move off again, they got their first tidings of the enemy. One of the pair of scouts they had sent on ahead rode out of the trees and dropped from his pony beside Alexios with a weary salute. "A big war-party of Picts, Sir, moving south-east. Amlodd has gone after, to keep them in sight for a while."

"Any White Shields with them?"

"No, Sir."

"Votadini?"

"No, Sir, not yet."

"How many Pictish?"

"Difficult to say, Sir, among the trees. About two hundred, to judge by their tracks after they'd gone by."

"Let's hope they and their kin are not such skilled trackers as the Frontier Wolves," Alexios said. "Get out your bannock. You'll have to eat on the move; we're pushing on."

"It's a hard life, Sir," the man's weary face split into a grin.

"A hard life," Alexios agreed. "No justice."

Through all the short daylight hours they pushed on, roughly south-east, after crossing the track of the war-party, scouts out ahead, and behind them every man riding on the alert for any unusual movements of birds or beasts, any sound on the wind that might tell of enemies nearby, for the forest country must be full of war-bands by now, and every opening among the trees might show them the glimmer of lime-washed Attacotti shields, or the tasselled cat-skull standards of the Painted People; every gust of wind from the North might bring them the hunting cries of the Votadini on their trail. But after the passing of that first war-band they might have ridden through a deserted world. The decoy party had done their job well; Alexios's thoughts kept reaching out to them, and he pulled them back, each time. However things were with the decoy party, there was nothing that he could do by worrying about them, and he needed all his wits for the men of the main force in which he rode.

The forest began to fall back, which meant that now, on the open moorlands, they had much further sight of the country round, but meant also that the hunt would be able to see them from much further off. They rode well stretched out, but careful never to lose contact between company and company, keeping well up the hill slopes and watching always the skyline, while taking care never to get skylined themselves. Time and again they had to ford small hill burns, with every ford bearing with it the possible danger of an ambush; but still they might have been riding through an empty land.

The short daylight was fading into an iron-grey dusk, and with the dusk the foul mixture of sleet and rain came on once more. Soon, while enough light lasted, they must find a suitable place to make camp. Make camp, with men drenched through and dog-weary with a forced ride of more than thirty miles behind them, and a good few of them wounded besides. A proper fortified camp to be made before they could rest and eat their pared-down ration; though he was sure enough the Votadini would not attack after dark. Of the Painted People he was less sure; they might ambush men caught in the open, but probably they would not attack a camp. What the Attacotti might do, he had no idea. His old nurse, he thought with a sudden flicker of weary humour, had neglected his education.

Finn, the native optio, drew up beside him. "Sir, if we turn south at the loop of the burn, and head round by Red Horse Glen, it would add only a mile or two, and we could be at the Rath of Skolawn by full dark."

"Might be dangerous," Alexios suggested.

"We're off Votadini territory now, Sir. The Selgovae won't hold back the hunt on our trail, but they'll look on it as something between us and Cunorix, and take no interest themselves, not even enough to send word to Cunorix that we're drying off by a hearth fire of theirs. Besides, they'll be having too much thinking of their own to do with the woods crawling with the White Shields and the Painted People."

"Still, we don't want to risk stirring up a hornets' nest behind us."

"We could always try asking in all courtesy, Sir?"

Alexios took a quick decision. "So we could," he said, and turned to his galloper who rode immediately behind him. "Take the word up to Centenarius Hilarion, we are turning south for the rath of Skolawn." He laughed. "With luck we'll find us a fire to dry our wolfskins by tonight!"

Before the dusk had fully deepened into the dark, he was rather wishing he had not said that, as he crouched shuddering with cold on the edge of a hazel thicket, his arm looped through Phoenix's bridle, with the rest of his men; looking down towards the smoking ruins still glowing dimly red in places, in the valley below them, and waiting for the scouts he had sent in for a closer look, to come back.

Somewhere an owl hooted among the trees, and a shadow darker than the sleety darkness that surrounded them slid up to his side.

"The Painted People have been here before us," said the shadow at half-breath. "But the fire is sinking, the thatch was too wet for it to take a proper hold."

"Anyone left alive down there?" Alexios asked.

"They have maybe driven off some of the cattle. Otherwise … it is not the custom of the Painted People to leave anything alive behind them on the war trail through a place of living men."

Alexios was silent a moment. Then he said, "Nor, I think, would they be like to come back to such a place, once they had passed through it."

And so at dark they came down to the smouldering ruins where dead men and cattle lay among the charred thatch that had been the Rath of Skolawn. At least they could have fire here, under cover of the fire that the Caledoni had left behind them; and meat from the slaughtered cattle, and maybe grain from under the fallen granary roof.

They fed the ponies and tethered them in the remains of the corral and the steading forecourt, and cleared the dead out of their way, and huddled close about the small fires that they made, under the charred thatch of hall and byre and barn. Sodden wolfskins steamed in the warmth; and they stripped off rawhide boots and showed their feet and hands as the optios went round inspecting for chaps or chafing or broken chilblains. Maybe another night if the weather hardened, frostbite too; but not that as yet. Anthonius was busy among the wounded again. Men unslung the cooking-pots and began to brew up a mixture of meal and chunks of freshly slaughtered meat in water from the burn—better keep clear of the well—for something warm to stay their clemmed bellies.

Alexios, coming back with one of the optios from a round of the pickets, almost fell over a dead man in a dark corner, and met foraging parties of Frontier Wolves. For himself, he did not much fancy anything from the Rath of Skolawn, but they were still three days from Bremenium, and you couldn't afford to be squeamish; and the first whiff of the heating broth brought the soft warm water to his mouth as freely as to anyone else's.

But he had barely entered the half-ruined house-place and was shaking off his wet wolfskin before the fire, where Centenarius

Lucius had arrived just ahead of him, when he heard quick voices outside. "Is the Commander in there?" someone was asking.

Alexios swung round. "I'm here. What is it?"

"Sir," one of the scouts appeared in the doorway. "We've found something—someone—"

"Someone alive? Bring him in here, then."

"Better, if you come to him—her—it's a woman, Sir. We found her hiding among the grain, where the fire didn't get a hold."

"You could still bring her here," said Alexios.

"Not without getting rough with her, Sir. And we are none of us feeling like that, if it can be helped." The scout held up a bleeding hand. "She has bitten my thumb to the bone, as it is."

Alexios gave a sound between a curse and a snort of laughter, and flung on his sodden cloak again. "I should have thought the Frontier Wolves could be handling a she-wolf! Well enough; I'm coming."

He went out into the dark again, and followed where the man led.

By the light of a straw-plait torch held by one of the optios, he saw the woman as he ducked in through the low doorway of the store-shed. She was crouching back against the far wall; her teeth were bared as though she were a wolf indeed, and she clutched against her a thing that he thought in the first moment was a bundle of some kind, until as he moved forward he saw that it was a child, horribly dead, and with the broken shaft of a javelin sticking from the midst of it.

She pressed herself still further back against the wall, snatching at her breath as he drew nearer; and he said quickly, "Don't be afraid."

"Afraid?" It was only a whisper, but it could have been a scream, it was so harsh and shrill. "Why should I be afraid? What can you do that you have not already done—you or your brothers from the North?"

"Listen." Alexios tried to reach and reassure her, thinking that she was too far out of her wits to know who they were. "The Painted People did this thing. We are soldiers of Rome. There is no need for fear."

She let out a high wailing cry, staring up at him through tangled and bloodstained hair. And he saw that her hair was golden, and that once, no more than a few hours ago, she had been beautiful. "Oh kind and gentle soldiers of Rome! The Red Crests killed my man. Last year he went south to the Wall with horses to trade. He struck an officer who called him evil names—from the other horse-traders I heard it—they took and flogged him until he spewed blood and died under the lash. Now the Painted People have killed his son. Which of you then, should I love the most?" She bent forward, quick as a dagger-thrust, and spat on Alexios's feet. "My heart is glad that there is war between you and the Painted People! Aye, and the White Shields from over the Sunset Sea. I hope you tear each other's hearts out!"

And she curled herself in over the dead child in her arms, and began to rock herself to and fro, keening to it, seemingly unaware that anyone else was there.

"What are we to do with her?" one of the men asked, looking on.

Alexios was silent a moment. They could not leave the woman here, both for her own sake and because it was very clear that if the chance came her way she would put the hunt on their trail. They would have to take her with them, adding one more problem to the more than enough problems that they had already. There was only one alternative, and that was an ugly one.

The optio touched his dagger in a gesture that there was no

mistaking. "No!" Alexios said, as though the moment before he had not been thinking the same thing himself. "She'll have to come with us when we march in the morning. Give her some food, if she'll touch it. Keep her here and set a guard over her."

"The bairn?" said the optio, who had had bairns of his own, once.

"We shall have to part them when we ride on," Alexios said, with the low keening in his ears. "Leave her the bairn for tonight."

And he went back to the fire and the ruined steading.

The night crawled by, the watches changed and changed again with no familiar trumpet call, only the low-muttered word, the brief touch passing between man and man in the darkness. The fires had been deliberately allowed to sink low. Alexios, who had lain awake most of the night, had fallen asleep at last when he was roused by someone pressing just below his left ear; the old hunter's trick for waking a man quickly and thoroughly, without sound.

"Sir," someone was saying, "Sir—"

Alexios rolled over and sat up, "Yes? What is it?"

"The woman. She's gone. When we changed the Guard—"

Alexios scrambled to his feet and made for the gaping door hole. All around in the dark, men stirred and roused, weary as they were, for the Frontier Wolves had learned over many years of practice to sleep easily but not deep.

Outside the store-shed, the guard lay sprawled full length, and bending over him, Alexios saw by the light of a burning branch that somebody had pulled from the remains of a nearby fire, that he had been stabbed in the right side of the throat by somebody creeping up on him from behind.

Of the woman and the dead child there was no sign.

"She was not armed," the man with the light said.

"Oh yes she was. She had the spearhead from the child's body." Alexios was silent a moment; they were all silent; looking down at the sprawling body that had bled its life out into the sodden ground, and cursing himself. But it was too late for that now.

"She couldn't have got past the pickets; she must be somewhere in the rath, still," he said. "Turn out the men and make a search."

But the woman was not still within the rath. "She is of my people," said Optio Finn, reporting the vain search, when there was nowhere left to look. "It would be hard to hold a woman of my people in any place against her will. And this was her rath; she would know the bolt-holes as we cannot know them."

Alexios looked at him, aware yet again of the griefs of old links and old loyalties that must be among his men. "*Your* people? You are of the Frontier Wolves, you are of the Family," he said quietly.

"Nevertheless, I ran wild through such a rath as this in my cub days, and knew the ways in and out that would not be known to the Frontier Wolves."

Alexios nodded. "See to the ponies, Optio. They should have their nosebags now if we are to be away two hours before daylight. See they are issued with as much extra corn as you think good for them. We can't carry much away with us, but beasts and men, we can leave this place with a good square meal in our bellies." He looked down at the dead man. "Get him decently buried. He was of the Dalriads, wasn't he? Let him lie apart from the rest."

Inside the Family, the men of the Votadini and Dumnoni, Selgovae and Dalriads lived and fought and drank together, and in death were buried together, nothing counting but that they were Frontier Wolves. But outside the Family it was another thing altogether. The Dalriads among his men would not take kindly to one of themselves being laid in a common grave with men and women of the Selgovae who made their dance-prayers to gods with different names and different faces.

Once, Alexios would have had to have that explained to him. Now, he knew it without even having to think.

13 | *Orion's Sword*

WITH TWO HOURS OF DARKNESS STILL LEFT, THEY RODE OUT from what had once been the Rath of Skolawn, leaving behind them slaughtered cattle and the bodies of men and women and children with the charred thatch pulled down over them to cover their resting place; and one grave by itself. Presently the wolves would come ...

But now there were other things to think of, and one was the woman who had escaped with her dead child and the knowledge of their whereabouts; and another was the decoy party, who should surely have rejoined them by now.

Alexios spoke his anxiety in a low tone, pushing forward to join Hilarion for a while at the head of the Fore Guard. "It's been a day and two nights, could we have missed them, heading round by the Red Horse Glen instead of holding straight on?"

"Sir," said his Senior Centenarius, mock-serious, "You are speaking of the Frontier Wolves, not dull-nosed legionaries. Do you really think that two or three miles' change in the line of march would lose them our scent?"

"No. That was stupid of me. I'm short of experience in this kind of game." Alexios broke off short, hearing what he had said.

"Heart up, you're playing it none so badly, so far," the Centenarius told him; and Alexios could hear the lazy half-mocking smile in his tone.

"Thanks," he said tersely, and turning his pony aside, dropped back to take his place at the head of the Main Guard.

And indeed anxiety about the decoy party did not weigh on his shoulders much longer, for with the distant promise of daylight no more than a bar of sodden primrose far down in the southeast, as they came down the flank curve of a lightly wooded valley, they heard the long-drawn cry of a wolf far ahead. For a moment it seemed to Alexios that all the blood in his body kept tingling back to his heart. Then the cry was repeated, and repeated again. And from somewhere in the Fore Guard a she-wolf answered. Alexios felt a warm rush of relief. And a while later the optio of the decoy party appeared through the hazel scrub, with a half-seen flicker of riders behind him.

"Reporting back for duty, Sir."

"How did it go?" Alexios asked. As though they had been gone an hour, and he had not been sick with anxiety on their account.

"Well enough." Optio Vedrix gave a low grim chuckle; if there had been light enough to see his face it would have been grinning. "We left them a trail that wouldn't have shamed a wounded bull halfway to Trimontium, and then we—confused things somewhat, at the river ford below Battle Rocks, and doubled back a bit and took to the heather."

Alexios nodded. "Leaving no trail at all."

"We-ell, it is in my mind that they will be hunting on downstream a good way, thinking that we have taken to the water like a hunted stag. They will pick up our scent again in the end, I think, but not yet."

"That was well done," said Alexios softly. "That was very well done, Optio. You have baited and rested the men and horses?"

"In a sheltered hollow of the moors over yonder."

"So. Then fall back now and join on to the Main Guard."

They kept well over to the west, holding to the rolling moorlands and the narrow wooded valleys of swift streams, far from the run of the old half-lost roads; and after the forced march of that first night and day, their pace, with the wounded to think of, seemed maddeningly slow. Several times that day they saw the smoke of burning steadings on the skyline; and all day long, whenever the hills opened eastward, Trimontium rose against the sky, its three peaks from that angle almost hidden behind each other, and scarcely seemed to move. And they rode always with ears pricked and eyes straining for any sign of Pictish war-bands or the hunt on their trail.

In his desperate sense of their need for speed, Alexios had never been so aware as he was now, of the shortness of the northern winter days. And when one of the optios dropped back from the Fore Guard with word from Hilarion, "Sir, there's a level space just below the ridge yonder. It would serve well enough for the night," he shook his head impatiently.

"It can't be much over two hours past noon."

"But it will be dusk in little more than another hour, and we'll need that time to make camp—shan't be able to show a light to work by after dusk."

"Very well; I'll come forward and take a look at this place."

So on the level patch of high moor, they made camp, digging the narrow sleeping trenches that were better shelter than nothing, when you had no tents with you, and lining them with last year's bracken, while the cut clods were stacked into a low protecting wall topped off with thorn bushes. Sixty paces one way, thirty the other; one quarter for the ponies, picketed close, the other three for the sleeping trenches and the general business of the camp. While the daylight lasted, they risked small fires, as smokeless as might be, to make warm stirabout and heat some water for the wounded; and the wounded were tended and the ponies watered and given their meagre rations of corn, as their riders checked again for the condition of feet and hands. And all the while the pickets kept their watch, covering the men as they worked. So much to do, and not much time to do it in, but with every man knowing exactly his own job and getting on with it, somehow all was done before the dusk deepened into the dark and it was time to douse the fires and let the cold and dark and the wind-haunted stillness of the winter night take over.

Lying among his men at the heel of one of the long bracken-lined sleeping trenches that even on peace-time patrols had always seemed to him uncomfortably like a grave, Alexios thought that seeing the Frontier Wolves in off-duty hours, drunk and ribald, cock-fighting, wenching, scrapping among themselves, wild and insubordinate, you could easily enough imagine them turning hero against an enemy from outside, standing by each other in the last ditch, but you couldn't imagine this well-drilled and efficient making of camp in hostile territory. "If we don't get through," he thought, "if I don't get them through—if I don't get out of this— by the Lord of the Legions I've known what it is to command men worth the commanding!"

Above him the sky was breaking up, by morning it would be freezing hard; and suddenly Orion swung clear of the drifting cloud into a great lake of clear. He looked up at the three stars of the hunter's belt and the straight jewelled line of the sword hanging from it. He had never noticed before how bright and beautiful Orion's sword shone on a winter's night. He heard the faint stir in the close-packed horse-lines, and the dark soughing of the wind across the dead heather. "I have served with *men*, and I have seen Orion's sword in the sky," he thought with an odd feeling of content; and rolled over in the harsh bedding, pulling his wolfskin closer about him, and fell into a quiet sleep as peacefully as when he was a boy in his familiar sleeping cell at home in the Down Country farm.

Three times in the night he woke at watch changing, and made the round of the sentries on the turf banks and the little out-work that guarded the far corner of the horse-lines; and each time returned briefly to the same quiet sleep.

Again they broke camp in the heel of the night, with two hours of darkness still to run, and headed for the old marching camp at Ravens' Law. The wind had lessened, and there was ice crackling in the margins of the moorland pools; but the clouds had closed in again, low and leaden, and Optio Vedrix, who could smell the weather as a hound scents game, snuffed the wind and growled, "Snow. We shall have snow before the day's half through."

But before the snow came, the hunt was upon them.

They had expected it so long, every nerve on the stretch, for the first warning of its coming, that when the low whistling calls broke out behind them, and then the beat of hooves and the brush of flying shadows through the hazel woods, it was almost a relief.

"Here they come," Alexios said to the optio beside him. There was no need or time for a string of orders; the orders had been given in advance. The gaps between the three Guards were already narrowing, the escort closing up on either side of the wounded and the pack beasts, every archer slipping his bow from behind his shoulder. Better to keep moving; they were trained to shoot from horseback, and the tribesmen, even the Painted People, were not, which gave them an advantage on the move. But each man had only the ten arrows in his quiver, and no more could be issued before there was a halt; and Alexios sent up a prayer to Mithras that they would remember his orders that not an arrow was to be wasted; and then rather grimly laughed at himself. They had been on the Frontier much longer than he had.

And as the men of the Rear Guard turned in the saddle with

arrows ready notched to their bowstrings, the first flurry of snow blew out of the darkening north into their faces.

But the attack that could come at any moment did not come.

Hour after long-drawn hour the Frontier Wolves pushed on, the enemy on their rear and flanks loosing a stray arrow into their midst from time to time, filling the woods with the menace of their low whistling call and answer call; while the snow, eddying more thickly as time went by, made the task of their own marksmen the harder.

"Wolf-pack tactics," Alexios thought to himself as time went by and no open attack developed. "They know they have today and tomorrow at the least, to get us in, and maybe they haven't enough men themselves to be sure of an attack; so they'll try to wear us down, and wait their chance—hang on our flanks like a pack on the flanks of the driven herd, ready to cut off stragglers, harrying our rear until their moment comes." And then he thought, "Only we aren't a driven herd, we are another wolf-pack with teeth as sharp as theirs—and they know that too."

The snow was flurrying across their left flank, a dry powdery snow that cut down visibility where the trees fell back, but as yet was not damping the bowstrings. And as happens with snowfall, everything was going very quiet. Too quiet. The low whistling calls had died away; it was a long time since a Pictish arrow had thrummed into their midst. It was almost as though the hunt had drawn off. Almost, but not quite, not only his sense but the feeling that he had once thought of as thunder brewing in the back of his neck told him that it was not.

"Are you thinking what I'm thinking?" he asked the optio of the Praepositus's escort who had ridden beside him since they passed from the country normally covered by their own patrols into the First Ordo's territory.

But before the man could answer, one of the scouting party appeared, heading back past the Fore Guard, and reined round beside Phoenix. "Sir, they've got ahead of us. They're waiting for us where the valley narrows about a mile further on, lying up in the scrub."

"How many?" Alexios said.

"Something over five hundred, the Votadini and the Picts together. Still no White Shields."

"No need, of course, to ask if they sighted you."

"No, Sir," the man said, simply.

"Then they'll think we're walking blind into a trap; that's one point to us in the game, anyhow. Take word to Centenarius Hilarion, to pull back to close the marching gap and join forces with us, and himself to come to me here a moment." Then over his shoulder to his galloper, "Cullen, get to Optio Garwin and give him the word to send twenty-six men back to Centenarius Lucius, to strengthen the Rear Guard. Ask the Centenarius to come forward to me while that is done."

"Sir." The galloper pulled out from his place, and wheeling his pony disappeared down the long line of the column.

"We could try to outflank them, Sir," said the escort optio.

Alexios looked up at the steep wooded hillside, the rocky outcrops breaking through the dense scrub. "The wounded could never make it."

When Hilarion and Lucius ranged up beside him, he gave them the facts and the plan of action. "Hilarion, you and I, with the Fore Guard and the Main Guard combined will keep going, straight ahead, as though we were walking into their trap; meanwhile you, Lucius, take the reinforced Rear Guard up round that way, to try to outflank them." Again he glanced at the steep rocky hillside. "Hook round behind them and wait for us to have made contact and be fully engaged, then drive in from the rear. If you get the chance to stampede their ponies, so much the better." The fact that you could not fight on horseback in wooded country would hold good for the enemy as well as for themselves; and on both sides the ponies would have to be left standing somewhere in the rear with only a few men to guard them. That was understood by everybody with no word spoken.

A few more details were quickly dealt with, and the two centenarii headed back to their own places. Alexios moved up with Hilarion to the head of the Fore Guard. The column moved on steadily. It was an odd feeling, he thought, to be advancing deliberately into a trap.

The snow eddied like white smoke among the hazel trees, settling in a fine dry powder on wolfskins and ponies' manes, beginning to settle on the rough ground. Still the silence held, save for the faint sounds of the column moving behind him. And then, somewhere ahead, the quiet was splintered by the alarm call of a jay.

Alexios flung up his hand, and was aware of the signal being repeated all down the line behind him.

The column slowed to a halt.

In the lee of a dense thicket, they left the ponies, the wounded and the baggage beasts with their escort. Arrow sheaves were taken from their pack bundles and quivers were re-stocked, and then they pushed forward on foot, the main force heading straight for the waiting ambush, while Lucius and his fifty men melted up into the hazel scrub and flurrying snow of the steep hillside to the right.

In the narrows of the valley the trees fell back a little, and among the rocky outcrops and the more open scrub, the tribesmen were waiting for them; no means of telling just where, nor whether there were smaller parties on their flanks. "Send me a flight of arrows over that scrub," Alexios ordered. "High trajectory."

It was odd how even trained troops would look up to follow the flight-path of arrows coming over them, he thought, odd how white and betraying even the darkest of faces could show in that moment. He heard the faint sound of movement as the archers pulled to each side of the column head, the twang of the released bowstrings; he was aware of the dark streaks of movement as the arrows soared on their way.

An old trick, but it worked. Among the scrub and the rocky outcrops a pale flicker betrayed hidden men. The archers of the Frontier Wolves had loosed at extreme range, before any arrows of the Painted People could reach them. There was time for one more flight; a killer flight this time that went on its way like a cloud of hornets, and somewhere among the scrub ahead of them a man cried out, choking on the cry, and somewhere on the flank a pony screamed. Then the men slung their bows behind them; they knew where to aim their charge now, and as the Pictish arrows sang in answer, the archers dropped behind, while the rest went in with drawn swords through the gaps they left, running low behind their bucklers. The tribesmen had lost the advantage of surprise, but as the narrows of the valley ahead and the steep flanks on either side erupted into waves of yelling warriors, Alexios's heart gave an unpleasant lurch as it came home to him how desperately outnumbered they were. Knowing it from the scout's report was one thing, actually seeing the rocky slopes spew fighting men was another. He heard the "tock" of a Pictish arrow finding its target in a wicker shield beside him, and somewhere close by a man fell and then another. A third flight of their own arrows thrummed overhead, and then they were under shooting range from either side, and the tribesmen leapt to meet them with naked swords and heavy stabbing spears; and they were locked together, blade to blade, shield to shield, like wild beasts grappling for each other's throats, while their mingled war-cries tore the snowy silence apart.

Alexios ripped his long cavalry spatha from its sheath, "When the Commander needs to draw his own sword in anger, he has failed in his job." He remembered being told that at training school. But maybe training school had not known about the Frontier Wolves. Ahead of him in the press he glimpsed Cunorix for one fiery instant, his war-cap off and his russet hair flying, his mouth wide as he yelled the war-cry, and he drove towards him, filled with the terrible drunkenness of battle. But the swirling press closed over between them. The final settlement was not yet.

In the first charge they had driven deep into the enemy mass, but they were still desperately outnumbered; and Alexios, tuned to his troops as a good Commander must be, as a musician is tuned to his instrument, felt the first strong thrust begin to lose impetus in the face of the sheer numbers against it.

Where in the Name of Light was Lucius and his lot? Had they got through? He raised his voice again in the long wolfish war-cry, and heard it taken up on all sides. Heard too, from somewhere ahead beyond the tribesmen's left flank, the same cry, and then the neigh of a terrified horse. A dark animal flood was sweeping across the enemy rear, ploughing through their hindmost ranks, and behind them again sounded the wolf-yell. Lucius and his lot had got through, and had contrived to stampede the enemy ponies.

The pressure against the main force began to waver. The Frontier Wolves gathered themselves and thrust forward again.

It was hot work for a while, and then suddenly it was over. The tribesmen, caught front and rear and forced in on themselves, had had enough for the moment. They were pulling back, running for the flanks of the fighting; they were disappearing into the white whirl of the snow. Gone like a dissolving dream. And in the midst of the dream Alexios and his Junior Centenarius greeted each other wearily across their shields.

Behind them the Frontier Wolves drew breath and gathered up their dead and wounded, enough and more than enough, though the tribesmen had lost many more; and got back to their ponies and baggage train; and in as short a time as might be, were pushing forward again.

"That should cool their blood for a while," Lucius said, swinging into his saddle while the Rear Guard formed up once more.

"And thanks to you, they'll have enough to occupy them till dusk, getting their ponies back again," Alexios said.

"I don't know. It was only one stand of ponies we stampeded. Still, every little helps," Lucius said in his pleasant voice, and saluted and disappeared down the column.

Even as he spoke, from somewhere among the woods to their left, the long whistling call of the Painted People sounded as though in mockery.

Through what remained of that day they saw no more of the Picts or the Votadini, but they heard long-drawn eerie calls behind them and on either flank; once or twice even in front, for the tribes, carrying no wounded with them to slow them up, were free to fling small bands ahead; and time and again from some wooded bluff or patch of dense furze-cover, the odd arrow came whistling into their midst. They lost five men killed and wounded on the rest of that day's march, but there was nothing they could do about it save press on; for any detachment sent out from the main force, Alexios knew would never get back to them again. The snow was coming on harder, changing from a mealy cloud to whirling white flakes, and the wind was getting up again, from the east this time, a black wind with an edge like a fleshing knife that drove it almost straight in their faces. Men and ponies were dog-weary, having made a long march over rough country and fought a gruelling action since they broke camp that morning; and they were slowed up and hampered by their wounded, hemmed-in and harried, with the pressures of the hunt close upon them; while the tribesmen, though they must be just as weary, had all the freedom of the country round them. The light began to fade to a whirling brownish dusk, earth and sky the same colour. And with the loss of the light it seemed again all too likely that the Painted People, even without the Votadini, might close in in the dark on a weary column still on the march ...

But at full dusk, with the open moorland—they had left the wooded country long since—opening out like storm swept sea all about them, they rode into the old marching camp at Ravens' Law.

They hauled in dry thorn bushes to block the empty entrance that gaped in the night like a dead man's mouth, and strength-ened the weak places in the age-eaten turf ramparts. They got the ponies watered under guard at the nearby stream, and picketed them close, each with his last scraped-out measure of corn. They scraped out the old sleeping trenches, those where the northern and eastern ramparts gave some shelter from the wind and snow for the living, others, where there was no shelter, to make graves for their dead. They risked a shielded lantern for a while, to see to the wounded and for the nightly inspection of feet and hands, and for the rest, huddled close about the small spitting fires of heather and dry thorn branches while they lasted, to clean their weapons; then when the fires sank, huddled together for the little warmth that their chilled and weary bodies had to give each other, while they ate the dry evening bannock and a handful of crumbling cheese. And with the sinking of the fires, not only the dark and the cold crept closer, but the sense of menace beyond the old turf walls.

Alexios, moving among the dark humped shapes, his own bit of bannock in his hand, sensed another kind of darkness lying heavy in the hearts of his men, and said to the nearest group of shadows, "Only twelve more miles to do; not even a full day's march; and tomorrow night we shall sleep warm and full-bellied in Bremenium."

"And what makes him so sure of that, I'm wondering?" muttered a voice behind him as he moved on.

Alexios checked, and swung back towards the speaker. "I will tell you. I am sure because we have made well over three-fourths of the way already, and sent the men who thought we would be an easy kill off to lick their wounds. Because we are disciplined troops of Rome, which gives us the pull over any tribal war-mob, however valiant; and because of all the troops of Rome, *we are the Frontier Wolves!*"

Someone gave a small crow of laughter, half breath in his throat. "We are the Frontier Wolves, and let nobody forget it!"

And it seemed to Alexios that the darkness-of-the-heart lifted just a little. But whether they would indeed sleep warm and full-fed at Headquarters tomorrow night, or cold somewhere on the high moors with the snow unmelting on their breasts, that was another matter.

Going on his way, he remembered something he had forgotten in the press of other matters that he had had to think of lately. Tomorrow would be Midwinter's Night. Suddenly and piercingly, he remembered last Midwinter's Night; the fight on the Dancing Ground, and himself wading into it; young Rufus beside him with the amber kitten clinging to the neck folds of his cloak; big guileless looking Bericus and his fellow evildoers in the Principia office next morning; Orion hanging over the southern ramparts of Castellum …

It all seemed much more than a year ago.

Late that night, in a corner of the old marching camp, he squatted with Hilarion and Lucius and the senior optios, discussing their last day's line of march.

"Your word first," Alexios said to the escort optio, "these are your hunting runs, not ours."

And the man spoke briefly and to the point of the country still between them and Bremenium; of hidden valleys that might give shelter to the marching column, of wooded patches at the bend of a stream that might cover an ambush; of the Roaring-Water that, whichever way they chose, must be crossed at one of two places—by the bridge where the old east-west road passed over, or by the ford an hour's march further west.

Alexios said, "No other crossing place? None that the Votadini might not think of, seeing that this is not their home territory?"

"None, Sir, unless you swing right over to the Trimontium road—more than half a day's march. The Roaring-Water did not get its name for nothing. It's not wide, but it's deep and it runs like a millrace."

"So—then which of those two crossing places would you put your money on?"

"Depends on the weather, Sir. If it's still snowing like this to cover our tracks, maybe I'd make for the ford. Less obvious, though it's further. If the snow slackens off, we'll leave a trail that a suckling babe could follow."

"In which case," murmured Hilarion, "I'd put my money on getting down to the old road, and make for the bridge like bats out of a burning barn."

"On the other hand," said Lucius, "they can't so easily destroy a ford."

"But if they get ahead, they can hold it against us," Alexios said. His head was aching, a small tense ache that started at the back of his neck. He bent his head into his hands, pressing the base of the palms into his eye sockets until the darkness burst into coloured clouds. "Optio Vedrix, can that nose of yours tell us what the weather's going to do?"

"Sorry, Sir. It can smell the snow coming, can't tell when it's going to pass. Not in a black murk like this."

"Right." Alexios dropped his hands and sat up, the snow feathering cold again on his lips and eyelashes. "We'll head for the bridge. That's about six miles, isn't it? If we break camp mid-way through the Fourth Watch, we should make it soon after dawn. Centenarius Hilarion, send four of your best scouts ahead to keep an eye on the bridge and send back word if it's been broken down or not. If they leave at the change of the Third Watch, that will still give them a few hours' sleep. And for the rest of us, I suggest that whatever our faiths, we pray to the Lady Fortuna, who was ever the Goddess of Gamblers."

They broke camp with four hours still to go before dawn; snow lying thick on the men's wolfskins as they rose and shook it off in clouds. It was still snowing, but not as hard as it had been; there was more light to see by, and a faint breath like smoke rose from the horse-lines into the pale-feathered air. Several of the wounded, the man with the belly-wound among them, had died in the night; and they left them lying in their sleeping-places, piling the turfs back over all.

And, each man eating half a dry bannock as he rode, the last food that was left to them, they headed down the old half-lost road to Bremenium, their one chance, to reach the bridge before the hunt caught up with them—supposing that the bridge was still there.

The bridge was still there. Alexios, seeing it through the thin snow-flurry as the road dipped towards it in the grey dawn light, was vaguely surprised at that. If he had been Cunorix he would have tried flinging forward a party to destroy the bridge. Maybe the Lady Fortuna knew a good prayer when she heard one.

Of course there was always the chance that it was a trap, but the advance scouts reported no sign of life within striking distance of the far bank. Anyhow they had no time to waste in thinking about it; a good mile back when the snow had trailed its curtain aside for a moment, they had seen a mounted figure on the skyline of a nearby ridge, and before the snow swooped back again, had known by the long-carrying view call answered from somewhere behind them, that they also had been seen. The hunt was once more close on their trail.

On the near bank, there had at one time been a small posting station and the fallen remains of turf and timber walls, Alexios saw, could give cover to a Rear Guard party, while the rest got on with cutting the bridge behind them.

The Fore Guard were already crossing, then the wounded and the few pack beasts brought up from their usual positions towards the rear. Then the Main Guard. Wheeling his pony aside, Alexios sat while they went, the ponies' hooves ringing hollow on the bridge timbers, until on the far side the next snow-squall turned them into ghosts and swallowed them. But his senses were strained the other way, probing for the first sign of the enemy above the rush of dark water coming down in spate and through the swirling whiteness that blotted out the way they had come. The crossing seemed to take an interminable time, but the end-riders of the Main Guard were on the bridge at last, leading the

Rear Guard ponies with them. Now only a dozen or so men of the Rear Guard remained, crouching behind the stone footings of the ruined posting stable, each man with his bow sheltered under his wolfskin to keep the string dry; not that there would be visibility for more than one flight of arrows before "Swords Out," Alexios judged.

He glanced at Lucius standing beside him, and set his hand for an instant on the quiet man's shoulder. "Right, we'll not waste time. When you hear the horn, run like redshanks. We'll give you what cover we can from the far bank, and have men standing roped-up and ready in case anyone goes in the water."

Lucius smiled round at him, his eyes quiet as they always were, in his filthy and exhausted face. Somewhere in the white murk, they heard the low eerie whistling call of the Painted People.

Alexios swung Phoenix round and clattered across the bridge.

On the far side, men had already fetched axes and crowbars from the pack ponies who carried them, while others were fixing picket ropes across the breast-straps of the freshest and toughest beasts to serve as hauling lines. "Quick!" Alexios called. "Not much time!"

But almost before he had turned Phoenix back to face the river, they were hard at their desperate labour, for they too had heard the wood-wind call of the Painted People. The wind-hush, snow-hush above the hoarse voice of the river was lost in the shouting of orders and the ring of axes on heavy timbers. Men were swarming all over the bridge; axes blinked in the dawn light as they rose and fell, while below, thigh deep, waist deep in the dark swirl of the icy water, half-clinging to snowladen alder branches as they worked, men fought to secure the hauling-lines onto the timber bridge supports on the downstream side.

The whistling call of the Painted People sounded again, very close now, and suddenly it was joined by the hunting call of the Votadini. Across the river there was a stirring in the white murk, faint shadows growing stronger as they came at the run. A flight of arrows leapt out from the cover of the ruined walls, and a high yell echoing out of the snow-swirl was cut off short. The ring of axes took on a redoubled urgency. Across the bridge, the bank was suddenly alive with battling figures half-lost in the mealy cloud; and in the same instant Alexios heard Hilarion's shouted order, and a splintering crash and splash as one of the bridge timbers went down in a fountain of freezing spray. The bridge shuddered like a live thing in agony. It was beginning to go.

With his gaze on the small valiant band that had risen from the ruins to fling themselves between the swarming warpainted hunters and the bridge head, Alexios said to his trumpeter beside him, "Sound the Break off and Recall."

And for the first time since they marched out from Castellum, the bright harsh notes of the hunting-horn gave tongue, "Break off! Fall back! Ta-ran, Ta-ta-ran-ta-ran…"

The wolf-cloaked men were coming, falling back onto the end of the tottering bridge. Alexios saw two of them go down to the Votadini throw-spears, the remaining nine reached the bridge and began the crossing. But the enemy were close behind—too close. The ponies were straining at the ropes, urged on by the yells of their drivers and the slash of reins across their necks and haunches. The bridge staggered like a drunk man, timbers falling, but the main structure righted itself and still stood. Six of the Rear Guard had reached their own side; but still on the far end of the bridge, the three last had whirled about, and stood, swords up, shields up, facing the swarm of tribesmen. And Alexios saw that the man in the centre was Lucius.

Their own archers stood loosing across the river into the thick of the tribal rush. He saw the three men give back one step on the tottering log-work, two steps, three, their chins driven down behind their shields, their blades slashing deep. A tribesman of the Votadini flung wide his arms and plunged down into the racing water; a half-naked warrior of the Painted People followed him, but the rush behind them thrust on.

"Pull!" Alexios yelled. "Pull! Fiends and Furies! *Pull!*"

Ponies and drivers strained again, and again, then came forward up the bank at a plunging scramble. The whole bridge had gone lax and limber; there was a whining and cracking of timbers, and with a rending crash the whole thing keeled over, and its centre and near end swept down-river in a tossing welter of beams and planking.

Alexios saw the three men—no, there were only two now—spring back and to the left making for the water above the fallen debris. He saw the howling struggle as the tribesmen on the stump of the bridge tried to check and were driven on by the rush behind them, to plunge down among the wreckage. One of the ponies had been swept away before they could cut the hauling line that held him to his baulk of timber, the rest, hacked free, were plunging up through the alder scrub; while the men, who had been standing roped up and ready waist-deep, in the whirling spate, were making for the place in mid-stream where the Frontier Wolves had gone down. In the yeasty turmoil, Alexios could make out little of what was happening out there. He was down the bank with half-a-dozen of his men, braced against the icy drag of the river, taking the strain of one of the swimmer's ropes. There were two men now on the end of it. Hand over hand, they began hauling in.

"All right," someone said, "I've got him." Arms reached out

to take the sodden man-shaped bundle from the swimmer; and Alexios, one foot on the bank, reached forward in his turn to get hold of the limp body and heave it further up the bank to the man above him, saw with a jab of shock that it was Lucius.

Lucius with a great red spear-hole gaping juicily below his collarbone. He must have taken the thrust in over his guard in the very moment that the bridge went.

A few yards further downstream, they were hauling ashore the second man. The third had gone downstream with the dead of the Votadini and the Painted People and the tumble of lesser bridge timbers.

On the level ground at the top of the bank, Alexios was squatting beside his Junior Centenarius, holding him propped against his knee to ease his breathing. Blood was pumping from the hole under his collarbone in little jets; the bright blood that carries a man's life with it. He pressed a handful of his own cloak over it, but he knew that it was no good; not with blood that colour. Lucius opened clouded eyes, and looked up into his face. "Has—the bridge gone?"

"The bridge has gone," Alexios told him. "We'll be in Bremenium by noon."

"Just—let me get—my wind back—think I—must have swallowed—half the river—"

"No hurry," Alexios said, his throat aching.

Lucius was silent a few moments. He looked faintly puzzled more than anything else. "Tired," he said at last. "Stupid—feel so—tired."

"You've had a hard morning's work. Go to sleep now."

And like a tired child, he turned his head on Alexios's knee and settled his cheek. He gave a small dry cough, and that was all.

It was like Lucius, his Commanding Officer thought, to die so quietly and neatly. He remained a moment longer, looking down at him. Suddenly he wondered if Lucius had known, when he brought his beloved Georgics to be burned with the Castellum papers. Then he laid the wet body down, and got to his feet.

Nearby, the second man was vomiting up half the river, but seemed to have taken no other harm.

Beyond the river, the tribesmen had melted away into the snow-fog. Alexios knew they would be making upriver towards the ford. It would take them a good while to reach it, but still there was no time to stand while the grass grew under one's feet.

"Get the Centenarius across his own horse," he said to the nearest wolf-cloaked figure. Then lifted his voice in a sharp general order, "Back to the ponies."

And the bridge-breaking party, together with what was left of the Rear Guard, headed at a run for the place a little back from the river where their mounts waited, the few men who had been sent back with them already swinging into the saddle.

They were too spent for the steed-leap, and scrambled anyhow into their saddles. The two carrying Lucius's body slung him across the back of his own horse who snorted in fear and tried to put his head round to snuff at his master grown suddenly strange, until another man grabbed his bridle. And they broke forward.

The land rose gently from the river left behind them, and somewhere ahead, just over the next ridge, the Fore Guard and Main Guard and the baggage train with its weary wounded, would be plodding along, strung out, following the half-lost road under the snow.

"Now for Bremenium! Ride!" Alexios shouted, and settled down into his saddle.

14 | *Midwinter Night*

THEY REACHED BREMENIUM AHEAD OF THE HUNT, AND WITH a couple of hours of leaden daylight left. The snow had eased off from the whirling white fog that it had been earlier, and the world had opened out again, so that they could see the great fortress while they were as yet some way off.

So that they could see what was left of it.

The walls stood up blank and dead, no sentries' heads moved along the rampart walk; only the heads of the great catapults stood up from their emplacements like giant grasshoppers; and smoke that was not hearth or camp smoke rose from the midst of the place, and already the ravens had gathered and were sweeping to and fro on black wings above what was within.

Somehow that was the one thing Alexios had not thought of; that they would win through to Bremenium, and Bremenium as a living fortress would not be there. It seemed impossible that the great stronghold could have fallen; not Bremenium with its massive walls and powerful catapults, its full garrison of Cavalry and Artillery as well as Frontier Wolves.

Lying up in the shelter of a patch of thin woodland, waiting for the return of the scouts he had sent in for a closer look, Alexios could still not quite believe it, despite the cold black pit that seemed to have opened in his belly.

Maybe this was why the Votadini had not tried to destroy the bridge ahead of them. Then why the fight at the bridge itself? Maybe Cunorix, having joined spears with the Caledoni, was suffering from a divided command? He would never know, and it did not much matter now, anyway. But it wasn't possible that Bremenium had fallen. There was something crazily wrong somewhere.

The scouts got back; and their report made it clear that there was no mistake. But there was indeed something crazily wrong, some kind of horrible mystery. Both Sinister and Dextra gates were wide open, the scouts reported, and casting round the eastern side, they had found the tracks of many ponies. Driven ponies, not ridden, for the most part. There were a few Pictish dead outside the walls, but nothing like the number to be expected. But inside the gateways it was another matter. There had been hard fighting within the gates; many bodies of Picts and men of the White Shields, but for the most part Roman.

"The gates," Alexios said, frowning, "had they been fired? Battered in?"

"No Sir," said the leading scout, "just standing open."

"Some kind of trap, with us for the quarry?"

The man shook his head. "Just a massacre."

And the second scout said shakily, "The place reeks of death and emptiness."

"It seems we are fated to camp on the spoor of the Painted People," Alexios said.

Beside him Optio Brychanus said urgently, "Sir, not in the fort!"

Alexios looked round and met his haggard gaze, and beyond that the cool half-mocking face of Hilarion, showing as usual nothing of what was behind it. "No, not in the fort. Too many ghosts, and too great a length of wall to be held by not much over a hundred men. But there's more snow coming, by the look and feel of it; and we've got to get shelter for the wounded—for all of us. Maybe somewhere among what's left of the settlement outside the walls."

Hilarion's mouth quirked at the corners in his grey and filthy face. "The bath-house, say, there should be enough of us still in fighting trim to hold that."

But in the end, out of all the wreckage of the settlement, it was not the bath-house that they took over for their strong-point, but the waggon park close by the Dextra gate. The walled open space where the supply waggons had been used to stand, and where the levied corn and drafts of local ponies had been checked by Quartermaster or Horsemaster, and much of the local trade between the fort and the country round had been carried on. The breast-high freestone walls still stood, and along one side, what was left of stables and warehouses would give some shelter to wounded and exhausted men through the bitter winter's night. Probably they would not be able to hold it indefinitely, Alexios thought, with a dull sense upon him of having come to the end of the road; but at least there would be shelter for a while, and a few hours' rest, if the tribesmen did not come up with them before dusk— and somewhere to make a last stand.

Leaving his Senior Centenarius—his only centenarius, now— to take over the camp-making, he ordered twelve men including those left of the Praepositus's escort—a scouting detachment, a foraging party, hard to say what—to enter the fort, and himself went with them.

The snow lay thick over dead men, making them all seem alike where it had drifted into corners and against walls, though in the more open places they could still be seen for what they were, Roman cavalryman, painted Pictish warrior, man from across the Western Sea with his lime-whitened shield splashed now with dried blood; brindle cloaked Frontier Wolf. No sign of any of the

Arcani. So the attack must have come yesterday, though the faint smoke still rose here and there from charred and sodden timbers towards a sky that was the colour of a fading bruise, heavy with more snow still to come. The dead lay clotted thick about the Principia where the garrison must have made its last stand. The ponies had all been driven off, and the picket-lines were empty save for a few contorted carcasses of beasts that had been speared in the fighting, and one wretched hamstrung cavalry pony still struggling up and falling as he must have been doing for many hours.

The Frontier Wolves loped questing here and there; in one of the burned-out granaries they found a little scorched corn bursting out of its sacks, and scooped it up as best they could into the hollows of their shields. The hamstrung pony was put out of its misery with a dagger thrust. Alexios spoke aside to the optio. "Have that poor brute butchered; we'll eat meat tonight for our Midwinter Feast."

"Horsemeat, Sir?" the optio said doubtfully.

"Horsemeat, Optio. We will make the proper sacrifice to the Lady of the Foals, and she will forgive us in our need."

They were back at the Dextra gate, the slaughter-house smell of Bremenium clogging the backs of their throats despite the cold, when they heard a faint groan. As they checked, it came again, seemingly from below the stair that led up to the nearest catapult platform.

"Someone's alive—come!" Alexios shouted, and they ran.

At the foot of the stair the sprawling dead were piled; and something stirred faintly in their midst. They hauled the dead aside, and a man's face opened its eyes at them and groaned again.

"Cognos!" one of the escort men said in recognition.

Alexios knelt down beside the man, who wore the sodden rags

of an artilleryman's uniform. "Softly now, we're friends," he said; and to the Frontier Wolves who had crowded after him, "Cloaks and spearshafts—make a stretcher."

The wounded man shook his head very slightly. "I'm just about—broke in half. If you move me—I'll be on my way. Thirsty, though."

"Bring water," Alexios said, and as one of his men turned away to fetch it, "What happened here?"

"The Painted People—painted devils—and the Attacotti—they've joined spears. Wiped us out—Frontier Wolves and all."

"What of the Arcani?" Alexios asked.

The man's mouth twisted. "D'you think we'd have been overrun if—somebody hadn't—opened the gates?"

His head rolled sideways.

Alexios got up. "No need now," he said to the Wolf who came with his helmet half-full of water.

Back in the waggon park they had got the ponies picketed close and the wounded into shelter, and made small fires under the broken roofs of the warehouse row. Alexios ducked in under the sagging thatch into the faint warmth and the fire-flicker, and the smoke caught at his eyes and throat. It was coming on to snow again.

They had found a little meal to make warm stirabout for the wounded; the scorched corn must go to the ponies.

"Presently there will be fresh meat for all of us," Alexios said, and saw spent and famished faces lifted, the ears of his Wolves almost visibly pricked.

"Have the Painted People spared the Commander's cow, then?" somebody asked.

He shook his head. "They left one of the cavalry ponies hamstrung."

About him in the fitful flame-light he saw the faces change; now they had the look of men with the warm hunger-water drooling into their mouths; but in their eyes a sullen blankness. They were being asked to break the taboos of their kind, and they thought that he did not understand. For that one moment, so far as they were concerned, he was on the outside again, as he had been when he first took over his command.

"We will make an offering to the Lady," he said. "The Mother of Foals will not hold it against us, for we also are her sons and she knows our need."

And the moment passed.

Men grinned back at him out of gaunt and filthy and wind-cut faces; men so grey and far-gone in exhaustion that it seemed they could get no warmth from the fires to which they huddled. The smoke billowed back on them, and mingled with the smoke the first flakes of the new snowfall that flecked their hunched shoulders and fell hissing into the flames.

Men came out through the Dextra gate and scrambled across the low wall carrying great lumps of raw and bleeding horseflesh; fresh meat, horribly fresh; still warm and faintly smoking in the bitter air. Alexios pulled his thoughts back from that wretched pony maddened with pain and fear. "Hack that lot up small and set it to the fire," he said. "Keep the left shoulder for the atonement offering."

And he went off to see to the next thing that must be dealt with.

The men of Lucius's own Centenary had scraped out a shallow grave for him in the ditch that divided the waggon park from the wall of the fort. They had made it slantwise instead of following the line of the ditch, and for a moment, Alexios, scrambling down to join the little burial party, wondered why; then he remembered, the ditch would be running too much north and south, and it was important to the Christians to be buried east and west. Maybe, like the Votadini, their spirits needed to know the direction of the sunset. That would have been Anthonius's doing. The first of the new snowfall was eddying round them, large flakes like the soft breast feathers of white birds; there were a few of them already lying at the bottom of the grave-scrape when they lifted Lucius's body into it, and a few more settled on the harsh hairs of his wolfskin and on his lips, before they piled in the half-frozen clods and pulled down more from the steep side of the ditch to make him a good mound.

Anthonius, with a drip on the end of his long twisted nose, looked questioningly across the rough grave at Alexios. And Alexios made a small gesture to him to carry on.

The Medic began to speak the parting words for a man of his own faith. "Oh Lord God, receive into Thy loving hands—"

But Alexios never heard the end of the short prayer, for at that moment, between gust and gust of the wind, a low whistling call, far off yet and on the outmost edge of hearing, reached him from the world outside the makeshift strong-point. One of the lookouts shouted something, and a pony in the picket-lines flung up its head and whinnied. As he clambered back out of the ditch heads were turning to listen, men reaching for weapons as they scrambled to their feet. From all round the fringes of the ruined settlement came the whistling calls, and joined with them now the deeper and fuller-throated yell of the Votadini on the bloodtrail.

"Man the walls," Alexios ordered. And to the wounded men about the fires he said, grinning, "Anyone with an arm to use, carry on with the cooking. It may be that they will not attack today—they must be as weary as we are. But if they do, then assuredly we shall fight the better for the smell of supper cooking behind us!"

A few moments later, crouching behind the barricade of half-charred timbers with which they had closed the gate-gap of the waggon park, he saw movement among the half-walls and fallen roof beams of the buildings beyond; figures slipping low from cover to cover in the fading light. The whole settlement was suddenly alive with moving shadows, closing in. So many shadows. The Frontier Wolves were still so desperately outnumbered; and in their spent and famished state, their Commander knew with a cold certainty that the next attack, if it came before they had had time for food and rest, would finish them. The half-ruined waggon park at Bremenium would indeed be the place of their last stand.

The pony whinnied again, and was answered from somewhere on the outer fringe of the settlement, where the tribesmen must have left their own ponies before closing in on foot. Alexios had hoped desperately that they were only scouting, but they were too many for that. Too many shadows moving in, gaining substance as they drew near. It looked as if they were going to attack at once, hoping to finish the thing before the last of the fighting light was gone—while the spirits of those who died would still be able to find their way Westward by the hidden sunset.

But meanwhile there was a kind of pause; the Frontier Wolves crouched behind their makeshift breastwork, swords in hands, eyes arrowed into the flurrying snow. The light was already too unsure for marksmanship, and they had too few arrows left in their quivers to risk wasting any of them. Among the ruined buildings ringing them round, the shadows crouched like hounds in leash. Soon, maybe in the next heartbeat of time, the leashes would be slipped and the attack would break upon them in a howling wave; but for the moment there was the pause, the waiting, the hush under the gusting wind.

And in the waiting hush, as though from somewhere outside himself, the knowledge came to Alexios of what he had to do. It was a crazy idea, he knew that even as it came to him, but he knew also that there was just a chance it might work; might gain for his exhausted men the time to eat and regain some strength from the food, time for a few hours' rest that would give them a better chance when the fighting came in the morning.

He spoke to the optio beside him, "Ask the centenarius to come to me."

And as the man went off, he began to unbind from his waist the stained and tattered silken rags of the Ordo dragon.

He had barely finished when the tall shape of Hilarion slipped low along the breastwork to his side. "Sir?"

"Take charge of this," Alexios said, holding it out to him.

Hilarion looked down at the flattened mask and bright rags, then up into Alexios's face; and for once there was no trace of mocking in his own. "What would you be thinking of doing, Sir?"

"I'm not quite sure. Playing for time, I suppose—no time to go into details; but if anything goes wrong, it will be for you to take over the command, so in Mithras's name take this now and don't argue."

But Hilarion argued all the same, briefly and urgently. "Better let me do it, Sir, whatever it is. Not supposed to be the Commander's job to get his throat split open playing some lone wolf hero-game of his own."

"Unfortunately," Alexios said, "I am the only one who can play this particular game."

Their eyes met: and Alexios answered the unspoken question in the other's gaze. "Because I am the one who killed Connla."

There was a sudden stirring among the settlement ruins; and

all along the waggon park walls an answering tensing, a faint ruffle of sound that was scarcely sound at all, as men altered their stance and tightened their grip on their weapons. Hilarion took the wreckage of the Ordo dragon and began quickly to bind it round his waist.

A long war-spear with a tassel of marten tails flying from its neck came in a high arc over the wall and hung quivering with its point in the ground close by.

"Hold your throw!" Alexios shouted, as all along the breast-work the spearmen's arms went up and back in reply. He was running low for the place where the corner of a small shed built against the wall beside the gate-gap would give him a certain amount of cover.

Standing in the shadow of it, he called "Cunorix, Lord of Six Hundred Spears!"

There was a moment's pause, and then the familiar voice shouted back, "I am here, Alexios of the Frontier Wolves!"

"And of your spears? How many still to run forward to the killing-ground at your call?"

"Not all that once there were; that you know; but with us a war-band of the Caledoni who have joined their spears with ours—enough to finish the thing." His voice turned mocking. "How many still of the Wolf-kind?"

"Enough to finish the thing," Alexios flung back at him. "But first there are matters that must be spoken of between you and me."

"Na! There are no more words for speaking between you and me."

"A few. Come out into the open space before the gate-gap here, and bid your men to hold back their spears, as I will bid mine, that we may speak together."

"And why would I be doing this thing?"

"Because if you do it not, the Children's Children of the Clan will tell it round the fires on such winter evenings as this, how Cunorix the Chief dared not stand out from among his warriors, risking his neck in a certain matter—as a mere captain of a few score Frontier Wolves dared to do!"

And even as he spoke, Alexios stepped clear of his meagre shelter and swung himself up onto the wall-top, and stood there, his belly clenched within him as he wondered whether the next thing he knew would be a flight of spears or a Pictish arrow. But nothing moved on either side of the breastwork. All he felt was the freezing feather-touch of snow on his face. And then out into the open space below him stepped Cunorix, with no spear in his hand, and his sword still in its wolfskin sheath.

Alexios greeted him, holding his own hands well clear of his weapons. "You breed fine hunting dogs, and closely you have hunted on our trail these past two days; why then were you not swifter to pick it up at the outset?" He was talking at random, anything to make the talk last as long as possible, aware with every word, of the light of the snowy day fading towards dusk …

"We would have picked it up sooner—as soon as we found that the trail we followed at the outset was a false one—but that one sent us astray."

"So—and who was this one, that I may speak of him in gratitude to the Lord of Light?"

"Speak then of a woman who we found by the Ford of the Rowan Trees. There was a dead child beside her, and she was washing its bloodstained clothes."

Alexios felt the hair rise at the nape of his neck, remembering old stories of the Washer by the Ford; remembering also the woman at the Rath of Skolawn. "I hope you tear each other's hearts out," she had spat at them.

"You have dreamed a dream," he said. "That woman would have put you on no false scent for love of us."

"Na, no dream," Cunorix moved a pace nearer, and stood swaying a little on his heels and looking up. "A strange story though, and I will tell it you before we kill you. She cried out like a hawk, and caught up the child against her, and pointed eastward and said, 'They went that way, towards the Sunrise. Follow swiftly, oh hunters of Annwfn, and when you come up with them may you tear each other's hearts out!' And then she caught sight of our brothers the Painted People among us and she began to scream and scream, and turned to run and caught her foot in a tussock and fell, and went on screaming. And we knew by that that she was not—what at first we had thought she might be. So we killed her to stop her screaming, for she was putting fear upon the ponies. And then we cast eastward a while, until we picked up a trail. But it was two days' old, and a trail of the Painted People at that. I am thinking she must have been one with her wits astray."

"I also," Alexios said, "so far astray that she confused even the hatreds in her heart, and mingled the Painted People, who killed her child and went on eastward, with the Frontier Wolves who came later and headed by another way."

"Och well; whatever the way of it, behold, the hunting is ended now, and the quarry stands at bay," Cunorix said. And looking down at him, Alexios saw in that one moment a likeness to Connla that he had never seen before, the same shimmer of laughter like summer lightning. But Connla was dead, and for that one moment it seemed to him that he was looking at a dead man.

The moment passed, and out of the corner of his eye, he caught the sudden forward start of another figure, tall and black-cloaked and hooded like a gore-crow; and a high voice cried, "There has been enough of this! Kill! Kill!" and a low growling murmur broke from the waiting warriors.

Cunorix glanced that way and made a fierce gesture, "Back, old father! It is I who say when there has been enough!" But to Alexios, he said scornfully, "Were these the words that we must speak together …"

"No," Alexios said, still playing his desperate game for time, "no mere telling of tales, but a question that is for me to ask and for you to answer."

"What question?"

"This: How long have the Clan of Cunorix of the Votadini, run as one pack with the Painted People, calling them their brothers?"

Again there was a muttering among the warriors, and from somewhere the hissing wild-cat anger call of the Caledoni.

"Since the People of the Eagle who once called themselves their friends slew Cunorix's younger brother, for the mere matter of a horse-stealing that was half in jest."

"Nay," said Alexios, "but for the slaying of two Frontier Wolves and the breaking of the Frontier peace that was no jest at all."

"No matter! The thing is done. There is blood between us."

"Kill! Kill!" cried the priest, his arms upflung, his hood fallen back so that Alexios saw clear as by the white light of its own malice, the skeleton face and huge brilliant eyes of Morvidd the Druid. There was a shifting and a slipping forward of the shadow warriors. But the daylight was fading every moment, and the snow falling more thickly…

Alexios said, "It was I who killed Connla. I killed him to save him from an uglier death, and that you know. Nevertheless it was I who killed him, and his blood is between you and me." He knew that the moment was upon him, and he gathered himself to meet it. He was no longer talking at random. "Your warriors are as spent as we are. If you attack us now, it may be that you will overwhelm us. But whether or no you overwhelm us, many of your men will die."

"Those who die will go West of the Sunset by the Warrior's Road! Do not heed him!" screamed the priest.

"Try telling that to the women beside the fires that they do not return to!" Alexios flung at him, then turned back to Cunorix. "There is Blood Feud between you and me. So be it. Then as two who settle a Blood Debt, let us fight it out, here and now, your sword against mine; and if you kill me, then my men shall avenge me if they can; but if I kill you, then let the debt be wiped out, and I and my men be free to go our ways."

"Free to go your ways? Do you not know that the Painted People, and the White Shields too, by now, are between you and Habitancum?"

"I do not ask that you promise for the Painted People, nor for the White Shields. We will take our chance with them, afterwards. I ask that you promise for your Votadini following." Suddenly his voice warmed, and he was speaking as friend with friend. "Cunorix, we have hunted together and eaten bread together, and laughed together at foolish jests, our arms laid across each other's shoulders. Shall we not now do this last thing together, you for your warriors and I for mine?"

And again there was silence under the booming wind. The shadow warriors made no further move nor murmuring; and behind the breastwork of the waggon park, the Frontier Wolves crouched tense and still. It was as though both knew that the thing had gone beyond them. Even Morvidd the Oak Priest had ceased his savage outcry, and the Painted People stood silent; this was no concern of theirs, they would make their own red trouble later.

And, one standing on the low wall, his wolfskin hood hanging loose behind his war-cap, one standing just below, his tawny head flung far back on his strong neck, his thumbs in his belt, Alexios and Cunorix looked at each other as though they were alone on the high moors on a good hunting day.

Then Cunorix said almost gently, "Now here indeed is a thing for the Children's Children of the Clan to tell round the fire on winter evenings. So be it, Alexios of the Frontier Wolves. This last thing we will do together, you and I."

It did not take long to make all ready. The gateway barricades were heaved aside just far enough to allow one man to pass through the gap. Torches of roughly plaited straw or brands pulled from the cooking-fires were passed from hand to hand. An odd sense of ritual had descended on tribesmen and Frontier Wolves alike, as they lined the makeshift breast-work and drew closer from among the settlement ruins to ring with torch-flare the open space before the gateway.

Alexios flung off his cloak and tossed it to the nearest man. There was a feeling of unreality on him as he drew his sword and hitched up a borrowed buckler on his left arm, and walked forward through the narrow gap.

In the centre of the open space, Cunorix stood waiting for him. He too had flung off his cloak; his tawny hair was bound back into the warrior-knot, and the traces of war-paint showed red and black on cheeks and forehead, and the wind-ravelled torchlight played fierce and fitful on the naked blade in his hand.

The trampled snow was yellow where the torchlight fell, blue beyond its reach, blurring away into the dusk that spun and whirled with falling flakes; and the flakes hissed when they eddied into the torch flames. Otherwise there was no sound in the long trough of quiet between gust and gust of the wind. The fighting-space was ringed with watching faces that hung like painted masks against the dusk behind them, a huddle of wolfskin cloaks, oxhide shields, fur or feather tasselled spears with the light catching jagged on their tips, the snarling wild-cat head on its spearshaft that was the ensign of the Painted People; the face of Morvidd the Oak Priest hawk-hovering over all. In one quick raking glance about him Alexios took it all in. Then deliberately turned his whole awareness to the man waiting for him sword in hand, and shut out all the rest; shut out, too, the memory of the high moors beyond Credigone and the shared hunting fires at the day's end.

He slipped one foot in front of the other, crouching a little, his eyes on the eyes of his enemy.

"Watch the eyes," said his old drill instructor's voice in his ears. "Don't forget the sword hand, but always watch the eyes." The leaden weight of weariness had fallen away from him, and he felt light on his feet and very cold, with a bright inner coldness that had nothing to do with the east wind and the eddying snow.

Cunorix crouched also, eyes wide above the bronze rim of his shield, swaying a little on the balls of his feet. Slowly they began to circle, each waiting for the other to make the first attack. Alexios was realizing suddenly that he had no idea how good a swordsman Cunorix was, for they had never crossed blades before; and it would be the same for Cunorix also. So at the outset they fought delicately, warily, exploring each other's skill, seeking for each other's weaknesses; moving about each other with small padding footsteps as precise as those of a dance, with now the sudden bright flicker and ring of blades in slash and parry, and again the long watchful pauses in between.

Beyond the ragged torchlight it was almost dark now; but Alexios had forgotten that he was playing for time; he had come near to forgetting that he fought as champion for the Frontier

Wolves, with maybe the lives and deaths of his men hanging on his sword point. This was another thing altogether; a thing between himself and his friend, his enemy, with the stain of Connla's blood lying between them.

Cunorix made the first lunge in earnest, and sprang back as Alexios parried; and the wary circling began again, until Alexios sprang forward, his blade striking out an arc of light from the torch flare, and Cunorix sprang out sideways with a narrow thread of blood springing out of his forearm.

A shout broke from the watchers. "First blood!"

Again and again their blades rang together and broke clear, each had the other's measure now, and the play was growing quicker and more deadly.

Utter silence held the watching throng. The only sounds in Alexios's world were the ring and rasp of blade on blade that sent a tingling jar all up the sword arm, the pad of their own feet on snow that was becoming every moment more slippery as it was beaten down, the whistling of breath snatched through half-open mouth and flaring nostrils. Weariness was creeping back upon him; his guard wavered for an instant; and in that instant Cunorix's sword leapt from nowhere in a vicious down-cut, and before he could spring clear, shored away the outer edge of his buckler and seemed to grate against his shield arm leaving a wake of white fire from shoulder to elbow.

There was a stirring among the men behind him, and from the tribesmen a roar of "Second blood!"

The light skin-covered wicker shield became suddenly as heavy as though it were made of forged iron; and something warm and sticky was running down inside it, making the strap slip on his forearm as he heaved it upward and pressed in with his own answering blade.

There was red on the snow now in good earnest, making it yet more slippery underfoot; and he knew that if he was going to win this fight he must do it quickly, before the strength went out of him. There seemed to be a flicker of cold iron all about him; his own blade and his enemy's, scoring a kind of bright and deadly tracery upon the air. The snow whirling in the torchlight had begun to make a dizzying dance that spun at the corners of his eyes. He gathered himself and got in a powerful side-swing and felt his blade bite Cunorix's thigh below his shield guard. Then as Cunorix lunged wildly in reply, he sprang sideways to avoid the thrust, and his feet went from under him on the treacherous mingling of blood and hard-packed snow, and he went crashing down.

He twisted over, covering himself as best he could with what was left of his buckler, and as Cunorix's blade swept down, flung himself sideways and stabbed upward beneath the other's shield, and felt the hard-driven point go in under the breastbone.

The Chieftain's sword flew wide in mid-stroke, and with a defiant yell that ended in a horrible choking sound, he crumped on top of the man who had been his friend and heart-companion.

Alexios felt him twitch once, and lie still. He dragged himself out from under the dead weight and lurched to his feet, aware of a roaring like a wild sea in his ears. And slamming his reddened sword back into its sheath, he stooped and turned the other onto his back. He lay hacked and twisted, a red gash gaping to the bone of his thigh, the jagged hole under his breastbone oozing out a soggy blackness. Even so, Alexios thought that he was still alive; but a mass of blood and vomit came out of his mouth, and it was only the streaming torchlight as men crowded closer that flickered in his eyes and made them seem to move.

There had begun to be words in the sea-roaring; someone shouting, "Kill! Kill!" But he had already killed his friend.

"Kill! Kill! Though the sun be down, I, Morvidd can guide you beyond the sunset. Kill! Kill! *Kill!*"

He tried to pick up his shield, but his arm was numb and dripping red. Red everywhere on the snow, his own blood and Cunorix's mingled. And glancing down he saw his leather sleeve slashed away, and a long gash that snaked down his upper arm, laying bare the bone.

Hazily he was aware of a rush of shadows, and fighting all about him. Hands were on him, the hands of his own men, dragging him back towards the narrow gap in the barricade. And then he was inside, and men were heaving the timbers back into place. He was sitting on the ground and somebody was jabbing the neck of a leather bottle against his teeth, while somebody else lashed a strip of filthy cloth about his arm. He managed to stop his teeth juddering, and swallowed. Some of the barley spirit ran down his chin and some down his throat. It burned like fire, but started his head clearing, so that awareness of what was happening all around came back to him.

A savage struggle was going on all the length of the breastwork and the barricade; and still, above the tumult and the howling of war-cries and the weapon-ring and the plunging and neighing of frightened ponies, he could hear that terrible long-drawn blood-shriek of the Oak Priest. "Kill! Kill! *Kill!*"

A leaden despair crushed down on him. He'd failed, then. He'd played his desperate game for time; he'd held them off until the last light went, banking on the surety that the Votadini would not attack in the dark; and they were attacking in the dark after all, sicked on and maddened by that accursed priest and maybe by the Painted People who were with them. They were breaking their Chieftain's promise and their Chieftain's honour with it.

"It was a good try, Sir," somebody shouted in his ear.

He found that he was on his feet again, lurching back into the thick of things. At full pitch of his lungs he raised the Wolf Cry, and heard it caught up all about him. He saw Morvidd the Priest standing on the rubble-pile of a fallen building, arms upstretched above the tossing torches, shrieking the tribesmen on. And in the same instant the man beside him, taking a chance in the torch-light, nocked an arrow to the bow he had taken from under his cloak. Close to his ear Alexios heard a throbbing twang, and the bow sprang from its tense curve. And the mad figure on the rubble mound stood rigid for an instant clawing at the arrow in its throat, then pitched over backwards with a bubbling scream.

A fresh howl rose from the tribesmen as they saw their priest go down. And as though in answer, rising clear above the uproar, from somewhere in the wild night beyond, came the clear ringing notes of a hunting-horn sounding the charge; and a fresh yelling as of all the black hosts of Ahriman, and a smother of hoof-beast sweeping near over the snowy ground.

15 | Return to the Wall

THE PRESSURE OF THE TRIBESMEN SEEMED TO WAVER AND lose impetus as the yelling newcomers crashed into them from the rear; and with an answering yell the defenders of the waggon park rose and poured across the breastwork. Taken before and behind, in the storm and darkness they had no idea how many or how few were the wild horsemen crashing in upon them. Their Chieftain and their Priest were dead; and now that the screeching voice no longer cried "Kill! Kill!" from somewhere deep within the Votadini the knowledge of broken faith rose to sap their fighting powers.

They crumbled and turned and fled, the Painted People with them, for the place where they had left their ponies. Many of them never reached it, with the Frontier Wolves howling on their heels. Those who did, flung themselves in something near panic upon the waiting beasts, and streamed away like a broken dream into the night.

"Seems it was worth playing for time, after all," Hilarion shouted.

Later, the optio of the relief force, such as it was—a double patrol of the Frontier Wolves, twenty men in all—stood before Alexios, as he sat by one of the cooking-fires nursing his tightly bandaged arm across his knees, and made his report. He made it woodenly, his eyes fixed on the air above the other's head. He had been used to report each time he returned, and at times such as this training was something to hold on to; so he made his report to Alexios because none of his officers were left alive to receive it.

"The Attacotti are landing all along the West Coast, and some of the Damnoni and the other Western tribes have joined them. They say some of the Arcani, too, but we've no proof of that; the Attacotti we saw. Segontium has fallen, but the rest of the Wall forts are still in our hands, though the trouble is still spreading. We were on our way back—forced riding—when we got word of Bremenium …" His face twitched and crumpled, then turned wooden again.

"Sit down, Optio," Alexios said.

The man shook his head. "Rather stand, Sir."

"Sit *down!*"

The optio folded up beside the fire. "Sorry, Sir. We sent a couple of scouts forward at sunset, while we lay up, and they brought back word of what was happening out there in the settlement; and we made all the speed we could. Didn't know who it was holed up here in the waggon park. The scouts reported Frontier Wolves but could tell no more. We thought it might be some of our own lads."

"About a dozen of us are—what remains of the Praepositus's escort. The rest of us—no, we're not your lads; we're the Third Ordo, down from Castellum," Alexios spoke gently. "I'm sorry."

The optio managed the shadow of a grin. "No need to apologize, Sir." Then with a sick weariness, "How could it have happened? The strongest fort north of the Wall?"

"The Arcani opened the gates."

"You—know that, Sir?"

Alexios nodded. "We found one man still alive. He lived just long enough to tell us."

"So it was true about the Arcani."

"Seems like it."

"Oh God, oh God, what a mess!" said the optio.

"Have you lost any men from the patrol?"

"Two dead, five wounded," he jerked his head towards the battered range of ware-sheds where all the wounded lay in the shelter of the half-fallen roof. "It was hot work, just at first."

Hilarion loomed into the firelight, unwinding bright rags from his waist. "Sir, may I return to you the dragon of the Third Ordo, Frontier Wolves."

Presently the meat was scorched rather than cooked, and when chunks of it had been taken out to the sentries at their posts and issued to those of the wounded who could eat it or drink the broth, the rest crowded about the fires, gnawing at it like famished dogs.

The optio of the returned patrol looked at the meat and then at Alexios.

"The Painted People drove off most of the ponies," Alexios said, "but they left one poor brute behind them hamstrung but still alive—it's all right, Optio, we have made the offering to the Mother of Foals. Bid your lads to the Midwinter Feast."

They kept a strong guard that night, changing it at two-hourly intervals instead of the usual four, for the sake of the cold and weary men. But in truth, Alexios thought, there was not likely to be any further attack before morning, from the Votadini anyway. The Picts were of course another matter, a different danger. But there would not be enough of them in this band to make an attack on their own.

The night wore away in quiet, save for the howling of four-footed wolves who caught the battlefield smell of the fort from far off but dared not come too close for the watch-fires. Crouching beside one of those fires, between visits to his guard posts, Alexios heard them, and thought, "Have patience, four-foot brothers, tomorrow the fires will be out." He wished that they could bury the dead, all the dead, not just their own, not just Lucius; but his job was to get the living down to the Wall.

The usual two hours before dawn, they marched for Habitancum.

A good deal more snow had fallen in the night, covering the blood on yesterday's snow, covering the dead with a gentle white coverlet until the thaw came, or the wolves. Alexios wondered whether the tribesmen had carried off their Chieftain's body when they fled, or whether he still lay where he had fallen last night in the cleared space before the gate-gap, and took care not to look too closely at the pale hummocks that showed faintly in the snow-lit dark as they rode by. Better to remember the high moors beyond Credigone; better to remember the hunting fire and the shared laughter, and leave the rest to the wolves.

Some of the ponies had been killed in last night's attack; but men had been killed too, and now there was no need to use animals for pack duty, for they had scarcely anything save their wounded left to carry; so there were enough mounts still for their full remaining force, and even a few spares.

The survivors of the Praepositus's escort and the Bremenium patrol now formed part of the Fore Guard, and took over the duties of scouting ahead and path-finding through this country that they knew as a man knows his own kalegarth. Snow was still spitting down the wind as they rode out, but the sky was less full than yesterday; and presently as they rode, the low dawn showed a bar of cold daffodil-yellow through a break in the cloud-roof far down to the south-east.

Riding at the head of the Main Guard, Alexios was finding that it took quite a lot of concentration to sit up straight in the saddle, not hunched forward over the pain in his left arm. Anthonius had re-dressed it and made him a sling from a strip torn from a dead auxiliary's cloak; but every snow-clogged beat of Phoenix's hooves under him seemed to go through him with a sickening jar, and from shoulder to finger-tips his arm felt as though it was made of hot lead, except that lead does not throb. Heavy, so heavy, despite the sling. Again and again he straightened up as the sheer weight of it seemed to drag him down. Not a good idea to let the men see him riding hunched over as though he should be with the wounded in the rear. He straightened his shoulders yet again.

Presently, exploring under his cloak, he felt warm stickiness coming through the sling. Curse! He was bleeding again. Once, Hilarion ranged up beside him and asked under his breath, "Are you all right, Sir?"

"I was never better," Alexios informed him through shut teeth. And Hilarion saluted, and fell back to his own place again.

By the straight military road, Habitancium was not much over half a day's foot-march; but they were following ways known to the Bremenium men, which had nothing to do with roads; secret ways among the hills that almost doubled the distance. So it was sunset when they came in sight of the fort. But though twice they had crossed the tracks of sizeable companies, and once they had lain up in the birch below the crest of a ridge, each man with his pony's muzzle strap twisted tight to prevent it whinnying, while a large mixed war-band of Picts and West Coast tribesmen passed along the valley below them, they had stayed clear of all encounters on the way. The Painted People, who had hunted them down from Castellum in company with Cunorix's war-band, Alexios reckoned, had probably got tired of the hunt, which was not really theirs, and gone off in search of easier prey.

From a long way off, the fort showed dark and stubborn, but it was not until they were close enough to see the Roman standards floating above the gatehouse, and the heads of the sentries moving along the wall, that he really knew that yesterday's nightmare was not going to be repeated. They had come to a living fort.

A while later, Alexios found himself in the lamplit office in the Principia, standing before the table stacked with papers, at which sat the fort Commander.

"Third Ordo, Frontier Scouts, reporting in, Sir—also a double patrol of the First Ordo—what's left of them."

He wished the floor would stay still under his feet, instead of floating gently like the deck of a galley in a calm sea. You didn't mind it in a galley, but on dry land it was disconcerting.

The Commandant added the paper he had been reading to one of the piles, and looked up, showing a narrow hard face with a humorous mouth that had at that moment no time for humour. "Ah yes, Ducenarius—"

"Aquila, Sir, Alexios Flavius Aquila," said a familiar voice out of the shadows. "My successor at Castellum." And a figure that he had not noticed before stepped forward into the lamplight. He had almost forgotten that Julius Gavros would be here.

"So. You have reached us just in time, Ducenarius Aquila. We pull out at dawn—this lot to the fire, I think ..."

"Pull out?" Alexios said stupidly.

"Yes. When the order for recall went up to you, our own orders were to remain here—close in to the Wall defences, as we are; but now, in view of the worsening situation, we are ordered back." The Commandant finally abandoned the papers, and leaned forward on his elbows, giving Alexios his whole attention. "I must say it is a pleasant surprise to see you. I very much doubted if the order would ever reach Castellum."

"It didn't, Sir," Alexios said. "In view of the circumstances I pulled out on my own initiative."

He was aware of a small quickly suppressed movement from

Ducenarius Gavros, and turned his head a little to meet the other's eyes. He felt suddenly very much older than he had done when last they stood face to face.

"Circumstances?" said the Commandant.

And Alexios heard his own voice making some sort of report, of the breaking of the Frontier peace and the happenings of the following days. Odd to think that only ten days or so ago, life had been normal, and apart from the feeling of thunder brewing at the back of his neck, there had been nothing to worry about beyond the problems of satisfying Praepositus Montanus on his visit of inspection.

In the silence when he had finished, he heard the steps of the sentry outside, drawing nearer along the colonnade, passing by, growing fainter. A very orderly sound, belonging to an orderly world that seemed strange to him just now.

The Commandant's voice sounded out of the silence, its tone suddenly sharpened, "You're wounded."

"A sword cut in the arm, last night, Sir."

The Commandant turned to Julius Gavros. "He's one of yours. Take him across to the sick block for patching up. He's bleeding all over my floor."

Later, much later still that evening, having had his arm re-dressed by the camp surgeon, having seen his own men safely bestowed and forced down an evening meal that he was by then past wanting, Alexios was sitting on the edge of the narrow cot in Gavros's sleeping quarters, trying one-and-a-half handed to do something about the flattened head of the Ordo dragon, which he had just unbound from his waist.

Gavros, just back from rounds, was standing in the doorway that gave onto the outer chamber, throwing off his wolfskin cloak and slipping his sword-belt over his head.

"How is the arm?"

"It is for aching when the wind blows from the east." Alexios frowned at his task, and quoted a veteran of the Third Ordo, whose old weather-wise spear-wound was well known to both of them.

Gavros turned to lay his sword on the chest. "Ask a fool question … Your lads are crowing it through the fort how you came by that wound. Strange, in the old Chief's Hall that day, I could have sworn there was to be friendship between you and Cunorix."

"There was."

Gavros stood for a moment as though making up his mind about something; then he came across the room and stood, his arms along the high window-ledge and looking out into the night. "Do you think you could tell me the things that you left out of your report to the Commandant?"

Alexios looked up. "Where would be the point?"

"The powers that be will ask for more details than the Commandant did, he having other things to occupy his mind, tonight."

Alexios felt as though all the blood jumped in his tired body. "Not another Inquiry?"

"Ach, no. But they will ask for more details. And I think that you may find it easier to give them if you have first gone through them with me."

"Get them straight in my mind, you mean?"

"Partly; but more than that; I think that there have been things in the past few days that you will find it harder to speak of, the longer they remain unspoken, until maybe you cannot speak of them at all."

And somehow, in a dead-level voice, Alexios found himself telling what Julius Gavros asked. He was so tired and his arm hurt so much that he could not remember what he had told the Commandant after all, and so he told it all again; from the horse-stealing half in jest and his own killing of Connla. "The light was going—he'd have been torn to rags. It seemed the only thing to do."

"It probably was the only thing to do," said Julius Gavros. "Go on."

And Alexios went on. "So the Praepositus relieved me of my command and put me under arrest—and then the first attack came, and he was killed. So I took over the command again. Hilarion will bear me out in all this. And then—well I told the Commandant about the further attacks and my decision to pull out." How drab and pointless it all sounded.

"That can't have been easy."

"It wasn't. The Lord of the Legions knows it wasn't," Alexios said.

They looked at each other in the light of the lamp in its wall niche; and all that Alexios had not told even now, seemed passing to and fro unspoken between them. Even the untold part about Cunorix. And for the first time since he had made the decision, though he had thought he was sure at the time, Alexios knew that it had been the right one. That even if the order to withdraw which never reached him had not been sent, it would still have been the right one.

He let out a little sigh, like someone letting go a physical strain, and turned the dragon head on his knee to come at another place with his knife point.

Gavros dropped his gaze to the bright bloodstained silken rags trailing across Alexios's knee, and the grotesquely flattened mask of bronze and silver wires he was holding in a hand half out of its sling. "What would you be trying to do with that bit of wreckage?"

"Get it back into parade-ground shape." Alexios tried not very successfully to work his dagger point between the crushed jaws to ease them open. "Number Three Ordo, Frontier Wolves isn't going to ride into Onnum tomorrow except under its own standard." There was a warm pride in his voice. "But I don't seem to have enough hands."

From the darkness outside came the clear well-ordered notes of the trumpet sounding for the Second Watch of the night. Marching feet went past; somewhere a voice shouted orders. The fort was still busy with preparations for marching in the morning. "We'll be back," Alexios said, without conviction.

Gavros did not answer.

An hour before daybreak the garrison of Habitancum, making what was officially a "Temporary withdrawal", marched out through the Praetorian gate. A very different march-out from the one Alexios had led five days ago from Castellum. A solid half cohort of Auxiliaries—Raetian spearmen—and four flanking squadrons of Cavalry forming the Main Guard, the Second Ordo, Frontier Scouts forming the Van; and behind the baggage train, forming the Rear Guard, the Castellum men and the few survivors of the First Ordo. Yesterday they had ridden like a grim skein of ghosts, but now after a square meal and a warm night, and with the knowledge that they were on the last day's march and every mile would see them closer in to the forward defences of the Wall, they rode like living men again, like the Frontier Wolves, the proud scrapings of the Empire who would not call the Praetorian Guard their equals. Alexios felt the renewed spirit in them as he rode at their head, Phoenix's rein twisted round his almost useless left hand—luckily he and his mount knew each other's ways so well that he really only needed his knees—and in his right hand a spear from the tip of which floated the bright bloodstained rags of the Ordo dragon, its mask now roughly opened out and wearing a somewhat drunken leer.

It was a bitter dawn, and the breaths of men and ponies smoked about them as they rode, but it seemed that at last the sky had emptied itself of snow. The sunrise came silver-gilt behind the tattered cloud-bars that were drifting away, and presently the shadows of horses and men and upheld standards and the birch trees of the hillside lay long and sharp edged, blue as hyacinths across the fallen white.

Rome was withdrawing yet again from the Frontier hills; but they were doing it in style, heads high and at their own pace, as a promise to all who saw them, that presently they would come again, as they had always done before. "But will we?" Alexios thought. "Will we—this time?"

He gave his shoulders the old familiar jerk, and sat up straight against the drag of his wounded arm, determined that at least he would do credit to the men following him, as they were doing credit to him.

Somewhere in a bare thicket of rowan and hazel a robin sang as though there was no sorrow in the world, and from the skein of men behind him someone whistled back.

All day they held straight down the great military road, with the watery sunlight glinting on the Cohort standard and the red horsehair crests of the auxiliary officers. Once there was a short sharp skirmish between the right-hand cavalry wing and a small war party who they put up much like a dog putting up game. But the column swung steadily on. Time and again a few Pictish war arrows loosed at extreme range thrummed into their midst from behind some scrap of cover, and a couple of men were wounded, and in the last ranks of the Rear Guard men nocked an arrow to their short Syrian bows, and turned in the saddle to return fire, though there was nothing visible to loose at. But it was clear that as yet there was no big war-host so far to the south-east, and so close in to the Wall. By tomorrow probably it would be another matter.

And when, some while past noon, they saw horsemen pricking up from the south, the shout that went up from the Fore Guard and spread back down the line was a cheer of greeting. And beside Alexios, Optio Garwin, narrowing his eyes into the snow glare as he pulled his pony clear of the column for a better look, came back grinning. "A full wing of the Asturians from Cilurnum! They're bringing us in style!"

"It's no more than we deserve," Alexios said, trying not to let the words sound blurred. He was feeling very cold, with a sick coldness that seemed to clutch at his heart and belly. Only his left arm was not cold, but throbbed like a forge fire. And the stickiness had come back, making his hand slippery on the reins.

There was a time of sun-dazzle on snow, and then a faint mist rising that might have been made of frost and evening fog and distant woodsmoke, or might have been in his own head. And then far ahead of them was the dark shape of the Wall snaking along the high ground, with a smoky sunset away to the right behind it, and the towers of Onnum with a shadow bloom on them like the bloom on black grapes, drawing nearer and nearer.

And then there were more horsemen; and torches, and the gates of Onnum standing wide. And already the head of the column was passing through. But the new horsemen had reined to one side to watch them pass; and as each Century and troop went by, standards were lifted high in salute, and heads turned and there was a flash of uptossed weapons in the mingled light of sunset and torches.

Nearer and nearer yet. Hazily Alexios realized that the new

cavalry were an escort of some sort. As the sunset faded and the torches began to bite, he could make out shields—incredible shields of Imperial Purple, blazoned in gold—and in their midst a man on a tall black horse, his helmet-crest of eagle feathers and his cloak of the same Imperial Purple. A man whose face he was sure he had seen somewhere on a coin.

He raised the tattered dragon in salute, and heard his men shout and the rasp and hiss of blades being drawn and tossed up behind him; and the face on the coin hovered forward with a look of quickened interest. And then the torchlit dark of the gate arch received them.

In the broad and crowded parade-ground within, that was already full of Habitancium men, he drew rein, his men behind him, and dropped from the saddle.

The ground rose up to meet him, and he heard someone say, "Hold up, Sir." And felt an arm round him before torch-light and dusk spun together, and he sank quietly into nothingness as into a pit.

16 | *The First Attacotti Frontier Scouts*

THE NEXT TIME ALEXIOS KNEW ANYTHING AT ALL CLEARLY
again, it was another evening—evening or early morning, just at
first he was not sure which, for the square patch of sunlight that
danced and trembled like golden water on the lime-washed wall
at the foot of the cot could have belonged to either. But then he
heard the trumpet sounding for Stables, and knew that it must be
evening because at that time of year morning Stables came before
sun-up.

He seemed to have just floated out of some kind of cloud, and
everything on the far side of the cloud seemed a long time ago.
Perhaps it *was* a long time ago. He had no means of knowing.
He felt cool and rather damp, which was pleasant, because the
cloud had been hot and scorching-dry. There had been daylight
and lamplight in it; and faces and hands that came and went, but
all blurred and hazy. He remembered a small yellow-faced man
with the winged staff and twisted serpents of a medic on his tunic
most often. Remembered him saying something about leeches
for the wound-fever, and a voice that had sounded surprisingly
like Uncle Marius's, saying, "Good God! Man, he's bled almost
white already!" Come to think of it, he seemed to remember his
uncle's face, too, somewhere in the cloud. But maybe that was just
a dream. Maybe it was all a dream …

He was lying under a striped native rug in much such a small
lime-washed sleeping cell as he had known, in one place or
another, ever since he joined the Eagles; or at least since he had

finished with the barrack rows of his time below the vine staff. In this particular cell the small high window was at the head of the cot. He made to roll over and look out of it, and a vicious jab of pain told him that the ache he had been vaguely aware of somewhere close by was actually centred in his own left arm, which was tightly bandaged and lying on the cot beside him like something that did not really belong to him at all.

He began to remember things before the coming of the cloud, chief among them the cleared space before the wrecked waggon park at Bremenium, and the dizzy whirling of snow in the torchlight, and Cunorix's face across the rim of his shield.

He put up his good hand quickly, as though to thrust that particular memory away, and saw with a detached interest how thin it was, the wrist bones showing like those of a gaunt old man and the tendons to the fingers standing out like cords. He opened and shut it experimentally, for the satisfaction of feeling that at least he had one hand that was still his own; and a shadow hand opened and shut on the sun-square on the wall. The old battered ring with its flamed emerald hung loose on his finger. Have to be careful or he'd lose it. It was on the wrong hand, anyway. Somebody must have shifted it over for him.

As he looked, the sunlight caught the stone, and far down in the heart of it woke a tiny spit of green fire. He played with it idly, turning his hand to watch the green spark wake and sleep and wake again. And suddenly just as he had done riding up the Castellum road nearly a year and a half ago, he thought of the men from whom that ring had come down to him: but it was a different kind of thinking. "You can't say I've failed you," he told them, "not now. Whatever happens to me now, however much my nice shining military career stays ruined, I got the Ordo back—well, we got each other back." But almost in the same moment he knew that not having failed his forebears was good but not really the thing that mattered. He had not failed something else, though he was not sure what; he had kept some nameless faith within himself; and that was the thing that really mattered. In his utter weakness he found to his horror that he wanted to cry, and rubbed the back of his hand angrily across his eyes.

The curtain over the doorway was pulled back and an orderly came in. But it must be later; quite a bit later, for the sun-square had gone and there was a lamp burning in a niche in the wall. The man carried a slab of bread and a bowl of something that smelled like broth; and the smell made Alexios suddenly aware that he was hungry. The orderly looked harassed and in a hurry. "You awake, Sir? That's the way then. If I give you the bowl can you manage—fresh batch of wounded just come in, and we're a bit pushed, tonight."

"I can manage," Alexios said. But he was clumsy with weakness and lying too flat, and some of the broth slopped over onto the blanket. He cursed, quietly but vehemently, and in the same instant the door-curtain that was still swinging behind the departing orderly swung back again, and the tall crane-fly figure of Hilarion strolled in.

"You'll live," said Hilarion. "Nobody could curse like that who wasn't on the mend." And then taking in the spilled broth, "Here, give me that."

He took the bowl, and sitting himself down on the edge of the cot, slipped an arm under Alexios's head to raise him and held it to his mouth, all with the most unexpected gentleness.

Alexios took a mouthful of the warm broth and swallowed, almost before he knew it. "How long have I been here?"

"More than a week."

Alexios was not surprised. It could have been anything from

an hour to a hundred years. But a lot of water could pass under a lot of bridges in a week. "What's—been happening?"

"Drink some more broth," Hilarion said, "and I'll tell you."

Alexios gave a small cracked laugh. "You sound like my old nurse."

"A worthy woman, I have no doubt—have some bread? I wouldn't, if I were you, it seems to be the consistency of old saddle leather."

"I'll stick to the broth, then—only in the Name of Light tell me what's been happening."

So, in the intervals of tipping warm broth into him, Hilarion told. "Well, we seem to have left the whole Frontier country going up in flames behind us—Habitancum burned out, the Damnoni swarming in from the West Coast along with the Attacotti, to join spears with the Picts—though I doubt they've any clear idea what they're fighting about."

"At least Cunorix's lot knew that," Alexios said, and there was a small silence.

Then Hilarion went on. "Anyhow, the Emperor has sent in the Legions now. The good old flat-footed Sixth from Eburacum and the Twentieth up from Deva. Gavros and the Second Ordo have been ordered off westward for scouting duties with *them,* so things should be quieting down soon."

"Emperor?" A confused memory was trying to shake itself clear of the fever-cloud in Alexios's mind: a flash of gold and purple—a face that he seemed to have seen on a coin—troops shouting the old out-of-date salutation that the army still hung on to, "Hail Caesar!"

He frowned at Hilarion, trying to get the memory into focus. "That was the Emperor? Constans? What was he doing here?"

"Come out to see the fun, I suppose."

"No, I mean—what is he doing in Britain? Didn't know he—was in Britain, did we?"

"No, we didn't. Communications haven't been all that good just lately, you'll remember; and he'd only just arrived—come over from Gaul to look for himself into rumours of incompetence and disloyalty among the officials left over from his brother's reign—we could tell him about that—and arrived just in time to see the North go up in flames."

Alexios abandoned the Emperor, and went back to something that mattered to him more nearly, "What about our own lot?"

"The Third Ordo is taking life comparatively easy at the moment. We have been temporarily added to the Onnum garrison."

"Why us? We're not much good at that kind of duty."

"The Onnum garrison are below strength, and—well I suppose the Dux your esteemed uncle thought we could do with a short spell in barracks to get our breath back and lick our wounds."

Again there was a small sharp silence, and then Alexios asked, "How many have we lost?"

"Twenty-seven killed since we pulled out of Castellum," Hilarion said, still with that surprising gentleness. "Something over thirty wounded badly enough to be out of action."

"So we're still—what—something over half fighting strength," Alexios said; and then, "Poor old Third."

"A good number of the wounded will be back on the fighting strength presently."

"But not the killed."

"No," said Hilarion, "not the killed." He set aside the empty bowl and lounged to his feet. "The survivors, however, are bright of eye and bushy of tail, and telling the world in general that any time you feel like setting up as Emperor on your own account, they are behind you in close formation. I do think it might be a good thing if you go to sleep now and make a rapid recovery, so that you can take over the command again before they make Onnum too hot to hold them."

"The devils!" said Alexios with affection.

"The devils!" agreed Hilarion. "Good night."

Time passed, and Alexios began to gather strength again, while the daily dressing of his arm became a less messy and less painful business; and news from outside the sick block and then from outside the fort began to drift in to him.

Everything was quieting down, as the old Sixth and Twentieth with the cavalry of the Wall forts took over, dealing with the Picts and the Attacotti, and breaking up the huge war-mobs of tribesmen without needless damage to either side.

"You know," said Hilarion, one night when he had lounged in as he generally did after the evening meal, to sit on the edge of Alexios's cot, "we're used, these days, to thinking of the old Line-of-Battle Legions as second-rate. Oh not hard bargains like us, just—outdated. But I doubt if any of our modern pared-down fast-moving light field forces could have done a better job."

Rumours drifted in, too, of the state of the Frontier hills left behind the fighting. The days of the outpost fort, it seemed, were over; from now on the Frontier would be held in a different way, with even the Frontier Wolves based on the forts of the Wall itself.

"Another strategic rearrangement," Cunorix had said, on the day that Alexios had killed his wolf. The first day that ever they had hunted together.

And then, a full month after Alexios had marched his tattered little army back to the Wall, the Emperor was in Onnum again, on his way south to Eburacum, and the Dux Britanniarum with him; and the old sprawling fortress where the road ran through to the North, and the forts and mile-castles on either side were crowing with trumpet calls; bulging with over many troops and horses and officials like a grass-snake that has just swallowed a toad too large for it, lying out on a sunny bank.

And the day after the Emperor rode in, the purple and gold of the Imperial dragon now flying in the light east wind above the roof of the Commander's quarters, Alexios, on his way back from the horse-lines, received a summons to the Imperial presence.

"Have I time to clean up?" he asked the young sprig with the purple crest of the Imperial Bodyguard in his helmet.

"I am afraid not. The Emperor does not care to be kept waiting."

So hurriedly straightening his worn and weather-stained leather tunic as he went, feeling that his belt buckle was central, and the brooch which held his wolfskin in its proper position on his shoulder—he still had his wounded arm in a sling, and that tended to make it slip crooked—he followed the Emperor's messenger up to the Commandant's quarters, past the young men with their purple shields propped beside them playing dice in the colonnade, up the stair to a big chamber full of low winter sunlight.

There were several high-ranking officers in the room; one lounging at a table on which were a great pile of papers, a dish of dried figs and a scatter of wine-cups; and among the rest, standing close by, the Dux Britanniarum. But in the first moment of entering, Alexio's quick gaze picked out the figure standing in the furthest window; a figure sombre by contrast with the rest, in wolfskin and weather-worn leather like his own. Ducenarius Julius Gavros. Only of course it was Praepositus Julius Gavros, now. He was glad Gavros had got the Numerus in Montanus's place. Glad for Gavros, and glad also for the Numerus. It would be good for the Frontier Wolves to have a Commander of their own kind again.

The young guardsman who had come up with him saluted. "Ducenarius Aquila, noble Caesar," and departed.

Alexios stood where he was, waiting; and the man at the table, the man whose face he had seen on coins, went on reading the document he held in one hand and eating the fig he held in the other. He finished the document and another fig at the same moment, and looked up, licking his fingers. Alexios was surprised to see how young he was. He knew of course that when he had originally been made Caesar by his father Constantine, he had been only seventeen and very much a younger son, but somehow when you came face to face with your Emperor you expected him to be more than six or seven years older than yourself. Constans's face was narrow-boned and long-nosed, and would have been better with a beard, for his chin was his weakest feature, but his mouth was wide and wickedly amused at life, and his eyes alert and bright. Hunting, drinking and wenching were the three things everyone linked with the name of Constants; but his young Commander of Frontier Scouts, standing in the middle of the room and steadily meeting his gaze, judged that there was a good deal more than that to his Emperor, and rather liked what he saw.

"Ah," said the Emperor of the West, after a long stare. "Ducenarius Aquila. You look somewhat changed since the last time I saw you."

"I *have* shaved, Sir," said Alexios, gravely, but with a glint.

"It could be that, of course." The Emperor's gaze dropped to the sling which showed at the parting of Alexios's wolfskin. "I hear that I have to congratulate you on your swordsmanship— how does the arm?"

"It will soon be as sound as ever, Sir."

"So, then allowing for a short spell of sick leave, you should soon be fit to return to duty; which brings us to the question of your future. It has come to my ears," Constans took up his wine cup and drank, then sat idly swirling the wine and looking down into the cup, "that your men are crowing it through all the wine shops in Onnum, that they are prepared to back you should you feel like promoting yourself to Emperor."

Alexios's breath caught for an instant, then he let it go carefully. He said nothing. He was not going to belittle or disclaim his own small disreputable band by saying that they made wild jests when the drink was in them, or hurriedly protesting that he had no knowledge of such foolish talk.

Then he saw the amusement glinting in the Emperor's face as he looked up from his wine cup, and his heart gave a slight lurch and returned to normal.

"What? No protests of innocence and undying loyalty?" said Constans. "Wild talk in jest can be taken for treason—on the other hand, it can suggest a good Commander whose men find something in him worth their following ... The state in which your men got back to Onnum suggests the second of these two things. They did not look perhaps in parade-ground trim, but their good discipline and good heart—obviously *extremely* good heart—were plain to see. I know that Praepositus Gavros, here, will forgive me if I say that marching behind the Habitancum troops, the Third Ordo Frontier Scouts had very much the air of the tail wagging behind the dog. For this, I offer you my congratulations."

"Thank you, Sir," Alexios said.

"And for this, I feel also—these are very pippy figs—that you have earned something more than congratulations. A crown or a military bracelet is after all just one more thing to keep clean, which leaves us with promotion, eh, Marius?"

"If you say so, Sir," said the Dux Britanniarum forbiddingly.

Alexios glanced quickly in his direction. Uncle Marius had had enough of trying to push his nephew up the ladder, but meeting the older man's eyes, he was startled and a little shaken, to see something very like pride in them, all the same.

"Oh I do say so; and not for his own sake alone. The army has need of the right men in the right places. So—" The Emperor stuck out three bony fingers, and turned down one of them, "Did you hear that I had a brush with the Sea Wolves on the way over? The present coastal defences are as my dear elder brother left them, which is to say they're a disgrace; and I have decided to leave the General Gratian here in Britain to take over the setting to rights of the Eastern shore forts and fleet. There's a place for you on his staff, with the rank of Tribune." The Emperor turned down a second finger. "Alternatively I should be happy to receive you into my 'Family,' my personal bodyguard—you will have seen some of them on the way up here. I daresay you will not really think of that as promotion; but they are officer cadets, and a place among them carries with it the almost certain prospect of commanding a crack field force one day. On the other hand—" he turned down the third finger. "Go and look out of the window."

Alexios had a feeling that the Emperor was playing a game he found amusing; playing with people as though they were pieces on a board, and watching the result. But he did not think that was all it was. He crossed to the window at the far end of the chamber, Gavros moving back a little to make room for him, and he looked out.

On that side the Praetorium faced towards the granaries, with a kind of yard between; and below in the yard, squatting on their heels or prowling to and fro or simply propping up the walls and staring straight in front of them, a couple playing knucklebones, one picking idly at a half-healed scar, one braiding his barley-pale hair as tenderly as a girl, another deep in conversation with a stray dog, were about a hundred of as wild looking tribesmen as Alexios had ever seen.

"You see those men down there?" said the Emperor's curiously light voice behind him.

"Yes, Sir."

"They're Attacotti prisoners. They *were* Attacotti prisoners. The Twentieth took a good many, and they seemed too good fighting material to waste on the slave market, so I offered them the choice between that and serving with the Eagles. Some five hundred of them chose the Eagles. The rest of them are at Cilurnum, and tomorrow they go down to Corstopitum to begin their six weeks' foot drill. When that's done, you can take them out to Belgica and make Frontier Wolves of them."

For a moment Alexios remained standing very still. Two chances of a really brilliant career—or this. He went on looking down at the men in the yard below; strangers and enemies, and utterly familiar.

"Do you wish for time to consider your choice?" said the Emperor's voice behind him.

He turned from the window, and for an instant caught the old Commander's eye cocked upon him. "Once a Frontier Wolf, always a Frontier Wolf," Gavros had once said.

He went back to his place before the Emperor. "No, Sir, I'll take the Attacotti."

"So-o," Constans said, "well, there's magnificent hunting in Belgica."

Alexios looked at his uncle, "I'm sorry, Sir."

"Don't apologize," said Uncle Marius. "After all, anybody can end up as Dux Britanniarum." And then he did a surprising thing.

He came round the table and took Alexios's free hand in both of his. "Your mother will cry again; but do you know, I believe your father would have been rather proud of you."

In the first-fading of the short winter's day, Alexios stood on the northern ramparts of Onnum, leaning his sound shoulder against the parapet, and looking out northward along the line of the road. He needed a little time to himself. A puddling of snow still lingered in the hollows; and far off, the higher hills of the Frontier country were still maned and crested with white; but nearer moors showed the sodden darkness of last year's heather, and the wind that always harped along the Wall had gone round to the west, and the green plover were calling.

Alexios's gaze followed the road that led on and on, out of sight and still on, through forts that were dead now, empty to the wolf and the raven. Habitancum and Bremenium, Trimontium that had died a long time ago; Castellum. The road and the hills ... They had seemed so different the first time he had looked out over them, and assuredly not because of the fire of autumn burning in the gold of birch leaves and the russet of bracken had given them warmth. They had been the wilderness of desolation waiting for him, then. Now they were the hills of his lost wilderness among which he would not go again.

He remembered the Lady at the turn of the track by the ford, and the cold empty feel of the stone, the last time that he had leaned aside for that passing touch. The Lady had known. He remembered the babble of wildfowl along the estuary shores and the way the river crooned to itself on quiet nights. He remembered faces strung out along the way; men left behind, Lucius at the bridge over the Roaring-Water, the Quartermaster among the dark stone dancers of the Chieftains' Death Place, Rufus and the Emperor's hard bargain back at Castellum. His mind twisted away from the memory of Cunorix as he had last seen him, and when he tried to lay hold of the young Chieftain's face in the light of a shared hunting fire, showed him instead the moment when he had held up his new son to show him to the Clan. Would the squalling and scarlet bundle be the new Chieftain one day, though his father would never be old and tired and full of sleep? Or did he and his mother with the gold drops torn from her ears lie now beneath the burned thatch of their hall? …

He remembered again the night the Frontier Wolves had danced the Bull Calves and fought a private war among themselves; and away back beyond that the grey autumn morning when he had walked with Julius Gavros up and down the lines of blank, guarded faces and looked each one of them in the eye as though he did not give a broken sandal-strap.

He had been so young then. It was he who had changed, and not the hills, after all. He was older now, and had wiped out the stain of that mistaken decision on the Danubius. He felt suddenly very tired, as though he had been on a long journey. He had got somewhere, but he was not quite sure where; only that he had learned a good few lessons and killed his closest friend along the way.

And now it was the start of another journey.

Footsteps came along the rampart walk, and he glanced round to see Hilarion strolling towards him.

"It's just as I always said," Hilarion draped himself against the parapet at his side. "No sooner do we get a Commander comfortably broken in to our ways than the higher command send him off somewhere else, and we have to start on some new cub, all over again."

"I was just discovering that it comes a bit hard on the Commander, too," Alexios said, not knowing it until the words were spoken.

"Well, you'll leave them in good hands, now that Gavros has the Numerus."

Looking out along the road again, Alexios said, "I'm thinking you'll get Number Three Ordo in my place."

The silence beside him made him look round, and he saw with surprise that for the first time since they had known each other, Hilarion was looking not completely sure of himself. "As a matter of fact," said Hilarion after a moment, "I was thinking of trying for an Ordo in another Numerus—the old Third will be split up and re-made, anyhow."

"You mean—?" Alexios said slowly.

"You'll need a couple of good experienced Ordo officers," his centenarius told him, "and the gods know what you'll get if you leave it to the authorities. Up here we break in our own officers as we go along, but now it won't be so simple; and this new lot of yours—they're not even from inside the Empire, they're barbarians from beyond the pale. *We* shall have to do all the training."

"*We?*" said Alexios.

"*We,*" said Hilarion.

There was a sudden warmth in Alexios. The tall mocking man beside him would never fill the place that Cunorix had left empty and aching, but the startled warmth felt good, all the same. "Hilarion, do you want to come with me?"

"Well if I don't, I really can't think what this conversation is all about," said the centenarius.

"Then go you and put in your application, and I'll back it."

His slow lazy smile drifted over Hilarion's freckled face. "I already have," he said.

They looked at each other a long moment, and then laughter took them both.

From below came a ragged tramping and a snatch of wild

and mournful song. And still laughing, the two young men on the rampart turned, each with a hand on the other's shoulder, and stood looking down. The last slate grey of the daylight was fading, blending away into the red-flaked smoke of unseen fires where they were burning rubbish down beyond the horse-lines, and along the open space below the Wall, the men of the First Attacotti Frontier Scouts were being marched back to barracks for the night.

Alexios wondered how often, round how many camp fires in Belgica, he would hear that wild lament out of Hibernia when the native beer went round and it had long since ceased to be truly a lament and become something that one sang for the memory of old griefs and old longings and the pleasure of twisting one's own heartstrings.

"There goes your new command," said Hilarion, "and to think there are rising four hundred more of them at Cilurnum! Mother of Mares, what a pack! What a rabble! I wish us joy of them!"

"I wish us joy of them!" said Alexios Flavius Aquila, their new Commanding Officer.